A Crushing Walk in Cornwall

Books by Nicholas George

A Deadly Walk in Devon

A Lethal Walk in Lakeland

A Crushing Walk in Cornwall

Published by Kensington Publishing Corp.

A Crushing Walk in Cornwall

NICHOLAS GEORGE

KENSINGTON PUBLISHING CORP.
kensingtonbooks.com

KENSINGTON BOOKS are published by

Kensington Publishing Corp.
900 Third Ave.
New York, NY 10022

All Kensington titles, imprints, and distributed lines are available at special quantity discounts for bulk purchases for sales promotion, premiums, fund-raising, educational, or institutional use. Special book excerpts or customized printings can also be created to fit specific needs. For details, write or phone the office of the Kensington Special Sales Manager: Attn. Special Sales Department, Kensington Publishing Corp., 900 Third Ave., New York, NY 10022. Phone: 1-800-221-2647.

KENSINGTON and the KENSINGTON COZIES teapot logo Reg. US Pat. & TM Off.

Library of Congress Control Number: On file

ISBN: 978-1-4967-4532-3
First Kensington Hardcover Edition: April 2026

ISBN: 978-1-4967-4534-7 (ebook)

10 9 8 7 6 5 4 3 2 1

Printed in the United States of America

The authorized representative in the EU for product safety and compliance is eucomply OU, Parnu mnt 139b-14, Apt 123 Tallinn, Berlin 11317, hello@eucompliancepartner.com

For Bert, always my main "crush"

Acknowledgments

As much as I love writing mysteries, it can sometimes be a frustrating experience. Have I fully explained that clue? Did I just paint my protagonist into a corner? Can someone really be murdered like that? When questions like these arise, it helps to break out of the solitary activity of writing and consult with others.

Helping me get through my adventure in Cornwall have been my awesome agent Michelle Hauck, my impeccable editor John Scognamiglio (and production editor Robin Cook), and trusty friends that include David Link, Cristina Stuart, Rodney Hoffman, and Frank Burgos. Thanks to all!

A Crushing Walk in Cornwall

Chapter 1

Monday, midmorning,
near Treen, Cornwall, England

At first, I only heard the shrill wails of lapwings. Above me, the birds were swooping in circles, their black-and-white, angular bodies contrasting sharply against the deep azure sky.

Jorge Campos's screams rang out, rising above the cries of the birds.

"Someone help me! *Now*!"

My attention snapped to Jorge, panic-stricken, clinging to the railing of the wooden bridge I had just crossed. It had broken with a horrifyingly splintering groan and now teetered dangerously over a deep ravine. Jorge was gripping the railing with one hand, his other hand swinging helplessly over the chasm below, as was his left leg. His right foot struggled to maintain its hold on what remained of the bridge.

I was just about to take action when our walk leader, Brian, dashed past those of us who had already traversed the bridge. The other side appeared to be intact and secure, still connected to both sides of the ravine, but the side to which Jorge was clinging had largely given way.

Grabbing the large limb of an oak jutting out from the side of the ravine to secure himself, Brian planted his feet along the railing of the side of the bridge still anchored to the ravine and edged forward, proceeding slowly so as not to cause any jolts that might loosen that side of the bridge. As he neared Jorge, he leaned toward him as far as possible, his free arm outstretched.

"Careful, now," he said to Jorge. "Swing yourself around, and I'll pull you in."

Wide-eyed with fright, Jorge began to angle his body toward Brian, stretching out his free arm as far as he could. We all watched breathlessly as their hands connected. Then we gasped as the bridge let forth another groan and lurched downward before stopping again. Quickly, Brian pulled Jorge toward him. As soon as both of Jorge's feet were on the bridge's planks, Brian led him to the rest of us. When they arrived safely on solid ground, we gave Brian a round of applause and cheers.

After our cheers died down, a woman's voice shouted out from the bridge's far side. "*Hello-o*? Does anybody care about *me*?"

Jorge had escaped a fatal fall, but three of our party were still on the other side of the ravine, and one of them—Jorge's wife, Luella—was on the bridge itself. Although Luella had just started across and that side of the bridge appeared secure, she was frozen in fright, clutching onto the railing for dear life.

"You didn't have a problem rescuing Jorge!" Luella yelled to Brian. "So why won't anyone come and rescue *me*?" She looked back at the two walkers still on the other side, Rachel Scattergood and her young daughter, Ivy.

"I—I don't think I can do it," Rachel said.

"Jorge?" Luella called across to her husband. "Come and get your Lulu!"

"No!" Brian shouted. "It's too dangerous. Luella, you

should be safe if you work your way back to where you came from. Just keep holding on to the railing. It's not very far."

"Let me get her!" Ivy said. "I'm not afraid." She stepped toward the bridge, but her mother pulled her back.

"Are you *nuts*? You're staying right here with me."

From our side, Luella's son, Ben, yelled out, "For God's sake, Mother, go back! Just do it, like Brian told you, and you'll be all right."

With no other option, Luella began inching her way back, eyes closed. We held our breath, hoping the bridge wouldn't break free of its tenuous hold and tumble wholesale down the ravine. But soon Luella joined the others. The three stood in a huddle, looking across the ravine at those of us lucky to have reached the other side intact.

Ivy couldn't wait any longer. "Scaredy cats!" she said. She ventured out, but her mother dashed forward to yank her back just before the bridge gave another groan.

"Please stay off the bridge!" Brian called out. "It's too hazardous. There's a way to cross the ravine farther up the hill. Wait a second. I'm consulting the map." He pulled his cell phone from his coat pocket.

Beside me, Ben said, "I should never have let Mother talk us into coming over here to England."

"Don't be stupid," Jorge said. "This was a minor setback. Happens all the time."

"Well, it doesn't happen to *me*," said Dave Langdon, the travel writer planning on writing a magazine article about this walk. "If I wanted to live life on the edge, I would have gone hiking in the Himalayas, not walking along the coast of Cornwall!"

I turned my attention to the break in the bridge. Although it was several feet away from where I was standing, I saw a few ragged spears of wood that indicated it might simply have given way under the weight of our group.

But a much cleaner break, just beyond that, suggested to me that the bridge may have been booby-trapped.

Brian perused his online map and looked up the hill. "Up a few hundred yards there's a spot where the others should be able to safely cross the stream without the aid of a bridge."

"What do you mean, 'should be'?" asked Roy Hemper, the seventh member of our group. "Don't you *know*? What kind of guide are you?"

Brian closed his eyes, took a breath, and opened them. "I'm the only guide you have, Mr. Hemper. I'm telling you what I believe will be the best way forward. I've never had to deal with this bridge having a problem before."

Roy looked chastened. "I'm sorry. I wasn't expecting this kind of thing on the first day."

Brian called out to Luella and the Scattergoods, "Make your way up the hillside! Look for a narrow trail. I'll go up and help you across." He told the rest of us to stay where we were.

Luella and the Scattergoods began making their way up the hillside.

As we waited, my walking partner, Billie Mondreau, nudged me aside and, out of earshot of the others, asked, "What do you think, Chase? Should we be concerned?"

An accident occurring this early in the walk was not a good sign.

The birds above continued their wailing. Dave looked up at them. "You know what they call a group of lapwings?" he asked. "A deceit."

Billie and I exchanged looks. I wondered if she was remembering, as I was, something our guide, Brian, had mentioned the previous night at dinner. "I want you to enjoy our walk," he'd said, "but please be careful. Unfortunate things can happen."

Unfortunate things can happen.

Brian was most likely speaking about sprained ankles or insect bites, but Billie and I traded anxious glances across the dinner table after he made this comment. We'd both participated on walks on which far worse things had happened. Surely nothing like that could happen again, could it?

Chapter 2

Sunday, early afternoon,
St. Mawes, Cornwall, England

When I'd reached Cornwall the day before, my heart beat fast with excitement. There I was, back in my favorite place on the planet—the glorious isle of England—about to embark on another walk, this time along a coastline I'd never explored.

Unlike on past visits, I was being driven to meet the group by my British boyfriend, with whom I'd just spent two days at his home in Devon.

Thinking of Mike as my "boyfriend" sounds juvenile. I'm a man in my late sixties, and so is he. We'd been "dating"—another awkwardly inadequate word—for two years, at first through FaceTime and phone calls (I live in Temecula, California, north of San Diego, while Mike lives in Exeter, Devon), and recently more closely. Mike had just spent three months with me in the States, and now it was my turn to reciprocate and spend three months with him in England. I'd been in the country a couple of days, but our time together would officially start in a week, after the walk concluded.

Mike, unfortunately, couldn't get the time off from

work to join me on the walk. That was just an excuse, I realized. He could have arranged it, but truth be told, Mike was not a fan of country walking like me. I was born with the innate desire to move my legs and let them take me wherever they wanted. When I was a child, this annoyed my parents, who constantly had to search for me as if I was lost. But I never got lost. I always knew where I was; I just wanted to walk much farther than they did.

So I looked forward to being with Mike at his home after the walk ended, and I was heartened to know he was close by. He didn't live far from the starting point for the group's walk, the town of St. Mawes, at the end the Roseland Peninsula on Cornwall's southern coast.

I was looking forward to my stay with Mike, but not without some reservations. His stay with me in California had had its bumpy moments. He didn't like being so far from home, and in a very different climate. Like me, he had developed routines and habits through the years—reading certain newspapers and frequenting local restaurants—that couldn't be as easily accommodated in another country. He also hated American food. I wrote these irritations off as normal, mostly certain we were going through an adjustment period.

We had many good moments too. Some, naturally, involved physical intimacy (there's simply no substitute), and others involved sharing stories of our past. Mostly, we just enjoyed being together. Now it was my turn to live in Mike's world, and I was facing the same issues. I'd never spent three months away from my home, with its reassuring sights, sounds, and smells. I began to question whether my decision to spend so much time with Mike was a sound one.

Easing the transition was my decision to take part in another group walk, this one along the southern Cornwall coast. My good friend Billie, always on the lookout for guided walks in Britain, had suggested it. I'd never explored Cornwall, with its gorgeous coastline that has been the locale for many films and television shows. Best of all, Billie would be at my side.

As Mike drove, I studied his face, youthful still, framed by a bush of brown hair. He had a lively sparkle in his eyes. But I saw the sparkle dim. Slowing his well-worn MG, he pulled to the side of the road and brought the car to a stop. He began studying the GPS mounted on the dashboard. "According to this, I'm heading the right way, but it can't possibly be right, can it? It seems as if we're heading inland rather than toward the sea."

I looked at the green hills around us. We were still in England, of course, but other than that, we could have been anywhere. "Trust the directions. This road has taken so many twists and turns that it's impossible to tell north from south."

He nodded, but with clear misgivings. "Right, then," he said and pulled back onto the road. Around the next bend, we spotted the small, tasteful sign announcing The Carne, the hotel where my group was booked for the first three nights. He slowed, and we viewed the white façade of the hotel's main building, beyond which a small blue bay presented itself, surrounded by rocky bluffs. The subtropical breezes made conditions perfect for huge, solid, and fleshy succulent plants; large, spiky cabbage trees along the bluff looked somewhat incongruous beside the red valerians flowering beside them.

Mike found a parking space near the entrance. When he switched off the engine, he looked at the hotel and gave a whistle. "You won't be exactly roughing it, will you, Chase?"

I smiled. "You still are more than welcome to join me, you know."

"Can't do," he said. "You know that."

Further discussion about this would grow contentious, so I said nothing. Mike claimed that because he'd just taken a three-month leave to be with me in the States, he couldn't afford to take any additional time off from his job. Given his tenure and reputation as county coroner with the Exeter Police Department, I doubted that was true.

We stepped out of the car just as a dapper man in a blue waistcoat walked up from the hotel entrance to get my bag. He noted the luggage tag and said, "You're with South Coast Walkers, is that right? Three of your lot are in the sitting room."

He carried my bag off as I remained with Mike.

"Want to come in and have a look around?" I asked.

He gave me a nervous smile. "Thanks, but I should be getting home. Do you mind? First day back on the job tomorrow, you know. Lot of catching up to do."

We'd been together for the past three months in the States. This would be the first night in months that we'd be apart. A tear welled in my eye.

Mike smiled, stepped forward, and stroked my chin. "Be strong, Chase. I'm only half an hour away."

I led him to a private spot beside a berry-laden dogwood tree where we could hold one another without being seen. "I'll miss you," I said.

"And I'll miss you. But it's only for a week. After that, you'll see so much of me, you'll grow tired of my face."

I looked into his eyes. "I don't believe I could ever do that."

We shared a longer kiss than usual, and I promised to phone him later that evening. He gave me a smile and walked back to his car. Before getting in, he said, "Remember my advice. No murders this time!" He was referring, of course, to two murders that had occurred on previous group walks, both of which he became involved with in his professional capacity.

He drove off, passing a dark-blue Volkswagen Golf coming up the road and stopping at the spot that Mike had just vacated. I noted an Uber sticker on the vehicle's window. A slim Black man in his midforties stepped out of the back seat and eyed his surroundings before smiling at me. "Are you with the walking group?" he asked in an accent I pegged as American Southern—perhaps Louisiana.

"I certainly am," I said, returning his smile and extending my hand. "Rick Chasen."

"Roy Hemper," he said with a smile. "Brother, it's nice to hear an American voice. I'm having trouble understanding a lot of the people over here."

The Uber driver brought out Roy's suitcase and backpack. He thanked him before looking at the hotel's white stone façade, with its graceful arch and front walkway. He formed an appreciative smile.

"I was expecting something grim and castle-like," he said.

"This part of Cornwall is more like the French Riviera," I said. Taking a deep breath, I added, "Can't you smell the salt air? It's almost like we're in Monte Carlo."

Roy nodded and chuckled. "I spent the last two nights in London. I figured it would be better to hire an Uber instead of having to deal with the trains over here."

"The UK rail system is pretty good," I said, "but overall, I think you made the right decision."

Roy picked up his bags, and we walked toward the hotel entrance, a small whitewashed building roofed in shiny blue shingles, when a large van pulled up—the shuttle from the Truro rail station, according to a sign on the windshield. The driver hopped out and slid open the side door. A sandy-haired older woman emerged, dressed stylishly in a yellow linen top and white slacks. Dangly bracelets adorned her arms. She removed her sunglasses to survey the hotel as three others stepped out—a tall, physically imposing dark-haired man with a thick, dark-bristled moustache; a shorter, less imposing clean-shaven man; and a man with dark blond hair who maintained his distance from the others.

The last one off the shuttle was a welcome sight: a familiar older woman with tightly coiled gray hair. Billie grinned when she spotted me. "Chase!" she exclaimed, and rushed forward to give me a hug.

The stylish woman stepped up to Roy. "The bags are in the back of the van. Be very careful with the yellow one, that's mine. Which way is the hotel reception? We'll meet you there." Her voice was a mix of whiskey and tobacco.

It took a moment for Roy to understand what she was getting at. "I'm sorry, ma'am," he said. "I don't work here."

She cocked her head, confused, and the waistcoated young man who had taken my bag appeared. Catching on, she repeated the same instructions to him.

"This is quite a spread, isn't it?" the tall man said in a husky, deep voice as he eyed the property. "Four-star, I believe."

The woman was more concerned with the manner in which her suitcases were being handled. She watched the bellman wheel them off before saying, "I suppose. Come on, Jorge. Let's get inside. I need a drink."

The two walked off, the shorter, clean-shaven man following. The blond-haired man stayed with me and Roy.

"You haven't met Mr. and Mrs. Campos yet, have you?" he asked Roy and me with a strong trace of disdain in his voice. "Boy, do you have a treat in store."

"Are you here for the walk?" Roy asked the man.

"Yep, but I'm not with that bunch," the man replied. "Dave Langdon. From New York. How do you do?"

"Rick Chasen, California."

Roy introduced himself. "Looks like we're all here then. Nine of us, aren't there?"

"Ten, if you include our guide," I said.

The bellman returned for the remaining bags. As we followed him into the hotel, I put my arm around Billie. "Great to see you, my old friend. How have you been?"

"The usual. Fighting my advance into the golden years tooth and nail. My left knee has some arthritis. What about you? How is the torrid love affair going?"

I laughed. "The 'torrid' part wore off pretty quick, but the rest of it is going just fine."

"Will I be hearing wedding bells soon?"

My face clouded. Mike and I hadn't discussed formal recognition of our relationship, although I sensed it had been weighing heavily on his mind. Same-sex marriage was now common in both his country and mine. He knew I hadn't married my previous partner, Doug, who had passed away a couple years before, even though same-sex marriage had been legal in the States for some time. That was Doug's hang-up; he regarded marriage as a heterosexual institution, even though his devotion to me, I knew, could not have been more solid.

"We're taking things one step at a time," was all I said to Billie. My focus went to her sweater, one of her own creations. I looked closer at the images repeated in the pattern. Were those . . . parrots?

Before I could comment, we reached the front desk, where our bags had been placed to the side. A trim young woman, hands clasped before her, greeted us with a smile. "Welcome to The Carne," she said in a crisp Cornish accent. "I'm Lily. Your rooms will be available shortly. In the meantime, I believe your group is convening in our sitting room. It's right through there." She motioned toward a small room on the other side of an alcove.

The others' eyes turned toward us when we walked in. Besides those who had arrived via the rail shuttle, there were three others—an attractive, brown-haired woman I assessed to be in her late thirties; a teenage girl with long, straight, black hair and big, round, black-rimmed glasses; and a balding man with a broad smile, who turned to the group and said, "Good afternoon and welcome! I'm Brian Teague, your walk leader. I appreciate everyone arriving so promptly. Now that we're all here, we can toast to the start of a memorable week on the South West Coast Path. Please, help yourself to wine over there on the sideboard."

Most of the group had already collected their glasses of wine; the rest of us quickly got ours. The young girl came and wedged herself in between Billie and me.

"Ivy, come back here," the brown-haired woman said. "You know I'm not comfortable with you drinking wine."

"How can I toast with an empty glass?" the girl replied. "Besides, Father lets me drink wine all the time. Harder stuff too—scotch whiskey and vodka shooters."

The woman—her mother?—frowned. "All these people are going to think you're . . . oh, never mind. I'm in no mood to argue right now."

The girl smiled devilishly up at Billie and me. She whispered, "She's not really my mother. I'm actually a long-lost member of the royal family. We've come to England to reclaim my place in the line of succession. But it's a secret."

I traded looks with Billie as Ivy helped herself to the wine. Once we had ours, Brian walked into the center of the room.

"Everyone have their wine? Very good. Again, welcome! I've lived my whole life in this part of England and know Cornwall very well, so trust me that you'll be in good hands. I'll review what's in store for us in the next few days over dinner, but at the moment, please join me in a toast to a wonderful week!"

We raised our glasses and said, "Cheers!" before sampling our wine. To my amazement, Ivy downed her entire glass in one go.

"Perhaps we can introduce ourselves?" Brian prompted. He nodded to the brown-haired woman beside him.

It took her a moment to get the hint. "Okay then. I'm Rachel Scattergood, from Chicago, in the US. I'm an attorney."

"And what prompted you to come here to England, Mrs. Scattergood?" Brian asked.

Rachel gave a start. "Oh! Well. I thought it would be an educational experience for my daughter, Ivy, here. Also, it will get us on our feet and make us move around. That's so important, you know."

"Mother, *honestly*," Ivy said. She turned to us and said, "If you must know, my parents are in the middle of a divorce, and it's gotten really ugly. Mother plans to take Father to the cleaners, and he wants to make sure she doesn't get the chance. So she dragged me as far away from him as possible—"

Her mother's eyes widened. "Ivy! Stop, please!"

"—because he can be pretty nasty himself when he sets his mind to it. So, as long as we are halfway around the world until the actual divorce proceedings begin, we'll be out of harm's way. Isn't that right, Mother?"

Rachel looked as if she was in shock. I wondered if this tale had as much veracity as Ivy's assertion that she was a forgotten member of Britain's royal family. Her mother collected herself with a sigh. "You'll have to forgive my daughter. She has a very active imagination. Yes, I am in the middle of divorce proceedings, but it is nothing as dire as Ivy makes it sound." She looked down and glared at her daughter, a clear message to hold her tongue.

After the uncomfortable silence that followed, Brian said, "Right. Let's move on then. Mr. Campos?"

"Don't I get to introduce myself?" Ivy asked.

Brian laughed uncomfortably. "Oh, certainly, young lady. We already know your name and . . . and why you've joined our little group. Do you have anything to add?"

She thought a moment and said, "Not really. Just that I've Googled everyone here and know a lot more about all of you than you'd think."

"Ivy, please," Rachel said. "You'll make them uncomfortable."

"Why should they be uncomfortable? Unless"—she gave a slow scan around the room—"any of them have something to hide."

The tall bearded man to Rachel's left smiled, revealing a set of impossibly white teeth. "Well, I have nothing to hide! I am Jorge Campos, and I currently live in Naples, Florida, with my beautiful wife, Lulu, and my stepson, Benjamin."

"And what prompted you to take a walk in Cornwall, Mr. Campos?" Brian asked.

Jorge's smile faltered briefly but reasserted itself. "Who wouldn't want to stretch their limbs in such a beautiful spot? My wife and I are newlyweds, and because I'm an outdoors enthusiast, I wanted Lulu to experience the wonder of nature. We've always wanted to visit this corner of the world."

"What is your profession, Mr. Campos?" Brian asked.

Jorge's smile again faltered. "I didn't know this was going to be a job interview."

"If you don't wish to share that information, you don't need to, of course," Brian said.

"Why shouldn't I? I'm retired. For much of my career, I was a commercial airline pilot."

Ivy gave a sharp laugh.

"Mrs. Campos?" Brian encouraged.

Luella executed a deft slow head turn toward us and displayed a dazzling smile. At first, I assumed she was much younger than her husband, but, on closer inspection, the years were evident. Tightened skin around the eyes and mouth suggested surgical assistance more than good genes.

"Hello, everyone," she said. "I'm Luella Campos, from Naples, Florida, as Jorge said. I've never been on a walking tour before. And in England with my new husband! I can't tell you how exciting this is."

"I'm sure you'll be able to contain yourself," the younger man at her left said.

"Please be nice, Benjy," she said.

"And do you work, Mrs. Campos?" Brian asked.

Luella was momentarily thrown by the question. "Do I . . . what? You mean a job? Well, of course I do! I am one of the most prominent fundraisers for philanthropic activities in southwest Florida. I have raised millions to improve the lives of the homeless, the indigent, the poor—"

"Don't lay it on so thick, Mom," Ben said. "They might begin to wonder if it's true."

Luella's eyes narrowed, and her mouth stretched into a catlike snarl. She held up two fingers a micrometer apart. "Don't forget you're this close to being cut out of my will, Benjamin." She then mimicked a scissors cutting with her fingers. "Snip, snip!" she said in semi-jest.

One look at Brian told me that, like myself, he hadn't been prepared to deal with a bunch like this. Haltingly, he turned to Ben. "And you, Mr. Campos?"

Ben said, "My name isn't Campos. It's Purdue. Ben Purdue. I was the unfortunate product of Mom's second marriage." He turned to her. "Or was it the third? It's so easy to lose count."

Luella flashed a tight-mouthed grin and again made the scissors motion with her fingers.

"And . . . and . . . what appealed to you about a walk in Cornwall, Mr. . . . Purdue?"

"Not much, to be honest. But Mummy decreed that I should be here, so here I am."

This didn't generate a response from Luella.

"And what is your profession?" Brian asked, keeping to the script.

"I'm a color designation specialist."

Brian blinked a few times. "A . . . a what?"

"He comes up with the names for paint," Luella said. "Seven years of college, and he names paint for a living."

Ben gave her a sardonic smile and turned toward Brian. "There's much more to it than Mother realizes. Finding the right name for a new paint color involves research, testing, and creative brainstorming. I've won awards for my designations. 'Marshmallow mist' was one of my biggest successes. I won an award for it."

"That's fascinating," Brian said, turning quickly toward Dave, next in line. "Mr. Langdon?"

Dave smiled. "I'm Dave Langdon, from New York. I'm a journalist researching English walking paths for a magazine article."

"Indeed?" Brian said, clearly pleased. "Will your article include this walk?"

"I sure hope so. Of course, I won't mention anyone by name. If I do include any of you in photographs, I'll be sure to get your written authorization."

"Which magazine will this appear in?" Luella asked.

"I don't know yet. I'm freelance, so I write the articles first and then shop them around. But several outdoors publications have expressed an interest."

Roy was next. He stood up from the chair on which he was seated and smiled modestly. "Roy Hemper. This is my first time in England. I've always wanted to see it and figured a walk like this was the best way. I prefer to stay away from cities when I travel."

He went to sit down, but when Brian asked him about his job, he shot back up. "Oh, right. I . . . I own a couple of restaurants." He sat.

"Where are they located?" Dave asked.

Roy stood back up. "Um . . . Memphis. In Tennessee." He sat back down.

"What kind food do they serve?" Billie asked.

Roy got to his feet again. "Barbecue." He sat back down.

I was getting a little dizzy watching Roy's jack-in-the-box routine and hoped there would be no more questions. I nudged Billie to introduce herself. She hesitated a bit as she stood, perhaps because of her bum knee.

"Hi there. I'm Billie Mondreau, from Burlington, Vermont. I'm a retired librarian, and I love the English countryside. I try to walk over here every year if my budget allows or, as is the case this year, if my knees hold out."

"Your knees?" Brian asked.

"Just the left one, actually. I'm wearing a small brace. I'm not anticipating it will slow me down." She smiled and sat.

Finally, it was my turn. As I'd be talking with these people all week, I saw no need to provide a ton of information on the first day—just the basics. "My name's Rick Chasen, although everyone calls me Chase. I live in Temecula, California, and, like Billie here, come over to England frequently to walk. I'm also retired. In my working life I . . . I worked in law enforcement."

I sat, hoping there would be no questions. But luck wasn't on my side.

"Law enforcement?" Jorge asked. "You were a cop?"

Uh-oh. "Police detective."

I braced myself for a follow-up question, and was happy

when Brian said, "Very good, then! I'm sure we'll get to know one another better over the next few days."

With the introductions over, there were a few moments of silence. Dave walked to a display of ancient weapons mounted on the wall. "Look at all of this!" he exclaimed. I spotted a musket, a longsword, a battle-axe, a mace, and one particularly nasty piece I knew as a flail: a spiked ball and chain I remember from some of the bloodier comic books of my youth.

Brian gave a laugh. "That is a somewhat exaggerated collection of local weaponry, supposedly from Cornwall's storied past. Never underestimate the willingness of local establishments to exploit the darker corners of our history."

"But there were pirates around here, weren't there?" Ben asked.

"Yes, and smugglers too," Brian said. "Some of you might be familiar with Gilbert and Sullivan's *The Pirates of Penzance*. Many of these stories have a basis in fact, but, of course, they have been heavily embellished over the years."

Luella Campos stepped close to the wall and began singing, in a wavery but half-decent voice:

Go, ye heroes, go to glory
Though you die in combat gory
Ye shall live in song and story
Go to immortality!

"You know your Gilbert and Sullivan," Brian said. "Very good."

Luella gave a small bow. "I played Mabel once. When I was much younger. To very good reviews, I might add."

"Oh, come now, Mother, that was community theater, hardly Broadway," said Ben.

Now I understood the parrots on Billie's sweater. Parrots . . . pirates. She always wears patterns that relate to our surroundings.

We continued examining the weapons when the front desk clerk came in and announced that we could check in and get our room keys. I was about to turn when a loud *thunk* echoed through the room.

Dave was crouching beside a flail that had fallen onto the floor. "Sorry," Dave said. "I just wanted a closer look."

"Please move away," Brian instructed. "I'll notify the front desk to get someone to put it back. They really should secure those weapons better, shouldn't they?"

Ivy walked up to the fallen weapon. "How cool!" she said. "If I wanted to murder someone, here's what I would use!"

"Don't joke about something like that," her mother said. "It's not polite."

Her daughter turned toward us. "Polite! Who wants to be polite? It's so *boring*."

Chapter 3

Sunday, early evening,
The Carne

Ivy's mention of murder stuck with me as Billie and I made our way to our rooms.

Billie may have been pondering it too. On our way down the hallway of the main building, she asked, "So what do you think of this group, Chase?" Her tone indicated she was not very impressed.

"What you mean is, are there any potential murderers in the bunch?"

I was expecting her to laugh, but she was dead serious. Given that murder had darkened two of our previous walks, I couldn't blame her for being on the lookout for trouble.

"Yes, I suppose that is what I mean," she replied.

"That would be bucking the odds, don't you think?"

This time she did laugh. "Who knows? But if I have to buck the odds, why can't I win the Powerball lottery instead?"

As we proceeded toward her room, I detected a slight

limp in her left leg. We reached her room, and she began fishing her room key from her bag. "Are you sure you're going to be okay to walk with that knee?" I asked.

"It's no big deal," she said, as she inserted the key in the door. "Just a bit of arthritis. My brace takes care of it." I studied her face to see if she was making light of a more serious problem.

"Our bodies aren't the indestructible dynamos they used to be, you know," I said. "If your knee gets too painful, walking on it will only make it worse."

She looked up at me and smiled. "My orthopedist okayed me to come on this walk. This one isn't terribly rigorous—mostly mild elevation gains along the coast. But you're right. If my knee gets worse, I'll ease up."

I doubted she would give up on a walk that easily, but I let the matter drop and told her I'd meet her in the dining room at dinnertime.

My room was on the second floor of the main house, an elegant, whitewashed structure with lead-framed windows and wooden shutters. A more modern adjacent building and a smaller tangential cottage housed other rooms.

I was surprised to find I was booked in a suite, with a bedroom separate from the seating area and a spacious balcony staring out to the sea. It was comfortably decorated with little of the stuffiness one often finds in British seaside hotels. That could likely be attributed to the exposure to the southern coast, as the décor was airy and welcoming: a sisal carpet, curtains and throw pillows with bold stripes, and a large nautilus seashell on top of a bookcase. A vase of lavender and poppies adorned the other end. A large, yet not intimidating sleigh bed dominated the bedroom, with king-size pillows I wouldn't need. (Mike prefers firmer, heavily stuffed pillows, while I like the softer kind. Please don't read too much into that comment.)

Even though our group would be in the hotel for just three nights, I unpacked everything so I didn't need to live out of my suitcase. When I finished, I nervously took out my phone to check the results of that day's ball game in Boston. *Damn!* The Sox had lost again. They'd done that a lot this year. Had the Curse of the Bambino returned?

I checked the small clock by the bed. Two hours until we were to gather for dinner—just enough time for a brief nap.

I awakened just in time to take a quick shower, dress for dinner, and join the others in the downstairs sitting room. They'd changed into evening wear as well, although Luella, who had looked fittingly elegant when she arrived earlier, now seemed overproduced in a low-cut black dress and gaudy sapphire necklace. There was a strong citrus-and-vanilla scent about her detectable from several feet away.

I'd met everyone, but this was my first opportunity to take a closer look. They seemed like what I expected—Americans, somewhat uncomfortable on their first night in a strange country—and yet they were standing apart, as if they didn't trust one another.

Knock it off, Chase.

There I was, being too analytical, a common habit, given my police background. Nevertheless, experiences on previous walks had conditioned me to be suspicious of everyone. Any further speculation was broken when our guide Brian arrived, looking resplendent in a bright green shirt and aqua trousers, as if he'd been plucked from the harbor itself.

"Everyone here?" he asked, and without waiting for a response, said, "Brilliant. Let's head into the dining room. Once we're seated, I'll briefly go over our itinerary for the week."

The hotel's restaurant made good use of its best feature: an expansive view of St. Mawes harbor and the English Channel beyond. Lights from a few boats were beginning to twinkle in the early-evening light. The room wisely didn't compete with the view—simple, white-clothed tables beside bone-white, planked walls. As my pun-loving ex-partner Doug would have commented, it was nautical, but nice. Billie and I took seats across from one another at one of the two reserved tables.

Brian clinked his wineglass to get our attention. "You'll find the menu cards for tonight's meal right before you. There are two options to begin—a pea and mint soup and a wild garlic and nettle tart—and for the mains, you can select either a fresh lobster linguine or a John Dory with mussels."

"Nothing else?" Luella queried in a loud voice. "What if we don't want seafood?"

Brian's smile dimmed. "It's unusual, but I'm sure the cook can find something else."

"Be a sport, Lulu," Jorge said. "When in Rome and all that."

"I have allergies," she said, and extracted a large bottle of pills from her bag.

A young man in a blue shirt that reflected the seaside décor approached to take drink orders. He announced that a house Sancerre rosé wine would accompany the main course. Regardless, we all ordered cocktails.

When the server left, Dave looked out the window and said, "This is really breathtaking. Look at that view! Why do we need to go out walking? I could spend the whole week right here."

"Well, you can certainly choose to do that, if you wish," Brian said. "The Carne is famous for its relaxing quality. But you'll be missing out on scenery even more spectacular than this if you stay behind."

Our drinks arrived, and Brian stood with his glass raised high. "Our week of walking begins!" Here was someone who clearly loved the spotlight. He took a celebratory sip, as did the rest of us. "As you know, we won't be walking the entire South West Coast Path or even all of the southern coast. That would be an ambitious, although enjoyable, sojourn of two or three weeks. Instead, we'll be visiting highlights of the coast over the next five days. Let me briefly review the areas where we'll be walking."

We all knew the planned daily routes from the website and other materials we had received, but it was good to hear Brian explain them with his innate enthusiasm. His face lit up as he described each day's scheduled journey, excitedly detailing the many coves, ancient ruins, beaches, hidden harbors, cliffs, and landmarks we would encounter. We would be transported to the beginning of each day's walk, and from its terminus, by a van. It all became a muddle to me, and I expect to the others as well, as (to my knowledge) none of them had ever walked in this part of England. Still, Brian accomplished his unstated purpose: to get us keyed up for the week ahead.

When he finished, Billie whispered to me, "That was a bigger sales job than the description on the website. The walk also sounds more rigorous. I hope I can keep up with everyone."

"As I said, if you feel it getting too difficult, take a break. Don't overextend yourself." Billie nodded.

"Sorry for eavesdropping," Rachel Scattergood, seated beside us, said. "I confess I'm worried about the walk being difficult also. I probably should have trained a little, but I just didn't have time."

Her daughter, seated opposite her, looked at her. "You mean you didn't *make* the time." Turning to Billie and me, she said, "I ran up the stairs to the top of Hancock Tower without stopping. *Twice*."

"Ivy, honey," her mother said, with strained patience. "You couldn't have possibly. I know triathletes who can't do that."

"It's all on my Fitbit, Mom. Check that if you don't believe me."

"Don't worry," I said to Rachel, who was clearly at least thirty years younger than me. "You look plenty fit. And if you want to back off from any part of the walk, it's no badge of shame. I've done it myself on a couple of occasions." That wasn't true, but what harm was a little white lie?

"Mom hits the gym three times a week," Ivy said. "She's super buff."

"Ivy! Enough. Not everyone has to know my gym routine. Keep some things secret, please."

Ivy formed a smile I would have classified as "wicked." She reminded me of Wednesday Addams from the films and comics. "It's fun to have secrets. I know a big one about Mr. Chasen here. He's famous. He was a cop. He captured the Scorpio killer."

"That serial killer in California?" Dave asked, wide-eyed. "It was all over the news when he was caught a few years back. Was that you?"

I glared at Ivy and turned to the others. "I really don't want to discuss my past right now. Be assured that whatever I accomplished was the result of a team effort . . . not just me acting on my own. Anyway, that's all I'm going to say about it. I'm here for the walking, like the rest of you."

That, and the arrival of our starter courses, settled everyone down. Soon we were talking about our food, which seemed to meet everyone's approval. After a satisfying main course and a modest dessert of blueberry trifle, everyone was ready to call it a day and retire for the night.

That's when a grim-faced young man I'd noticed at a nearby table approached. "I couldn't help hearing you mention some walking you'll be doing. I hope you're not heading out on the trails around here, are you?"

"Why?" Luella asked. "What's wrong with that?"

The young man looked surprised. "You haven't heard? Someone has been sabotaging them. They simply are not safe."

His comment unleashed a buzz of conversation. Brian stood and asked everyone to be quiet before facing the young man. "I haven't heard of anyone being injured around here. Do you have any specifics?"

"Well, it's all everyone is talking about. We're afraid even to walk the streets of town."

"So," Brian said, "no specifics. Thank you all the same."

"But—"

"Thank you!"

The man walked away, and Brian turned to the group. "This rumor of booby trapping is nothing to worry about. It's very much overblown."

"I don't care how blown it is," Dave said. "What was that guy talking about?"

Brian took a deep sigh. "It's too involved to go into right now. A few months back, the administrative council that oversees the South West Coast Path approved some re-routing of some sections to avoid coastal areas that have suffered erosion. It was all done in the name of public safety. But some of the landowners whose property was affected were upset, even though it is all perfectly legal. For no reason other than sheer spite, there's been talk of harassing walkers so they stay off the path, although claims of any actual instances have been pure speculation. Trust me that nobody will be in danger."

"We weren't told about this when we signed up!" Rachel said.

"It made the news back home," Ben said. "That is, I saw reports of it online."

"What do you mean by 'harassing'?" Jorge asked Brian.

"That young man certainly seemed to know what he was talking about," Luella added. "Why should we trust you?"

Brian faced her straight on. "You'll trust me because I am your guide and I am responsible for you. I would never put any of my groups in harm's way. We can discuss this further tomorrow morning, but for now, I suggest that you get some sleep and prepare for a full day of walking."

After bidding everyone good night, I climbed the stairs, thinking about the possibility of trail sabotage on the way up to my room. I knew about Britain's unique protection of walkers' rights, which essentially allows anyone to roam wherever they please, regardless of who owns the land. Yet I'd always wondered how happy the property owners were with that state of affairs. I wouldn't be wild about strangers taking an unexpected stroll through my yard.

I needed to hear Mike's voice. He answered my call quickly but sounded sleepy. He told me how easy it was—frighteningly so—to fall back into the workplace frame of mind, as if he hadn't just taken three months off. Even though he hadn't yet reported to work, he knew there'd be paperwork that had piled up in his absence. Of course, most of a coroner's work isn't planned—it depends on people dying. But when they do, their deaths need investigating as soon as possible.

"And then there's Randall," he said.

"Your brother? What about him?"

"Chase, you know I've mentioned he's not doing well. I checked with his caregiver today, and it appears that he's gone further downhill than I expected."

Mike had spoken of his brother, who lived several miles away in Dorset, a few times. Randall is a few years older than Mike, and even though he'd once been married, he lived by himself and had been showing signs of mild dementia. He and Mike had never been extremely close—Randall didn't entirely approve of Mike's gay "lifestyle"—and Mike never seemed overly concerned about him. Was that changing?

"I'm going to pay him a visit tomorrow," he said, and let the matter drop.

I waited for him to tell me how difficult it was to face a night alone for the first time in three months. When he didn't, I made the comment instead.

"It will be strange, you're right," he said.

Only strange? What about heartrending, depressing, lonely?

"I will miss you," I said. "I miss you already."

"And I miss you as well." He seemed to mean it. We traded "I love yous" and bid each other good night.

I was drifting into a bout of melancholy when I spied the small desk opposite the bed. I'd forgotten to write in my journal. It had become a practice of mine on these walks to note the day's events each night before retiring. I'd developed the habit in my years on the force—a means of recording impressions of seemingly innocuous events before they disappeared from my short-term memory. My journal wasn't a diary, although some might consider it the same thing.

I got out of bed and sat at the desk in front of the small notebook, pen in hand. There wasn't much to make note of. I scribbled down brief impressions of each member of the group, as well as the disturbing news about possible sabotage on the trail awaiting us.

I turned out the light, my mind on the beginning of the walk the following morning. Why was I feeling anxious?

Chapter 4

Monday, late morning,
South West Coast Path, Cornwall

Whether intended or not, the timing of the partial collapse of the bridge the next morning couldn't have been worse. Once the group reassembled on the east side of the ravine, each walker was dishing out theories about what caused the bridge to fall apart.

Jorge, who could have been killed if the bridge had collapsed completely, shrugged it off. "You need to be prepared for anything in the wild," he said, although I wouldn't have considered this stretch of the coastal path "wild."

"Well, I didn't expect anything like that on the first day," said Roy. "I was looking forward to a leisurely, safe walk."

Brian said, "That is what we'll have, I assure you."

"How do you know?" Ben snapped. "What was it that guy at dinner said last night? Someone has been setting up booby traps along the trail!"

"Just because the authorities re-routed a few parts of the trail?" Dave asked. "That doesn't sound right."

Expectedly, Ivy said, "Of course, it was booby-trapped! Someone has it in for us. I can tell."

"Ivy, for once please stop letting your imagination run away with you," her mother said. "Listen to our guide. If he says the trail is safe, I believe him."

"I'm inclined to agree with your daughter," said Luella. "Didn't you see what happened? I could have been killed. We all could have been killed."

Brian raised his hands. "Trust me on this. I wouldn't lead you along this path if there was even the slightest possibility of danger."

His calm yet forceful assertion quieted everyone down.

"Let's proceed," he continued. "In a few minutes, we'll reach Penberth Cove, where you can avail yourselves of toilet facilities and midmorning refreshments. After that, we'll continue on to Porthguarnon, where we'll eat our lunch at a small farmhouse."

We fell into line behind Brian along the trail, which remained level as it veered from the sea and ran through a patch of bracken before entering a field enclosed by a short stone wall.

As we climbed the ladder stile over the wall and descended into another field, Billie said to me, "What do you think, Chase? Was what happened to the bridge just an accident?"

I hesitated a moment before responding. "No, I don't think so. I took a close look at where it had broken, and it certainly looked as if someone had cleanly sawed through the wood. It wasn't a rough break, as you would expect if the bridge had become weak with age."

"That's what I was afraid of. Will we need to fear for our lives for the rest of this walk?"

"Brian saw the break too. He was right beside me. But I can understand why he doesn't want to alarm the others."

"It sounds as if most are alarmed anyway."

We crossed the field to another stile, and beyond that into a forest of beech and chestnut trees. A gentle breeze, bearing a faint scent of the sea, had a soothing effect. The jarring incident at the bridge lost some of its horror as the walkers fell into a nice, leisurely rhythm in the peaceful morning.

Few things in life are both fun and good for your physical health, but walking is one. It lifts you up spiritually and emotionally, gives your heart and lungs a workout, reduces cholesterol, improves circulation and bone density, reduces the risk of diabetes, and burns calories. It also can be done practically anywhere, and the only equipment you need is a good pair of shoes.

Walking is even more enjoyable (at least it is for me) when enjoying the company of fellow walkers and discovering new places. Too many of us view the world through the windshield of our car. It doesn't begin to compare with experiencing the world on foot. While walking, you're not enclosed in an artificial atmosphere. The movement forces you to confront real-world elements: the feel of sun and rain on your face, the sound of the wind riffling through tree branches, the fresh and invigorating scents of sea and forest. One also encounters animals. In England, that usually means benign ones like sheep and goats, although you must be careful with cattle.

Then there are people. Like animals, they come in all shapes, sizes, and temperaments. Most of those I encounter on my walks are friendly, but even the challenging ones can be fascinating, sometimes even more so. That could be due to my curious nature. Like Ivy, I always wonder what someone might be hiding. However, based on my experiences on previous walks, sometimes I look too deeply.

Other than the mishap at the bridge, the morning's walk had been a good introduction to Cornwall. We started the day at a classic Cornish locale, riding in the van to the far western tip of the county's peninsula, home of the spectacular open-air Minack Theatre, carved out of a gully atop a cliff into a rudimentary Greek-style stage and seating area. It was created in the 1930s but looks like something from ancient times. Unfortunately, no performance of *The Tempest* was scheduled that morning, so we continued east along the coast.

The van then took us up the coast to the east, near Treen, where we began walking in earnest. The group quickly proved to be capable and non-complaining walkers. We weren't scaling the Alps, but I've been with groups who have groused at much less.

That was when we came to the bridge crossing a small ravine.

Now we were taking a short detour off the trail to view a massive seventy-ton boulder perched on the edge of a small headland, a few hundred feet above the rocky beach below.

"This is known as Logan Rock," Brian said, as we gathered around the imposing chunk of granite. "For many years, it amazed people with its precariousness—even a child could push gently and it would rock. Then, in 1824, a young soldier gave it a strong push and sent it crashing down to the bottom of the bluff. There was quite an uproar about this, and a couple of blokes made a living guiding visitors down to the fallen rock."

"How did it get back up here?" Dave asked.

"The Admiralty dispatched lifting equipment it used for sunken ships," Brian said. "They were able to restore it to its original position, but they never did restore the delicate balance. However, some say it can still be rocked if you push hard enough."

Dave, who was standing the closest, placed both hands on the rock and began pushing. When it was clear he wasn't making any headway, he grunted, planted his feet firmly, and gave it everything he had. Still no movement.

"Let me try," Roy said. Dave moved aside reluctantly, and Roy stepped up, spitting on his palms and assuming the same stance as Dave. The biceps in his arm bulged as he pushed—he was a short, slender man, but muscular—but to no effect. He might as well have been trying to move a mountain.

This contest had evolved into a senseless macho standoff, with each man in the group feeling the need to prove his masculinity. I felt no such urge, however. "My turn now," Ben said, taking Roy's place. Instead of placing his palms against the large rock, he leaned his right shoulder against it, huffed and puffed several times, but to no avail.

"You can see that this is more easily said than done," our guide said. "Let's continue on our way."

"Hold on," Jorge said. "I haven't had a chance." He placed his hands on the rock and leaned toward it at a sharper angle.

"Careful now," Brian cautioned.

Jorge was the largest man in the group, and his strength was evident in the contours of his upper body. But nothing happened. He pushed harder, his face straining with the effort.

"Please don't pull anything, my darling!" Luella said.

Finally, the boulder shifted, although barely noticeably. Jorge stepped back to regain his breath and the rock moved back into place. It seemed like a lot of effort for not much payoff, but he beamed as if he'd just performed a Herculean feat. "How 'bout that, huh?"

"Now I know who to call the next time I need my piano moved," said Dave.

Luella gave Jorge an admiring smile and moved in to give him a congratulatory kiss.

We returned to the coastal path, seabirds darting above and the surf crashing loudly on the rocks around us. I noticed some were plugging their ears.

"Quite deafening, isn't it?" I shouted to Roy, walking beside me.

He laughed. "I love the sounds of nature! I was born deaf and didn't have my hearing restored until I was a teenager. Nowadays, I appreciate all the sounds in the world!"

I thought of how wonderful it must have been to hear for the first time. I wanted to ask Roy what it was like to finally discover music, but he'd walked too far ahead.

The path continued to hug the shore, but not close enough to cause worry about the trail giving way into the water. The morning's incident at the bridge had my senses on alert, however.

Behind me I heard Rachel ask Dave, "You play the piano?"

"A little jazz, a few standards," he said offhandedly. "It helps me relax."

"I saw a piano at the hotel. You'll have to play something for us."

"Nah," he said with a laugh. "I'm not that good. And this walking is plenty relaxing."

It didn't take us long to arrive at Penberth Cove, a broad crescent of rough, rocky sand bordered by stony cliffs. A few fishermen were preparing to go out in their boats, a reminder of the important role the sea played in the local economy.

We gathered on the beach near a stream that flowed from the hills. Fortunately, there was no bridge we needed to cross.

"You see that piece of equipment out there?" Brian said, pointing to a large, rusted assembly of iron spars and chains that looked like a relic from a bygone civilization. "That's an old capstan winch, from the nineteenth century. It was used to haul boats up from the beach. Today the fishermen use portable winches mounted on their trucks."

I shot a nervous glance at Jorge, fearing he might want to test his physical prowess again on the winch. But he looked disinterested and joined Luella and Ben as they followed Brian back up the hill on the other side of the cove.

"You know who he is, don't you?" asked Ivy, who had appeared at my side, in a coy, conspiratorial tone.

"Who?"

"Mr. Campos! You really don't recognize him?" She leaned close to me as she walked. "He's really Tom Wakefield!"

"Tom Wakefield? You mean the *Hawaii P.I.* guy? From the seventies?"

She nodded. "He's got everybody fooled with what he's done to his hair. But it's definitely him."

With her wild ideas and odd appearance—her glasses and disdainful countenance made her look like a mature woman packed into the lanky frame of a young girl—Ivy was definitely unlike any child I'd ever encountered. I hadn't seen a photo of Tom Wakefield in years, but I supposed he could now look something like Jorge. Yet many questions came to mind.

"Why would a celebrity be pretending to be someone else?" I asked. "And how do you know about Tom Wakefield? He was popular long before your time. I barely remember him myself."

"I've seen him on reruns. I keep up on things like that. Everybody has secrets. You'd be surprised the kind of stuff I find out online."

"I advise you not to believe everything you read online."

"Oh, of course, I don't. Just the stuff that's believable."

We reached a modest wooden farmhouse on the path leading to Pendeen, where tables had been set up beneath an oak tree. Brian directed us to the largest. Two older men sat a nearby table, drinking tall glasses of ale. One wearing a wool cap eyed our walking sticks and backpacks and said loud enough for us to hear, "Look what we have here, Walt. Another bunch of bloody trespassers!"

We uneasily took our places at the table. A large woman in an apron appeared with a smile. "Good day! Before I bring out your food, would you like drinks? We've got a very nice local bitter. It's light, but it has a proper punch."

That sounded perfect to me, and judging by the nods I saw, it met with the others' approval as well.

"Don't give it to 'em, Sal!" the man in the cap said. "They'll just piss it all out on my field."

The woman marched over to the two men. "I'll not have you harassing my guests, Lawrence Hancock. You'd best be on your way."

The man downed the rest of his beer, stood, and eyed our group angrily. "Bah! There are too many of you fools these days. Turning my land into a bleedin' pleasure park! Let's be off, Walt."

As they walked away, the woman turned back to us and managed a smile. "Don't mind old Larry. He's all bark and no bite, as they say. But he's been a downright bear ever since part of the coastal path was routed deeper into his property a few months back."

"Was that because of erosion on the coast?" I asked.

"Right you are. Dinna know if it's global warming or whatever, but some of the bluffs have been giving way. You can't blame the government for wanting to keep people safe. Of course, some of the landowners don't see it that way."

"Could this Lawrence guy be the one who booby-trapped the bridge?" Ben asked Brian.

"Booby-trapped a bridge?" Sal asked. "What are you talking about?"

Brian told her about the incident that morning near the Treen cliff. "It seemed very suspicious, as if the bridge had been tampered with."

Sal nodded. "It's true that there have been a few odd accidents that are hard to explain. Larry's not the only local landowner upset by the changes to the coastal path. He and some of the others have even formed their own protest group—Landowners United Against Unwanted Aggression. LUAU for short."

I had to stifle a laugh. Whoever came up with that acronym overshot the region of its relevance by about seven thousand miles.

"It's all a load of tosh," Sal said. "That lot might not like what's happening, but the law's the law."

"She's talking about the Countryside and Rights of Way Act," Brian said to the group. "We've had a right to roam in this country for hundreds of years, but it didn't become a proper law until the year 2000. It gave full protection to the network of footpaths and trails in the UK."

"So the government can just take someone's land and turn it into a public trail?" Dave asked. "That doesn't sound very fair."

"It's not as bad as it sounds," Brian replied. "Nearly all these paths had been around for ages, in one form or another, but were only loosely protected by the right to roam. Landowners have lived with them for generations with few problems. Most walkers are respectful of their privacy and take care not to be a nuisance, such as by not making too much noise or littering."

"Well, I certainly wouldn't want a bunch of strangers walking through my yard unannounced," Luella said.

"Of course not," Ben said. "They might see you without your makeup."

Luella flashed him her joking-but-not-really-joking grin. "Just keep it up, Ben. Remember—I can disinherit you at any time. Snip, snip!"

Chapter 5

Monday, afternoon,
South West Coast Path, Cornwall

As we prepared to return to the trail, Roy called out, "Jorge! You left behind your sunglasses!"

Jorge kept walking. I went up to him. "Did you hear Roy? You left your sunglasses behind on the table." Jorge thanked me and went back to get them.

"I wonder if he's got hearing problems," I said to Billie. She shrugged as she kneaded her left knee.

"How are you holding up?" I asked.

She managed a smile. "Not too bad, I think. The brace helps, but it's about as comfortable as a girdle."

"Please don't overdo it, kiddo. If your knee starts to feel iffy, ease off for a bit."

"Give me a break, Chase! I know how to take care of myself." She raised her leg a couple of times to prove her flexibility.

"Everyone ready?" Brian called out. Geared up, we positioned ourselves behind him and followed him across a road. On the other side, someone had posted a small sign:

HEDGEHOG AWARENESS WEEK

How could I be aware of hedgehogs when I'd never actually seen one? I knew they could be road hazards, akin to squirrels darting out into the middle of traffic, but I didn't know what problems (or benefits) they might cause on a walking path. My puzzlement was interrupted when we encountered an angled, five-step stile traversing a stone wall. Climbing could present a challenge to Billie's knee, yet she had managed to climb the earlier ones and scaled this stile admirably.

"How many of these things do we have to go over?" Ben asked. From what I could assess, he was the least fit in our group; he definitely could shed a few pounds.

"Stiles are unavoidable when walking English country trails," Brian said. "But trust me. They make it easier than scaling the walls without them."

As we crossed another field, I marveled at how the permeability of English property lines had given rise to a fascinating suite of walking solutions, all dedicated to getting past walls and fences. There are step stiles and ladder stiles and squeeze stiles, as well as countless bridle gates, pedestrian gates, and kissing gates, small enclosures with a hinged gate that allows walkers to pass through while keeping livestock out (the gate "kisses" the enclosure on either side, rather than being securely latched).

"There's nothing like a brisk walk to get the old heart pumping, is there?" said Jorge from behind me.

I slowed so we could walk side by side. I snuck a look at him as he strutted beside me. Could he actually be Tom Wakefield? I struggled to remember what the actor looked like. It had been years since I'd seen him in anything.

Jorge turned back and called to his wife, "Keeping up, my dear?"

"You're walking too fast!" said Luella, several steps behind him.

He chuckled and said to me, "Dear lady, isn't she? What

a blessing she's been in my life. But she's a delicate thing. Has always been pampered. Needs toughening up."

"How long have you two been married?"

He thought a moment. "Four . . . no, five months. Her dear son introduced us. Now he's my son as well! Isn't life surprising?"

"Had you been married before?"

"Never! It always seemed too confining. But at some point, you need stability and consistency in your life, don't you think? What about you? Do you have a little lady at home?"

Okay, here we go. Again, I needed to come out to someone who presumed I was straight. Even though I'd done that a hundred times, it always was uncomfortable.

"No, I have a little *man* at home. A grown one, actually. He's a Brit."

Jorge smiled at me. "Good for you! I wouldn't have taken you for a . . . what are the letters they use nowadays? LBTQ?"

"Close enough," I said. "Mike and I have become very good at blending in and looking like everyone else." I hoped Jorge could sense the sarcasm in my remark.

We reached the stone wall on the other side of the field, and another stile. Not far away, a workman was repairing a damaged section of the wall. Brian led us over to watch.

"Notice how he uses no cement or bonding material," our guide said. "These workmen are true artisans. They know how to fit the stones together for maximum strength and durability."

The man gave a laugh as he tapped a stone into place. "We'll see how true that is in about fifty years. That's how long this stretch held up before last month's storm."

Ben struggled to lift one of the loose stones piled beside the workman. "Holy crap, this is heavy!"

This was another challenge that proved irresistible for

Jorge, who bent and picked up two stones, one easily with each hand. It made me wonder why he needed to continually prove his masculinity.

"He sure likes to show off, doesn't he?" Rachel asked Ben.

"That's just his old theatrical training coming out," Ben said. "He's a bit of a ham."

Theatrical training? Why would an airline pilot need that? As much as I hated to consider it, perhaps Ivy was onto something.

Dave snapped a photo of Roy holding one of the wall stones, and we moved on again, following the path as it meandered near the coastline, along the top of a bluff, and then inland again. Because most of it passed through private land, I stayed alert for any potential hazards. However, the terrain was pastoral and seemingly harmless, with many plots of vegetables and corridors of hedgerows.

As the trail traced the edge of a small forest, I fell into the familiar, calming reverie that often overcame me on my English walks. When I tell people back home that I'm passionate about walking in England, they picture the English countryside of film and fiction. Windswept hills. Lush valleys, cozy pubs in tiny stone villages. An abbey here, a castle there. Roughly a zillion sheep.

The truth is . . . England really is like that. It is James Herriot country. It is *Wuthering Heights* country. In the south of Cornwall, it is definitely Daphne du Maurier (as well as *Poldark*) country. All lazy becks and misty woodlands and drystone walls.

We passed through a shady oak plantation, and I looked around at my fellow walkers. They were mixing well, pairing with someone other than their usual partner. Ben and Roy were walking side by side, and ahead of them, Brian walked alongside Luella at the front of the pack. Behind me, Dave and Rachel were engaged in a pleasant conversation, both laughing occasionally. I wondered where Ivy had gone to—she was always at her mother's side—when I discovered her right beside me. Billie was not far behind her.

We walked in silence for a few moments before Ivy asked, "Are you mad that I Googled you?"

"I have no secrets, but I prefer to be the one who tells people about my past."

"Sorry," she said. "But I remember the news of the Scorpio killer when I was just a kid. And I'm walking with the guy who caught him!"

"My team assisted in capturing the man," I reminded her. "It wasn't just me."

"From what I saw online, it didn't sound like that to me. It just goes to prove what I was saying . . . you never know what people are hiding." She paused and added, "It's like that man who's walking with my mother."

"You mean Dave?"

"He says he's a travel writer, but I don't believe it for a second. Why doesn't he take notes on anything? And he shoots photos with his phone, not with a real camera."

I found that odd myself. "Everyone has their own way of working," I said. Turning to her, I asked, "Why are you so suspicious of people?"

"You need to be. I learned a long time ago that people lie all the time."

I wondered what had happened to Ivy to give her such a cynical view of the world so early in her life. Maybe she was simply a kid with an overactive imagination, as her mother said. Or maybe it was something worse.

The path veered back toward the bluffs lining the shore. Out at sea, several large rocks rose above the surface of the water, scattered as if the gods had dropped them. I remembered from a guidebook they were known as "gazells." I was enjoying the calming sounds of the water and the birds when a guitar and bass intro made me jump.

"Sorry!" Ivy said, pulling out her phone. "I forgot to

turn this stupid thing off." She quickly scanned the small screen, turned off the sound, and put it back in her pocket. "Taylor Swift. 'Willow.' One of my favorite songs."

We rounded a bend hidden behind a stand of oaks and caught sight of a group of men wearing bright yellow, official-looking slickers ahead. Not far away was an emergency vehicle with flashing lights.

"What's going on up there?" Billie asked.

"It doesn't look good," I said. As we neared the group, their slickers identified them as police. We gathered behind Brian as he asked one of the men what had happened.

"A section of the cliff gave way," the man said, nodding before him. "Unfortunately, a woman was standing on it at the time."

Behind him, two men were hoisting a stretcher up over the lip of the bluff. It was trussed with ropes and held a covered form that was unmistakably a human body. Our group watched in a stunned hush as the shrouded corpse was taken up the trail toward a waiting van.

"Oh my God, that could have been me!" Luella wailed.

"It could have been all of us," Ben said.

"I didn't sign up for a death march!" Roy fumed.

"It's like a video game!" Ivy said. "How cool!"

"I'm feeling faint," said Rachel. Dave moved forward and held her.

"What do you say now?" Ben said to Brian. "Do you still think this walk of yours is safe?"

"Please, everyone, remain calm!" Brian announced in his most authoritarian voice, which wasn't quite authoritarian enough. He asked the policeman, "Do you think this woman's death could have been planned?"

"Planned?" the man replied. "You mean, was the top of the cliff tampered with so that it gave way? I would have to say that is highly unlikely. Erosion is very common along here, but we almost always detect it and flag it—or repair it—before anything like this happens. You can see that the unstable area up there is blocked by ropes. That woman shouldn't have ventured beyond them."

"You see?" Brian said to us. "This woman wasn't even on the trail!"

"However," the policeman continued, "there have been sections of this trail, untouched by erosion, that have been reported to have been tampered with. This doesn't look to be anything such as that. Nevertheless, this incident will, of course, need to be reported . . . and investigated."

"Is it safe for my group to pass through?" Brian asked.

"As long as you keep to the trail and stay away from the roped-off sections, certainly," the policeman replied.

"Well, I'm sure as hell not going to walk any farther," Luella said.

Jorge put his hand on her shoulder. "What else can we do, Lulu? It would take us hours to go back to where we started. Trust me. I'll keep you safe."

"I'm with my mother on this one," Ben said. "It's too dangerous to go on."

Jorge spun to face him. "Grow a pair, boy! Take a chance for once in your life."

Ben stepped up to Jorge. "How dare you talk to me like that!"

"Calm down," I said. "I know something about coastal erosion. It's a completely normal phenomenon that happens all over the world. The Brits are good at conducting geological surveys to ensure trails here are safe. That's why this path has been re-routed at certain points, with the hazardous areas clearly marked. As long as we don't go beyond any ropes or warning signs, we should be safe."

The group regarded me in silence, absorbing my words. I'd basically restated what Brian and the policeman had just said, but I felt additional reassurance was needed.

"Chase is right," Brian said. "We need to move on and meet the van to take us back to the hotel."

In single file, we carefully followed Brian along the inside edge of the path. As we passed the spot where the woman had fallen, I noticed that the section of the cliff that had given way was indeed several yards beyond the rope barrier. She must have stepped off the path to get a closer look at the sea.

"Too bad about what happened, but this will really spice up my article!" said Dave, walking behind me.

"Isn't your article supposed to encourage people to come walking in England?" asked Rachel, walking beside him.

Dave paused before replying. "Well, sure. But people love adventure. A little scent of danger can be irresistible."

"Not to me," Rachel said. "If one more scare happens, I'm calling it quits."

"Nothing will happen. Brian and Chase are right. We'll be safe from now on. And I'll stay close to you just in case we're not."

I turned to see Rachel give Dave a grudging smile. Ivy was walking, stone-faced, behind them.

The trail dipped down a small slope to a beck that we easily crossed, stepping over two large, flat stones. Atop the slope on the other side was a gate, but the path veered toward a gap in the wall instead. We walked through and found ourselves on a bridle way.

"So, Chase, what attracts you most about walking over here?"

I'd forgotten that Dave was still beside me. Rachel and Ivy were now a distance behind us.

"Is this an interview for your article?" I asked with a smile. "Should you be recording this on your phone or something?"

"I don't work that way. I've got pretty good recall. I'm

not writing that kind of story anyway. There won't be any actual quotes."

His question was a familiar one to me, and I gave him my standard answer about the appeal of English country walking—the distinctive terrain, vegetation, and climate; the connection to history and literature; the picturesque villages; the plentiful pubs and intoxicating ales.

"You meet interesting people also, I bet. Have you ever become involved with any of your fellow walkers?"

This was such an unexpected question that I blurted out a laugh. "What, you mean romantically? Not with a fellow walker, no. But I am currently . . . seeing someone I met on one of my walks over here."

"I'm glad. This can be very romantic, walking with someone in such a beautiful setting."

"Am I detecting an attraction to the comely Mrs. Scattergood?"

He nodded and gave a small laugh. "She's really something, isn't she?"

Rachel was an attractive young woman, certainly, but she'd seemed on edge most of the time. Perhaps Dave found that alluring. "Does that story her daughter told us at dinner trouble you?" I asked. "The one about her and her mother coming over here to get away from her husband?"

Dave considered my question. "It sounds melodramatic, but I've chatted with Rachel, and there is some truth to it. She says that Craig—that's her husband—has a very mercurial temper, and this divorce business has really shaken him up. I don't think she actually believes he will do her or Ivy any harm, but she thought it was a good idea to make herself scarce for a while, and she's always wanted to bring her daughter over to England."

"Why?"

"They have relatives here, I think. That, and she's always been fascinated by British history."

That was a typical motive for Americans visiting England. I recalled my first trip many years before, dazzled by visiting in real life places I had only read about in history books. "What about you? Why are you writing an article about English walks?"

I was waiting for a reply when we rounded a bend and were confronted with the sight of a short, squat, white lighthouse at the bottom of a short path to our right, the waters of the Channel beyond it.

"Wow!" Dave said. "I need to get a photo of that." He pulled out his phone and paused to take a couple of shots. When we resumed walking, he fell back to walk beside Rachel.

He never answered my question.

Chapter 6

Monday, evening,
St. Mawes, Cornwall

The rest of the afternoon's walk was free of danger, real or imagined. After the van deposited us back at our hotel, Billie and I were ready to retreat to our rooms for a rest before dinner. As we paused before her door, she said, "I hate to say it, Chase, but I'm feeling the same nagging feelings as on our previous walks."

I tilted my head. "Nagging feelings? You mean you think someone's about to be killed?"

"I'm sure I'm just being overly anxious. But there was that bridge collapse this morning, and the incident on the trail this afternoon. I don't want to look for things to worry about, but in light of what happened on our last two walks, how can you blame me?"

"I don't blame you, kiddo. But, other than hazards on the trail, are you picking up any vibes from our fellow walkers?" Billie could sometimes be more intuitive than me.

She thought a moment. "I haven't picked up on anything directly. Yet there's something . . . something I may have heard or seen, or even just sensed. Those incidents on the trail are unusual, you must admit. I'm starting to think our excursions are cursed."

I put my arm around her. "There's another way of looking at it. We might be drawn to such crimes because we're so good at figuring out who committed them."

"Now, there's an irrational rationalization if I ever heard one! Anyway, right now I'm drawn to my bed for a quick nap."

Billie wasn't given to unsubstantiated premonitions. I knew her well enough to believe that if she was concerned about something, there was a plausible reason. The trick was not to let our imaginations get the best of us. I wished her a pleasant nap and went upstairs to my room.

Before taking my own nap, I texted Mike to report we had completed our first day's walk. I purposely left out telling him about the collapse of the bridge and the woman's death on the trail. I was afraid he might insist I bail on the walk and head directly to Exeter.

Or perhaps I was afraid he wouldn't insist.

He immediately texted me back.

Glad to hear it. Good day here too. Feels nice being home again and with my old workmates.

That wasn't what I needed to hear. It wasn't the first time Mike had spoken of returning "home" and to his friends, as if I had kidnapped him and taken him away from his real life. The devil on my right shoulder whispered in my ear. *Why can't you be his "home" now? Why can't he feel "nice" about being with you?*

The angel on my left shoulder assumed a disapproving grin. *Of course, Mike is going to miss the only place he's ever known. It's natural that he's going to want to be with people who've worked beside him and supported him.*

That angel had a point. Although I was looking forward to spending three months with Mike in Devon, I'd probably start feeling homesick pretty quickly myself. The longest I'd ever been away from California before this was a little more than two weeks, and even that had felt excessive.

Give it time, my left-shoulder angel said.

Don't get your hopes up, said the devil on my right.

Dinner that night was at a local gastropub, the Sea House, strategically situated at the forefront of St. Mawes harbor. The establishment's whitewashed stone walls, shining in the brilliant sunset, made it stand out like a beacon in the night. Gulls squawked and dipped before us, and a soft, salty breeze blew crisp and cool against our faces. Everyone wore casual attire (loose, cotton, short-sleeved shirts, lightweight pants) except for Luella, looking somewhat absurd in a rolled tweed jacket and a bright orange cotton dress. It couldn't have been her fashion sense that had attracted Jorge's eye, could it?

"I've heard good things about this place from the hotel staff," Roy said as we entered.

"I don't think they serve barbecue here," I warned jokingly.

It took him a moment to get the joke. "Oh! No, I like all kinds of foods. I'm something of a gastronomic slut, as one of my business partners calls me. I'll eat practically anything! My view is that travel is mostly about food."

We were shown to a long and high, scrubbed wooden table brightened with stems of yellow flowers in small glass pitchers. Windows evenly spaced along the walls provided a different view of the harbor, more expansive than the one we'd enjoyed the previous evening. That the pub was dog-friendly was evident by the hounds stretched out beneath other tables. We took our places on the high stools around ours.

Brian beamed at everyone after they were seated. "We can start with a round of drinks and enjoy the ambiance. Isn't this a pleasant room?"

Looking around, Rachel said, "I've never seen such white walls."

"They're not white," Ben said.

"They're not?"

"Well, yes, they're white, but there are about a million shades of white. To me they look somewhere between swans-down white and egret white."

Luella emitted a subtle, patronizing laugh. "Don't flaunt your nerdiness, Benjy. It only makes you look ridiculous."

"Yes, you would know about ridiculous," Ben said. "Especially wearing that outfit."

His mother flashed another of her withering smiles and held up two fingers. "Snip, snip, Benjy. Snip, snip!"

Please, I prayed, someone rescue us from this passive-aggressiveness. Our savior turned out to be Ivy, of all people.

"What are 'starters'?" she asked, looking at her menu.

Brian seized the opportunity to explain that "starters," to us uninformed Americans, meant the first course of the meal. In the US, that usually means salad or soup, but on the menu that evening were scallops with garlic bread-crumb topping, as well as a salad.

Ivy's question directed everyone's attention to the menu. It was a fairly standard pub selection—fish and chips were the specialty—yet it also featured seafood, such as locally smoked salmon, oysters, roasted shellfish, and hake on spiced dahl with cauliflower pakoras.

"What is dahl?" Billie asked. "And what are pakoras?"

"Dahl is an Indian lentil," said Roy. "And pakoras are battered vegetables with a strong curry flavor. I had them once in Delhi and certainly didn't expect to find them in Cornwall. What a treat!"

Maybe I was being overly analytical, but how did a restaurant owner from Memphis have such a working knowledge of Indian cuisine? There was more to Roy than met the eye.

"Can I have that?" Ivy asked her mother.

"It sounds too spicy, and we don't know what's in the batter," Rachel replied. "You'd better stick with one of the fish dishes."

Ivy gave an exasperated sigh. I wondered why Rachel didn't want her daughter to eat spicy food.

"I'm going to have a hamburger," Ben said.

"A hamburger?" Jorge exclaimed. "You can have that anywhere! You're in a seaside town, Benjamin—eat some fish!"

"It's what I want," Ben said.

"How common," his mother said.

"Just don't call it a 'hamburger,'" Brian counseled. "It says 'burger' on the menu, and that's how it should be ordered. Otherwise, they'll think—"

"They'll think you're a common American, just as I said," Luella repeated.

Fortunately, the server arrived at that moment to take our drink and food orders. When she left, Dave asked Brian if he'd learned anything further about the woman who had died on the trail that afternoon.

"It seems she got too close to the edge of the bluff," Brian said, confirming what we already had heard. "That's never a good idea. If she had stayed on the path, she would have been fine."

"Some people are too stupid for their own good," Luella said.

"I had a further chat with the police in Truro," Brian said. "It's true that a few of the local landowners, including that man whom we encountered at lunch, have been upset over the South West Coast Path incurring on their property. But other than boastful threats, there's been no evidence that they've done anything that's resulted in a walker being injured."

And yet there was the cleanly severed plank of the bridge I'd seen that morning. That seemed a clear hazard to me, but I didn't want to bring it up and get the others alarmed all over again.

"There's a first time for everything," Roy said. "I didn't like the way that fellow at lunch was threatening us."

"Neither did I," Rachel said. "Now I'll need to be on my guard every single second we're on the trail. That's not very relaxing."

"Mom, you're such a wuss," Ivy said.

"I assure you, such worry won't be necessary," Brian added. He must be growing tired of needing to provide these reassurances.

Dave, seated beside Rachel, reached his arm out and placed it on the back of her chair. "Don't forget there are some pretty strong men in our group. I'll look out for you."

She smiled at him. I caught Ivy rolling her eyes.

"That's very chauvinistic," Luella said. "We women are capable of looking after ourselves, you know."

"You didn't rescue your husband when the bridge collapsed," Ivy said. "If you're so 'capable,' why didn't you do anything?"

Luella's eyes flared. "Why, you're certainly a nervy little thing, aren't you? Are you trying to stir up trouble?"

"I can look after my daughter, thank you," said Rachel. Turning to Ivy, she said, "She's right, though. You're being awfully rude. Apologize to Mrs. Campos."

Ivy muttered a barely audible "Sorry." I was preparing myself for more fireworks when our starters arrived. This calmed everyone, and they focused on eating. Brian used the time to describe what we would see on the following day, beginning with a morning walk on the causeway out to the castle island of St. Michael's Mount and proceeding up the coast to the town of Porthleven.

I looked around the table as he spoke. Without intending it, I had one of my "deep dive" moments, when time slows to a crawl. These first began happening when I was a child, and I never could predict when they would occur.

Beside me, Ivy was dividing her attention between Brian and the screen of her phone on the table before her. More internet dirt? Rachel was gazing appreciatively at Dave. Ben's eyes were cast down to the table, but he was intermittently speaking with Jorge and drumming his fingers nervously on the table. Roy's eyes were traveling around, as mine were, but came to rest on Ben and Jorge. Luella was examining the utensils in her place setting. Billie was the only one who seemed to be totally focused on Brian, who assured us the next day would be full of visits to charming coves, windswept beaches, and majestic sea views.

Luella put down the knife she'd been admiring. "But how will you make sure we won't be attacked? If anything happens to me on this walk, I promise I'll turn my lawyers loose on you."

"Lulu, it isn't necessary to talk about lawsuits," Jorge said, in the kind of patient tone one uses with a child. "Be reasonable."

"Reasonable?" Ben said with a laugh. "*Mother*?"

Brian's amiable smile had melted, possibly because of the suggestion of litigation. In an icy tone, he said, "As I keep repeating, there's no reason at all for any of you to feel unsafe. But if you do, you're more than welcome to leave."

"No one is leaving," Jorge said, giving his wife a stern look.

Our main courses arrived. Like most of the group, I'd ordered the fish and chips—it was a tourist favorite, of course, but as it was the specialty of the house, I figured it might be a notch above the standard version served in most British establishments catering to travelers. Even before taking a bite, I could see that it was: the plaice filets were large and lightly fried to a golden crispness, and the fries looked perfect—also lightly fried and not drowning in oil.

At one point, Rachel extracted an ornate pillbox from her purse and swallowed two small pills with water. "This food is great, but it's so rich. I need to take something to calm down my stomach."

"You need to have the constitution of a Brit," Brian said. "We put up with all sorts of unusual foods, but we're weaned on them. Our systems adapt."

Mike had said the same thing to me. I'd warned him about the spiciness of Southern California cuisine—the confluence of Mexican chili culture and Pan-Pacific cuisine, their flavors often ramped up with unique spices. They frequently sent me racing for the antacid bottle. Yet I'd never had that problem in England.

Luella reached over, picked up Rachel's pillbox, and studied its intricate design. "How charming. What is it? Moroccan? Peruvian?"

"Nordstrom," Rachel replied.

"Mother, put that down," Ben said.

Luella flashed a look of mock astonishment. "What do you think I'm going to do, steal it?" She placed the pillbox back on the table and pushed it toward Rachel.

"This meal was fantastic," Dave said. "But then, I'm used to looking at food as an adventure. You need to explore everything. Don't believe everything you hear."

"You mean like you being a travel writer?" Ivy asked.

Dave's smile faded as Ivy's question sunk in. "What do you mean?"

"Enough of your fantasies," Rachel said to her daughter. "Why are you picking on Dave?"

Ivy assumed a smug smile and only said, "I know what I know."

The desserts arrived—sticky walnut tarts and baked lavender custard—which prompted a flurry of oohs and aahs. By the time we were finished, the rest of the pub had emptied, and most of our energy had waned. Brian stood and reminded us to assemble in the hotel foyer at nine the following morning. We all stood as well, except for Luella. Her head was bowed, and she appeared to be sleeping.

"Lulu?" Jorge asked. He touched her shoulder. "Darling?"

I froze, alert at seeing someone not responding to stimulus. Luella's eyes slowly batted open, and she raised her head. "Oh, my. I'm so sorry. I must have drifted off."

"Let's get you to bed, darling," Jorge said, as he helped her to her feet.

As we filed out of the pub, Rachel came up to Billie. "I adore your sweater, Miss Mondreau!"

Uh-oh. One mention of her sweater and Billie was off and running with details. "Why, thank you!" she said.

Rachel fingered a sleeve. "What is that pattern?"

"They're choughs," Billie replied, "the blackbirds that, to some, are the symbol of Cornwall. I actually wanted to pay tribute to the distinctive Cornish food like pasties and fairings, but those don't translate well to knitted patterns. So I had to settle for a bird."

Rachel looked taken aback, not expecting such a thorough explanation. She nodded politely and walked toward Dave, but Billie trailed after her to continue the discussion.

In Billie's absence, Ivy appeared at my side.

"What did you think of the dinner tonight, Mr. Chase?" she asked.

This was an unusual line of questioning. "I thought the fish and chips were delicious. Didn't you?"

"I don't mean the food. I mean the conversation. Which of them do you think is a killer?"

"You think one of our group is a murderer?"

"Why not? It's like I said. Everybody's got secrets. It's a good thing there's Google, so you can find out a lot about them."

I didn't like where this was going. "Who have you been Googling now?"

"Everyone! It's crazy what you can find out. That's where I learned that Tom Wakefield hasn't been seen for weeks, and that you captured the Scorpio killer."

"Now, I've explained that—"

"That guy Dave? His story is totally bogus. I can't find him on Google at all. Extremely weird for a so-called writer. And that Luella woman? I got nervous when she was fingering my mom's pillbox, so I checked her out. Do you know she's been arrested twice for shoplifting?"

"You found that on Google?"

"They don't share police records, but I found news reports. It seems she's a big shot in Florida, so it made headlines. Small headlines, maybe, but still headlines."

I grasped her shoulders. "Take my advice. Regardless of what you find on Google, don't mention it while you're on this walk. Everyone's here to have a good time. They don't want to be put on the defensive."

"Sure, I get it. But information is like money. Sometimes you can use it to get what you want."

This girl was definitely a piece of work. "Are you talking about bribery? Blackmail?"

"Course not. That's against the law, isn't it? Even over here? No, I mean . . . oh, what is the word I heard on TV the other day . . . *leverage*. Something you can use against someone who is using something against you."

I resisted the temptation to lecture Ivy as I might my own daughter, if I had one. That was her mother's job. All I could say was, "You want my advice? Knock off all this detective stuff. Enjoy the walk. Learn something about Cornwall and not who other people may or may not be."

She gave me a sly smile. "Why not do both?" she said, and walked off.

Back in my room, after brushing my teeth and washing my face, I dug out my journal and wrote down the events of the day, including the death on the trail, the possibility of landowner subterfuge over the incursion of the South West Coast Path on their property, the reactions of the group. Did it all add up to anything? Despite the imaginings of a fantasy-driven child such as Ivy, and the rumblings of Billie's intuition, I wasn't ready to surrender to doom and gloom.

But I needed to hear Mike's voice; his warm British-clipped tones did so much to soothe me. He answered my call immediately, but didn't seem as perky as usual. I asked him how he was doing.

"It's been a trying day, reacclimating myself and all," he said. "I went to see Randall, and he's not doing well at all. He forgot I'd been away for months. He believed we'd just seen each other last weekend."

"So, his dementia's getting worse?"

"I'm afraid so, although he hasn't been officially diagnosed yet. It's all happened so suddenly. He was in fairly good shape when I left for the States. Anyway, I need to take him to a clinic within the next few days."

"I'm so sorry, Mike." My mother had memory issues in her final years, and it's not an easy thing to witness.

"I'll get through it," he said with resignation.

"I'm here for you as well, you know."

"And that makes a big difference." He asked how the rest of my day went, and again I didn't divulge any of the mishaps. I confessed that the group was a very mixed assortment, difficult to figure out.

"Isn't that true of most people?" he asked.

"To an extent, I suppose. Maybe it's because we're all strangers, meeting up in a strange land. It makes some people bond together and others become more suspicious."

"Then shut out the negative ones and focus on the countryside. That part of Cornwall is remarkably beautiful."

Yes, I wanted to say—with remarkably unstable coastal paths. Instead, I said, "I'm sure I'll enjoy the week, But what I'm really looking forward to is spending time with you here on your home turf."

A pause. "Are you really?"

"Why wouldn't I be? I'll be with my two loves. You and England."

Another pause. "I hope you're being honest with me, Chase. I loved being with you in America, but I'm afraid I don't love America itself."

"You were in California," I reminded. "Some would say there's a difference."

"Whatever the difference, it made me realize how much England is a part of me. I don't think I could abandon it."

"I'm not asking you to abandon it," I said. "But if we're going to have any hope of continuing on together, we need to find a compromise."

"What about you? You love England, I know you do. Would it be that much of a sacrifice to move here full-time?"

We'd had variants on this discussion many times over

the past three months. My response had always been that, despite my anglophilia, I'd been an American for sixty-seven years and was perhaps past the point where I was willing to give that up.

And yet I hadn't figured on Mike entering my life.

I hadn't figured on falling in love.

Chapter 7

Tuesday, morning,
St. Mawes, Cornwall

Boats were heading out of the harbor on their morning run when I entered the breakfast room. Billie was already seated—no surprise; she's an early riser—nibbling on a breakfast pastry at a table by the window. As far as I could tell, the pattern on her sweater was . . . no, that couldn't be right. Pirates with eye patches? I filled my plate a tad too abundantly from the breakfast buffet. I couldn't resist the thick rashers of bacon and poached eggs.

Billie smiled and took a deep breath as I joined her. "Do you smell the sea air?" she said.

"A little. The smell of bacon is overpowering it. Your sweater this morning is, dare I say, provocative."

"Pirates! What else could I wear in Cornwall?"

"Did they really have those kinds of pirates here?"

"Who knows? So I exaggerate. You guessed it right off."

"You're right, as always. So . . . are you looking forward to today's walk?"

"You bet!" she said. "This morning we're walking to St. Michael's Mount. I've always wanted to go there—

it has so much literary heritage. Do you remember your Milton?"

I paused to think. "Berle?"

Billie raised an eyebrow. "*John* Milton, dummy. He based one of his most famous poems, *Lycidas*, there." She looked out the window toward the sea.

Look homeward Angel now, and melt with ruth;
And, O ye dolphins, waft the hapless youth.

I took a pensive sip of coffee, considering the challenges of having a librarian friend. "Sounds Greek to me. What does it mean?"

Billie turned back. "Basically, it's Milton complaining how his good friend Lycidas drowned and none of the gods or muses did anything to stop it. It's really about the meaning of life and death."

"And what conclusion did he reach?"

"Unclear," she said as she pasted butter on her breakfast roll. "As far as I can tell, either you wait for death to provide your happiness or make the most of your time on earth."

"Earth time sounds like the winner to me."

The others began arriving. Rachel walked in, trailed by a sullen-looking Ivy, clad in a jarring combination of a Goth-like black top and walking pants. They began arguing about the breakfast selections.

"Can't I have bacon? And one of those croissants?" Ivy whined.

"You had bacon the other day, and that's enough for this week," Rachel said. "Have some of the granola and skim milk."

Grumbling, Ivy went to the cereal selections. Rachel looked at us. "Ivy's diabetic. It's always a battle to keep her eating properly."

Dave walked in, followed soon by Roy, who scanned the line of breakfast items, sometimes leaning down, his face inches away from the food, as if he were studying for mold. I hoped eventually he would make his selection.

"He's a nut about food, isn't he?" Billie said to me as we watched Roy. "I can see why he owns a restaurant."

Jorge and Ben entered, in the middle of what seemed to be a friendly conversation, as Jorge was smiling.

Brian followed, did a quick look at the group, and saw that Luella was missing. "Where's your wife, Jorge?" he asked.

At that moment, Luella appeared from behind him, saying, "Very sorry. I overslept." One glance offered another possible reason for her delay: she looked as if she had taken hours to prepare herself. Her face was perfectly made up, and her outfit—a walking coat that looked like a bright red toreador's jacket—seemed as if something chosen for a fashion photo shoot.

"Good God, Mother," Ben said. "What is that color? Panic button red?"

Luella flashed one of her withering smiles. "Very cute, Benjamin. You may know something about color, but you know nothing about fashion."

"We're going on a walk today," Ben said, "Not a promotional event for one of your shady charities."

Luella speared a melon wedge and held it up to examine it before putting it on her plate. Without looking at her son, she said, "Don't be so tiresome in the morning, Benjamin. Save that for later when I have the energy to strike you."

"You're being mean again, Lulu," Jorge scolded.

She gave him a look of mock anguish. "I know, darling. Aren't I terrible? You'll just need to spank me."

They carried their food to their table. Billie and I traded

glances. "There's only so much of that I can take," she whispered.

By the time everyone had finished their breakfast and gathered outside by the van, the group was in good spirits. The morning was bright and the sea air crisp and invigorating. Brian reminded us that we were headed for St. Michael's Mount, approximately five miles to the south. Once we were safely seated in the van, he swung into his guide mode and told us about the site we were about to visit.

"The island has an astonishing history dating back to medieval times. St. Michael's Mount was originally known as Ictis to Greek explorers in the first century. The castle was constructed in the fifteenth century to house a Benedictine priory established in the thirteenth century. Years later, in 1645, during the English Civil War, it gained its St. Michael's Mount moniker and was one of the last royalist strongholds. It is the 'daughter-house' of the famous, much larger Mont-Saint-Michel in France."

By the time he finished his spiel, the van pulled into the car park, ready for the island. The morning was clear, and the castle loomed impressively in the distance, rising like something out of a fairy tale. We stepped out, suited up with our backpacks, picked up our walking sticks, and began following Brian up the broad cobblestone causeway to the island. He explained that it was only walkable at high tide.

"The tide turns in about three hours," he said. "So we must get back before it's impassable."

The rocky path before us, lined by large strands of seaweed, looked like the yellow brick road leading to the Emerald City. The scene inspired within me the kind of awe I often get when walking in spectacular environments. Awe, it is said, activates our vagus nerve, that big bundle of nerves at the top of the spinal cord. It can come about by pausing and noticing the world around us, or experiencing a great work of art.

Billie and I fell into stride, with me walking a few paces before her. Roy was behind us, stopping momentarily to pick up a stone from the nearby water. "Look at this," he said, showing us a cobalt-blue rock. "I like to find interesting stones as reminders of my travels." He slipped it into a pocket of his backpack.

Soon Ben was at my side, matching me step for step.

"Beautiful day, isn't it?" I said. "Look at that blue sky."

Ben looked up. "Blue has the most beautiful color range. There's robin's egg and cobalt, azure and indigo. I would call this . . . Cornwall cyan."

That didn't sound like a prizewinner to me, but I didn't comment. I was thinking more about his odd family. "I noticed your mother dozed off at dinner last night. Does she do that often?"

The question didn't faze him. "All the time. I told her that it's probably narcolepsy, but she refuses to see a doctor about it. She usually only does it after she's eaten. I don't think it's anything to worry about."

"It could be a symptom of something more serious."

"Don't get my hopes up."

This wasn't a comment a devoted son would make. "Why such animosity between you and your mother?"

We walked several paces before Ben answered. "That's a long story and one I share only with my therapist. Let's just say that I'm a constant disappointment to her."

The only response I could come up with was, "Parents often hold their kids to an impossibly high standard." This from a man who never had kids.

"No, that's not it," he said. "She's a mess. Been pampered all her life. She thinks she deserves better treatment than everyone else. When she doesn't get it, she pouts, she fumes, she threatens to sue."

"Yes, I noticed that last night also. Does she do that often?"

Ben gave a huff of a laugh. "Dear Mother must have about ten lawsuits in progress as we speak. None of them will go anywhere, but she keeps a lot of lawyers happy."

I let him walk ahead as Billie joined me.

"Did you hear any of that?" I asked.

"I may be getting on in years, Chase, but I'm not deaf. So what if Ben has mother issues? We know that already. Some men never get over them."

I didn't say that that's what psychoanalysts are for.

As we grew closer to the island, Brian told us of the legendary giant Cormoran, a tyrant of a man who was said to have lived in the island's forest. When the locals finally had enough of him, they killed him and buried him in a pit. As we passed through the walls circling the village at the foot of the castle, Brian showed us a heart-shaped rock set into the path, rumored to be where Cormoran's heart is buried. He told us that, if we stood on the rock, we could hear the giant's heartbeat.

Of course, we all tried this out. Any heartbeats we may have heard, however, were probably in our imaginations.

As we passed through the small island village, a collection of holiday apartments and tourist shops, a middle-aged woman enjoying a cigarette outside a pharmacy surveyed us. Her face lit up when she saw Jorge. "I remember you!" she said.

Were we about to learn that Jorge was indeed famed actor Tom Wakefield? He paused and regarded her with a puzzled expression. "Excuse me?"

"You were here last week, am I right?" she asked. "Asking for that sleep medication?"

Jorge's face melted in an acknowledging smile. "Yes, that's right. You have a good memory."

As we continued walking, he turned to Billie and me. "Ben and I came here last week to make sure the climb would be easy enough for Lulu. I was having jet lag and stopped in the drugstore here to see what they carried."

Soon we arrived at the castle gatehouse, where Brian gave us our day passes and guards allowed us entry. To reach the castle, we had to negotiate a steep climb up a rocky walkway to the castle doors. It didn't seem appropriate for Luella, but Jorge knew her capabilities better than me. Sure enough, she executed the climb perfectly with the rest of us.

When we reached the entrance, Brian said, "You are now free to explore the castle. But mind that you return back here in precisely one hour. Is that clear? We need to leave before the tide comes in, and I don't want to have to go searching for any of you."

After he handed each of us a map of the castle layout, we entered through a heavy medieval door. On the wall of the entrance hall was displayed the coat of arms of the St. Aubyn family, which has presided over the castle since the seventeenth century. From there, we passed through a series of large rooms, including a library (shelves of ancient, leather-bound books and tables set for chess), a smoking room (large humidors on polished oaken tables), the priory church (the morning light casting colored rays on the floor as it filtered through the stained-glass window), and a map room (featuring a mummified cat from Egypt).

It was all full of tradition and very medieval and British and everything, but a little of that goes a long way with me. The same goes for elegant English country manor homes, most of the more renowned ones managed by the National

Trust. Yes, they're magnificent examples of period architecture, but I much prefer exploring their expansive gardens, mazes, and walking paths.

From the patient yet slightly bored look on Billie's face, I could tell she was feeling the same. "What do you say we go outside for a bit?" I suggested.

She smiled gratefully at my suggestion. "I'd like to see how the Channel looks from up here," she said. We studied our maps to locate the stairway to the next level. After a brief ascent, we easily found the large portico leading out to a broad terrace, where we could view not only the sea but also Lamorna to the west and the Lizard Peninsula, where we would be walking later, to the east. A strong wind was blowing in from the Channel.

Rachel and Dave followed us outside as well, as did Ivy. We peered over the battlements at gardens clinging to the cliff face.

"Isn't this where they used to throw people to their deaths?" Ivy asked with relish, looking down, her long black hair whipping in the wind. "I wonder if they died the second they hit the rocks."

"For heaven's sake, why do you always think of the most grisly stuff?" Rachel said.

"The castle is mostly known for the Benedictine monks who lived here for hundreds of years," Billie said. "They spent most of their time in meditation, not throwing people over the walls."

Dave said, "Will you excuse me? All that coffee at breakfast has caught up with me. I'll rejoin you in a few minutes."

He walked off, and we continued along the terrace as it wound around a corner of the castle, which brought us to a walkway that continued up and over a crag in the granite rock on which the castle was built.

"I've read up on this place," Rachel said. "I don't know how spiritual you are, but the story is that this island is positioned over ancient ley lines."

"Ley lines?" Billie asked. "I should know what those are, but I don't."

"They're supposedly key spots that connect with the universe through various monuments, such as the pyramids in Egypt and Stonehenge. It is said they carry pockets of concentrated energy that you can tap into if you manage to plug into their wavelength."

"Some people believe anything," Ivy said dismissively.

Her mother looked ahead. "There's must be somewhere to sit around here—oh, there's a bench up there! Let's go sit and see if we can sense any of that energy."

We walked over to a rock carved in the shape of a bench. Rachel sat and assumed a transcendent pose of meditation. Billie and I sat beside her. Almost immediately, a strong wind started up, lashing against our faces.

"Come sit with me, Ivy," Rachel said. "Join Mummy, and we can become one with the cosmos."

Ivy narrowed her eyes. "Don't talk to me like that. What do you think I am, a child?"

"You are a child, and a very rude one," her mother said. She closed her eyes. The wind continued to barrage us in loud gusts. Billie and I exchanged glances. I wasn't feeling any cosmic charge of energy, but I was definitely sensing something else. Perhaps it was my detective's intuition, or the eeriness of the moment, but I was sensing . . . danger.

"Did you hear that?" Billie asked.

I listened more intently. Behind the rush of the wind, I made out the undeniable sound of a woman screaming. It was coming from above us.

"Up there!" Rachel said. "Look!"

High above us, outside an opening in a castle turret,

was a red-clad figure, desperately clinging onto the castle wall, poised to fall.

"Good God, it's Luella!" Billie said.

I darted into the castle, found the turret stairway, and started running up, two steps at a time. With the wind no longer howling around me, I could more distinctly hear Luella's screams. The staircase seemed to be endless. At intervals, passages led off to the turret's interior, and from one of them Jorge emerged, panic etched on his face. He looked up.

"Luella's in trouble!" he said. "I've been going around in circles. I can't find the right way up!"

"Follow me!" I yelled and continued up, Jorge close behind me. After a mazelike series of twists and turns that seemed to double inside themselves, we arrived at the top. What kind of maniac designed this? Luella's screams had ceased, which wasn't a good sign. We headed to the opening, turned a corner, and saw her, precariously perched near the edge, one hand grasping an ancient torch holder on the wall, her legs dangling over the side. Her eyes were shut in terror.

"Lulu!" Jorge cried. He started to run to her, but his feet slipped on the wet stones, and he toppled forward. I managed to steady him, and he was able to put out his arm and grab Luella's free hand. She stared at him, terrified, and screamed again, releasing her hold on the sconce. Though she slipped off the ledge, Jorge's grip held fast. I wanted to help, but feared that inserting myself might cause more harm than good. Jorge was finding it difficult to remain steady on the slick stones, but he slowly pulled Luella to safety, let out a sigh of relief, and guided her away from the ledge.

She backed away. "I nearly fell to my death! You . . . you pushed me!"

"Me?" Jorge asked. "I didn't even know where you were! How could I have pushed you?"

"Well, someone did," she said, looking around her. "I mean . . . it *seemed* like I was pushed . . ."

"Why would anyone push you, darling?" He looked around. "I know exactly what happened. This floor is slick and wet from the sea air, and it's slanted. Plus, the wind is strong. You most likely lost your balance and fell forward. Why on earth did you ever come up here?"

Luella looked around as if she was lost. "I . . . I don't know. You didn't bring me up here?"

"Certainly not!"

Luella struggled to orient herself, placing one hand on Jorge's shoulder and the other on the wall beside her. Jorge's explanation about her losing her footing sounded plausible. I too was having trouble staying upright. Jorge held Luella and kissed the top of her head. "I should never have left you, my love."

"But why did you?" she asked.

"Darling, we got separated, don't you remember? We were in those passageways that went all this way and that. Before I realized it, you weren't with me. I've been searching for you for what seems like hours."

Luella weighed his explanation, looking from where we'd come. "How do we get out of here? Do we still have more walking to do? Good God. I need a Xanax."

Jorge led her away, and I began to follow, but paused to look back at the turret ledge, trying to picture the scenario he painted leading up to Luella's brush with death.

Plausible . . . or unlikely?

Maybe both, I decided.

Chapter 8

Tuesday, late morning
St. Michael's Mount, Cornwall

Jorge led Luella off, his arm around her waist, and tried to calm her down. I returned to Billie, Rachel, and Ivy to tell them what had happened. Dave had returned and was seated beside Rachel.

Billie's mouth dropped open when she heard of Luella's brush with death. "Talk about a close call! But what if Luella is right? What if she was pushed?"

"We all know she's disagreeable," Rachel said, "but would somebody really do something like that to her?"

"Don't forget she was on that bridge when it gave way," Dave noted. "I'm sure it's all just bad luck, but it makes you think, doesn't it?"

"You guys are so dense," Ivy said. "Mrs. Campos was telling the truth! Someone tried to kill her!"

Rachel turned to her. "Honestly, Ivy. Who would want to do away with Luella?"

"Her son hates her guts. Her husband wants her money because his acting career is in the dumpster."

Rachel crouched to look her daughter in the eye. "Ivy, I mean it. Enough of your wild theories. Try to be more respectful of people you don't know. Where did you learn to act this way? From your father?"

"Mrs. Campos's husband and her son didn't try to kill her anyway," Ivy said. She looked up accusingly at Dave. "I know who did."

It took Dave a few moments to pick up on what Ivy was implying. "Me? You've lost your mind. I was in the men's room for the past five minutes."

"Sure, that's what you say. But was anyone with you? You were gone just long enough to rush up to the top of the castle, give Luella a shove, and hurry back down."

I'd been watching this conversation with a degree of detached amusement, but Ivy had finally gone too far. I crouched in front of her and looked her in the eye. "When I was on the force, I needed solid evidence before I could arrest someone. You just met Mr. Langdon, a man you know practically nothing about, and you're accusing him of murder. Not only is that irresponsible, but it's incredibly rude."

This dissolved the smug look on her face.

"Mr. Chasen is absolutely right," Rachel said. "You owe Mr. Langdon an apology."

Ivy's face hardened as she stared down at the ground. I wondered how many apologies her mother had needed to coax out of her.

"I mean it, Ivy," her mother said. "You apologize to him right now or we're going home."

Ivy lifted her head, directed a glare at Dave, and said in a flat tone, "I'm sorry."

Dave gave her a sincere smile. "I accept your apology, Ivy. Thank you."

Rachel laughed. "There! How hard was that?" She and Dave stood and began walking off, leaving me and Billie with Ivy. I placed my hand on Ivy's shoulder.

"Let me give you some advice," I said. "It's fine to have

a lively imagination and think up stories. That's a talent. But when your stories involve real people and you talk about them seriously, they can do a lot of damage. The best thing to do is channel that imagination into something else, such as writing. You'd make a wonderful author."

I was expecting an immediate rebuff, but Ivy appeared to give my comment consideration. "I've thought about that, but writing doesn't make much money, does it?"

"Neither does blackmail," I said. "Not in the long run, anyway."

We followed Dave and Rachel to join the rest of the group at the front of the castle and take the walk back to the van. The tide was beginning to come in over the causeway, but it looked like we could make it back okay.

Brian led the way, with Billie and me right behind. She hadn't said much since Luella was saved from a catastrophic fall, and I suspected she was rattled.

"How is your knee holding up?" I asked.

"My knee is doing fine. It's my nose that's the problem."

"Your nose?"

"It's sniffing danger."

I took a deep breath. "It smells like saltwater to me."

"I'm not joking, Chase. We're only on the second day, and already two members of our group have nearly been killed in so-called 'accidents.' Not to mention that poor woman on the trail yesterday afternoon."

Normally, I would continue to make light of this, but there was no denying that these incidents gave me pause as well.

"And then there are those threats the local landowners are making," Billie continued. "I don't like it. I don't like it at all."

We walked in silence for a few moments before I replied. "I don't like it either. So we have a decision to make."

"What's our decision?"

"We could call it quits, and I could go back to Mike, and you could go off to see some plays in London. Or we can stick it out and do what we do best—enjoy the walk and, just as important, pay attention. Keep our eyes and ears peeled. Between the two of us, maybe we can stop something serious from happening."

"That sounds like a lot of work for a holiday trip," Billie said.

I flashed her a raised brow. "Work? Don't bluff me, kiddo. You love sleuthing around just as much as I do."

This made her smile. By that time, we had reached the mainland. The rear hatch of our van was open, displaying an array of snacks and drinks for our midmorning refreshment. As we nibbled and drank, Brian announced that it would be a six-mile walk to Praa Sands, where we would have lunch.

"Six miles!" Luella said. "I . . . I don't think I can make it."

"That's not so far, Lulu," Jorge said. "You'll see. It'll pep you up."

After her brush with death at the castle, Luella did look worn out. Brian suggested that she ride in the van.

"She's walking with us!" Jorge stated. His take-charge attitude mustered a grudging smile from Luella, and soon all of us were marching along the trail as it led from the island along a beach and then twisted around low-lying cliffs and rocky coves. Several paths branched off to the left and right, which would have confused the hell out of me had I been walking on my own. Occasionally, a way marker with the familiar acorn logo would appear to assure us that we were, indeed, still on the South West Coast Path, but I was thankful for Brian's guidance.

On the trail, our group spaced itself out in pairs. Billie walked beside me, Rachel and Dave behind us, and just ahead were Jorge and Luella, with Roy and Ivy closely behind. Roy would occasionally try to start up a conversation with Luella, who turned and told him to leave her alone.

When Billie and I reached him, he fell into step beside us. "That woman is not very sociable," he said.

"You can say that again," Ivy chimed in.

"She's just had a bad scare," I said to Roy. "You heard about what happened at the castle, didn't you? She believes she was pushed. Who knows? Maybe she thinks you did it."

"Me?" he said. "I've been trying to be friendly with her, not do her in!"

"I'm not accusing you," I said. "But maybe you should give up the peace effort for a while."

I wondered if Luella's dislike of Roy had something to do with that incident on the first day, when she assumed—because he was Black—that he was one of the hotel's employees rather than a fellow walker. I hate to assign racist views to anyone, but that might explain her coldness. Of course, she had just had a bad scare, which could account for that as well.

The path became a long stretch through a farm that Brian informed us was devoted to growing market greens. Beside me, Roy surveyed the expanse of plants stretching to the horizon.

"I wonder what kind of vegetables those are," I said as we walked.

"It looks like endive," he said, pausing to take a closer look. "Or escarole, to be more specific."

"Is there a difference?"

He looked surprised. "Sure there is. Endive has narrow, curly leaves, while escarole's leaves are broader and a paler green." As we walked, he bent down and pulled up a handful of leaves, which he displayed to me. "See? I tell you,

you haven't lived until you've had a soup or stew made with this stuff."

"In Tennessee, I would think you'd have . . . what are those called? Collard greens?"

He laughed. "Collard greens are different, more of a cabbage. Trouble is, they don't taste all that good on their own. You need to cook 'em up with salted meat and lots of spices."

"You really know your food. I'll have to visit your restaurant sometime if I ever get to Tennessee."

Roy smiled. "Who knows? Maybe someday you won't have to go that far."

He walked ahead, and Billie took his place at my side.

"Why does Roy look so familiar?" she asked.

"You've met him before?"

"That would have been unlikely. I haven't been to Memphis since I was in my twenties."

"Some people look like other people. That happens all the time. A couple of months ago, some lady approached me at the grocery store and assumed I was her dentist. She started talking about implants she needed. I told her to call my office for an appointment."

Billie laughed. "Good thing she didn't ask you to perform the procedure there in the store."

Even though the six miles passed quickly and the walk wasn't particularly strenuous, when we reached the small coastal village of Praa Sands, everyone was more than ready for a hearty lunch. Brian led us to the Three Bells, a brightly colored café on the town's broad beach. Although its peak summer business was a couple months off, a number of tourists already occupied the tables.

We approached tables that had been prepared for us and took our seats. When Roy sat across from Luella, she told him the seat was already claimed by her son.

"But he's already sitting over there," Roy said, nodding to Ben, seated at the table with Billie and me.

"Benjy, sit over here with your mother," Luella said. Ben looked puzzled but did as he was told. Roy came and sat with us. Soon we were reviewing the lunch menu posted on a board nearby—mostly standard fare like Cornish pasties and fish and chips, although the Cornish sea bass with chorizo stood out to me.

Ben picked up one of three bells placed on the table before us. "Are we supposed to ring one of these to order?"

Luella picked one up and examined it. "This is quite nice."

"Mother, put that down," Ben said.

"Benjamin, please stop ordering your mother around," Jorge said. "She's not a child."

A large woman wearing a blue apron and a broad smile came to take our orders. Brian introduced her as Jessie, the proprietor of the establishment. "She makes the best pasties in all of Cornwall, trust me," he told us.

"Is that a fact?" Roy asked Jessie. "Do you use swede?"

Her smile broadened further. "That I do!"

"What is swede?" Rachel asked.

"It's rutabaga," Roy said.

"We call it a turnip over here," Jessie said. "And I use only a little, because its flavor is so strong that some find it overpowering. But it adds just the right touch to the meat and potatoes. It's grown on the farm just up the road. You probably went past it on your walk this morning. Just thank your stars that you didn't encounter the farmer."

"What's the matter with him?" Billie asked.

"It's a her . . . Jane Berry. She's one of the LUAU bunch. They're the landowners who have raised such a fuss about the coastal path pressing deeper into their property. Proper chuffed about it, Jane is, and she's not the sweetest of lasses to begin with. I've crossed swords with her on more than one occasion—her son and mine are in a private school, and her boy is a right bully. But I need to watch my tongue, or she might refuse to sell me her turnips."

Brian told Jessie about the hazards we'd encountered on the trail and about the woman who died the previous day.

Jessie looked surprised. "Jane is a tough lady, no mistake, and that whole lot she's associated with are determined to fight the land-management system, but I can't see her actually *harming* anyone."

Before we launched into another discussion about dangers on the trail, Brian asked us to give Jessie our lunch orders. Because of Brian's praise and Jessie's description, most opted for pasties, accompanied by pints of ale. I selected the sea bass. Roy asked Jessie if he could visit her kitchen, and she gracefully consented. He walked off with her.

"Small wonder that man runs a restaurant," Rachel said, as Roy went off with Jessie. "I've never seen someone who thinks only about food. I like practicing law, but it's not my whole life."

The meals soon arrived and proved to be every bit as tasty as their hype. It was pleasant to partake of good British food while gazing out at seabirds coasting over the English Channel. When we finished, Brian called us to assemble outside and resume our afternoon walk. Luella looked sluggish and leaned against Jorge. "Darling, I don't think I'm up for more walking. Can you take me back to our hotel? And to bed?"

Jorge wasn't having any of this. "You mustn't give up, Lulu! You're a strong woman, and a brisk walk will make you even stronger."

He was laying it on pretty thick, I thought, but it made me wonder if Luella wasn't correct. She was clearly ready for a long nap.

"He's right, Mother," Ben said. "When you agreed to come on this walk, you promised you would keep up with us."

Luella gave a deep, theatrical sigh. "Very well. If you insist."

Jorge helped her on with her backpack. As they were about to leave, Ivy went and stood directly before Luella. "You might want to put back the bell you stole," she said.

Luella paused, and cocked her head. "What did you say?"

"I saw you put one of the café's bells in your coat," Ivy said.

Luella reacted with a credible look of shock.

Ben began digging inside the side pockets of Luella's coat and pulled out a silver bell. Holding it up to Luella, he said, "What have I told you about this, Mother?"

Luella's eyes darted right and left before focusing intently on Ivy. "You put it there!" Luella said.

"I did not!" Ivy protested.

Luella wagged her finger at the girl. "You're always snooping around, trying to stir up trouble! You must have slipped that bell into my coat when no one was looking."

Rachel joined Ivy to face Luella. "Are you accusing my daughter of being a thief?"

Luella's eyes narrowed into smoldering slits. "Your daughter is a nasty, nasty child. You had better get her into a correctional institution soon or the rest of her life is not going to be very pretty."

"Now you're telling me how to raise my child!" Rachel countered in a very different tone than I'd yet heard from her—heated, yet completely in control. "Judging from the way you treat your son, I would say you're the last person to be giving parental advice."

"I don't have to listen to such slander!" Luella said. "I'm contacting my lawyer when I get home. The next time you'll be speaking to me will be in court!"

"You don't mean that, Lulu," Jorge said with a forced laugh.

Rachel stepped closer to Luella. "That's fine with me, lady, because I'm an attorney, and I'm as at home in a courtroom as I am in my apartment. I make mincemeat out of everyone who dares to cross me."

"Please stop this, ladies," Brian said. "I'm sure all this was just a misunderstanding."

"He's right, darling," Jorge said to Luella. "The young girl was . . . just playing a game with you."

"Playing a game, my foot! That child is a bad seed. She needs therapy."

Ivy was about to speak up but stopped when I gave her a stern look of warning.

Time seemed to stand still as we waited for someone to make the next move. Luella continued to glare at Rachel, who continued to regard her with cold command. Finally, Luella said, "I don't appreciate such games," took Jorge's arm, and let him lead her away.

Rachel turned to Ivy, who had pulled out her phone and was scrolling through a message board. "Put that thing away right now," she said. Ivy grudgingly obeyed. "I meant what I told you, young lady," her mother continued. "You need to come to me if you see something like that again, or maybe Brian. Let the adults handle it. If you don't stop voicing these theories and accusations to others, I'm taking you home."

"But she did steal that bell."

"What did I just tell you? Leave these things to adults."

I tried to read Ivy's expression, but she'd become good at not giving anything away. Maybe I was wrong to suggest that she explore a career in writing. She was better suited to be a spy.

The group went back outside to the trail, although without much enthusiasm. That confrontation over the bell had thrown a bucket of ice over everyone's spirits. As we began walking, I noticed that Rachel and Ivy, embroiled in what looked like a heated conversation, kept well away from the Campos family. Billie and I kept our distance from the Scattergoods so we could discuss the incident without being overheard.

"I'm inclined to side with Luella on this one," Billie said. "You've told me about the whoppers that Ivy has been tossing around. I wouldn't put it past her to pull a stunt like this and plant that bell on Luella."

I agreed that Ivy wasn't a person anyone would call trustworthy, yet, even for her, this seemed to be a bit much. "Luella gave up the battle a bit too quickly, don't you think?" I said. "If she had really lifted that bell—and Ivy claims she saw a story online of Luella once being arrested for shoplifting—then it would be in her best interests not to press it too far. She found someone to blame to deflect from her own guilt, and that was her objective."

We continued walking for several moments before Billie said, "Maybe you're right. But here we go again. Not only do I have to worry about our walks being sabotaged, but now we don't know what little brushfire Ivy will set off next."

I looked ahead at Rachel lecturing her daughter as they walked. "Ivy listens to me," I said. "I think it's because of my police background—she respects that—whereas her mother comes across as a prosecuting attorney. I'll try to talk some sense into her the next chance I get."

"Good luck with that," Billie said, with little hope in her voice.

We fell into a steady walking rhythm, but instead of focusing on the passing countryside, I couldn't stop thinking about Ivy's stories. If she was right about Luella, was she right about the others? Was Jorge really Tom Wakefield? Was Dave a serial killer?

And what stories had she been spreading about me?

Chapter 9

Tuesday, afternoon,
Tremearne Cliffs, Cornwall

Perhaps it was the gentle, salty breeze that enveloped us as we walked, keeping us cool despite the warmth of the afternoon. Or maybe it was the reassuring rhythm of the path itself, which proceeded in mild undulations across low-rise bluffs, down to beaches or coves and back up again. Whatever the cause, the group had gradually turned into a compliant if not harmonious walking brigade.

Our midafternoon rest stop was at a small cove where Brian distributed bags of trail mix from his pack. There was a drinking fountain at which we could get water. We rested on logs and rocks and enjoyed the soothing lapping of the sea on the shore.

As we were finishing our snack, Jorge stood and said, "That water looks too good to ignore!" He stripped off his jacket and shirt, and ran out into the sea.

"What does he think this is, a biathlon?" Dave asked.

Jorge swam out until we almost couldn't see him, swam back, and emerged dripping from the sea. Okay. I tried not to let my mind go there, but damn. He was one gorgeous man. The water and the midafternoon sun accentuated the curves of his upper arms, the slopes of his muscles, the . . .

"Did you hear what I said, Chase?"

I swung toward Billie. "I'm sorry. I must have missed it."

She gave a knowing glance toward Jorge, who was drying himself off rather conspicuously, I thought. "I can see why you were distracted. Not in bad shape for a man his age, is he? Anyway, I asked if you'd heard from Mike today."

"Not yet. We usually catch up at the end of the day." That was hours away, yet I already knew I wouldn't be providing Mike with any graphic descriptions of Jorge's anatomy. He hadn't yet exhibited any jealous tendencies, but I didn't want to plant any seeds.

"I was wondering how his return to his normal life is going," Billie said.

"Are you suggesting his life with me hasn't been normal?"

"I put that wrong, didn't I? What I meant was his old life, his familiar one. That has to be difficult to return to after three months."

"Apparently not," I said, with a trace of bitterness. "It sounds like he couldn't be happier, getting back with his old workmates and his job and all that."

"I can understand that. I don't like being away from my friends for too long either."

That was a good point, as much as I hated to admit it. There was no way I could expect Mike to completely throw away his old life for a new one, and I wouldn't want him to. Now that I was looking at spending three months with him in England, I wondered when I'd begin missing my friends back home and my daily routine. Fortunately, I could still catch the Red Sox games on Sky TV.

Billie studied my face as I became lost in thought. "Are you both committed to making it work?"

I pondered that for a moment. "Yes, I'd say we are. But

I just realized what I'll miss most about being away from the US. My memories of Doug. That's where we had our life together. Even when Mike was there with me, I could still feel Doug's presence. I keep wondering what he'd make of my life these days."

Billie reached out and patted my hand. "He'd be thrilled you've found someone."

I smiled, but my eyes traveled to Jorge, buttoning up his shirt. I asked Billie, "Do you know the actor Tom Wakefield?"

"I think so. Wasn't he the bartender on that TV show *Cheers*?"

"No, that was someone else. Wakefield was the guy in *Hawaii P.I.*"

"You know me better than that, Chase. If he never appeared on *Masterpiece Theatre*, then he's lost to me. Why are you asking?"

I took another look at Jorge, convinced that Ivy had invented the whole Tom Wakefield thing. Yet there was a resemblance, if I was remembering accurately. But that was of a man as he was many years ago.

"Nothing important," I said to Billie. "I'll explain later."

Brian crumpled up his snack bag and put it in his pack, then stood. "Time to be on the move again!"

We all reluctantly got to our feet; the cove had been so intoxicatingly restful that most of us just wanted to nap. Within a few minutes, I was following Billie up to the top of a bluff. Brian and Luella were ahead of her, and Jorge was far in front. When the trail flattened at the top and began a slow curve eastward, I found Ben walking beside me.

"How's your mother doing?" I ask.

Ben gave me a weary smile. "You mean in general, or at this moment?"

"Both, I guess. That was quite a scare she had this morning."

He nodded. "My dear mother is a survivor. She's screwed up her life in so many ways, but she always comes out on top. It's usually because she finds some guy to support her until she dumps him and takes half his dough. With Jorge, it's different, though."

"How different?"

"Different in every way. I think she really loves him. Let me tell you, that's a shocker. She's never had a marriage like this before. It could be the best thing that ever happened to her . . . except for one small thing."

"What is that?"

"The tables are turned this time. She's the one with money, and Jorge is flat broke."

This was news. "How is she handling that?"

"Oh, she's handling it just fine. You know why? She isn't aware of it. She thinks he's as loaded as she is."

"How do you know he isn't?"

"It wasn't hard to find out. I noticed he always lets Mother pay for everything. So I did some digging around. When he met Mother, he lived in a small rented apartment and drove an old used Ford."

"That doesn't mean anything. Some people don't flaunt their money. But how could he be broke? Wasn't he an airline pilot? Those guys are paid pretty well."

Ben grinned and nodded. "True. But he spilled the beans to me when I pressed him. He claims he lost all his money on some bad investments. He wasn't forthcoming with the details."

"Did you tell your mother about this?"

"No way. It's about time somebody does to her what she's been doing to others all these years. We'll see how she likes being the victim for once."

"But if they love each other, as you claim, what's the harm?"

Ben was about to respond, but paused. He looked around, as if just realizing where he was. "I shouldn't be telling you these things. Forget I said anything." He started walking faster to put distance between us.

We proceeded on the trail as it hugged the imposing southwestern Cornish coast. I thought of how much coastline the relatively small country of England has: more than 13,000 kilometers—nearly one-third the circumference of the earth. And all of that coastline that I have seen is, in my opinion, spectacularly beautiful. We passed the Megiliggar Rocks, three colossal chunks of granite sticking up off the shoreline. From there, the trail headed inland, through fields and farmlands.

After walking through a gate into a field sheltered from the sea by a line of alder trees, a broad meadow stretched before us, the trail barely discernible on the tufted ground as it continued forward. Cows gathered in the distance, lazily chewing or mulling over whatever thoughts might be on their little bovine minds.

Suddenly, one began running toward us. It became quickly clear that this was no cow—it was an angry bull.

"Mrs. Campos, remove your coat!" Brian shouted.

"What?" Luella asked.

The bull was almost upon her.

"Take off your coat! The red color is attracting the bull!"

"Bull?!"

Jorge sprang into action and rushed toward Luella.

"Jorge, don't!" yelled Ben.

Ignoring him, Jorge ripped off Luella's coat, moved aside, and held it out to the bull, who was about to plunge into it when Jorge whipped it away. The bull staggered forward, confused as to what had just happened. Jorge continued to wave Luella's coat and entice the bull to the side of the field.

The whole episode had happened so quickly that I was still trying to sort it out when Jorge returned to us.

"This is inexcusable!" Brian raged. "Warning signs are required if there is a bull in a field. I must report the landowner to the authorities. Someone might have gotten . . ."

He didn't finish his sentence, but Rachel finished it for him. "Killed?"

"Hey, look over here," Roy said. He'd walked back to the entrance to the field and reached behind a hedge to pull out a sign that stated CAUTION: BULL IN FIELD. "Someone threw this into the bushes."

"Inexcusable!" Brian roared again. "If that sign had been posted, I would have warned Mrs. Campos to remove her jacket."

"It's the work of our saboteur, isn't it?" Dave asked. It certainly seemed that way to me.

Billie turned to Jorge and said, "Kudos to you, Mr. Campos. You really took charge. It looked as if you've done that before."

Jorge smiled modestly. "I once took bullfighting lessons in Spain."

Why would an airline pilot take bullfighting lessons? It seemed a strange hobby. Had Tom Wakefield ever played a bullfighter in a film? Or did Jorge risk his life to save Luella simply because he liked her money? I immediately reprimanded myself for being so cynical.

Jorge wrapped his arm around Luella and held her tight. "I almost lost you again, Lulu dear."

After what she'd been through that morning, it wasn't surprising to see Luella in what appeared to be a state of shock. Her eyes looked unfocused, her mouth slightly open.

Brian approached the pair. "I promise I will follow up with the authorities. There are stiff fines for not adequately warning walkers of bulls."

"What if this was the work of the same person who caused that bridge to collapse yesterday?" Dave asked.

"We don't know whether that was sabotage," Roy pointed out.

"And what about the lady who fell on the trail to her death?" Rachel asked.

"That was likely due to her own carelessness," Roy said.

Billie nudged me aside. "What do you think about this now? Do you still feel safe continuing the walk?"

Two close calls in one day triggered my alarm bells. "You know how I feel about coincidences. But you also know how I feel about leaping to conclusions."

"I don't think it's much of a leap. The big question is whether it's just some disgruntled landowner behind all of this, or . . ."

I nodded. "Or one of our group."

Brian suggested that we leave the field, in case the bull, who had returned to munching on grass at the other side of field, had a change of mind. When we safely walked through the gate at the other end, he suggested that we stop for a while to let Luella get over her shock. Fortunately, there were rocks and logs nearby on which to sit. Billie and I took off our backpacks and set ourselves on a large rock. She began rubbing her knee.

"Is that troubling you?" I asked.

I could see her wince as she kneaded the joint. "Just a bit. I'm sure it will feel better later after a hot bath."

I gave her a reassuring smile. "I'm sure it will. You have that Daniel Bard spirit if anyone ever did."

"Who's that?" Billie asked, and then smiled knowingly. "Wait. Don't tell me. I'm about to hear another Red Sox analogy, aren't I?"

"Am I that predictable? But yes, you're right." I gave her a brief summary of Daniel Bard, a pitcher with the Red Sox several years earlier who set a team record with twenty-five consecutive games in which the opposing team didn't score at all. His speediest pitch was clocked at 102 miles per hour. "He was quite a superstar. But his pitching became erratic, until eventually he was unable to even throw the ball over the plate."

"What caused that?" Billie asked.

"That's what's weird; nobody really knows. He'd suffered a few minor injuries, but not enough to really bring about that kind of a breakdown. Some people said he was the victim of bad coaching decisions, or that he got the yips, a mental condition that can cause athletes to suddenly lose much of their skill."

"Wow," Billie said. "But I still don't get what my knee has to do with all of that."

"Just this. Everyone counted Bard out, certain his career was over. He was relegated to the minor leagues, but he wouldn't give up. He was determined to make a recovery, and sure enough, a few years later, he made it back to the major leagues with the Colorado Rockies. That year he was named National League Comeback Player of the Year."

Billie raised her eyebrows. "That's nice. But I don't think I've got the yips, Chase. It's just time taking its toll on my joints. If worse comes to worse, I can always have a knee replacement."

"Give it some time before you do anything drastic," I advised.

* * *

As we headed back onto the trail, the group had formed into two camps: those shaken by what had just happened to Luella but still willing to go on with the week's walk, and those vowing to bail.

"I can't take any more of this," Luella said. "It seems like something is around every corner, just waiting to do me in."

"Same here," Rachel said. "There's no way I'm going to risk my life and that of my daughter after what we've seen!"

"I agree," said Dave. "Something weird is going on."

"You're all overreacting!" Jorge said. "Have any of us been harmed? No!"

"We just need to be careful, that's all," Ben said. "There are always hazards when you walk in the countryside, aren't there, Brian?"

"Very true," said Brian, although even he sounded cautious. "But again, I must reassure you that the trails on which we'll be walking are perfectly safe. I've led dozens of walks along them."

"You guys have no spirit of adventure!" said Ivy. "I want to see what's going to happen to us next!"

As we continued, I felt the need to play the father figure again, and I maneuvered myself beside Ivy, out of earshot of the others.

"You probably don't want any more of my advice, but here it is," I said to her. "Try to stop and think before you speak. If what you're going to say is going to cause people needless stress or worry, then it's best to stay silent. Or, as your mother said, tell another adult."

We walked a few moments in silence. It seemed as if she was actually digesting what I'd said.

"You're right," she said in a complacent tone. "I'm sorry."

I never thought I'd hear Ivy apologize. "Good."

"But . . . I just can't help checking people out online. And this morning I found out something about Roy over there."

"What did I tell you about believing everything you see online?"

"Yeah, I know, but this is really serious."

For once, she seemed reluctant to spill the dirt. "Well, go ahead," I said. "Tell me what you found."

She stopped and looked at me, not in a gloating way, but troubled. "He once served time in prison. For attempted murder."

Chapter 10

Tuesday, afternoon,
Porthleven and St. Mawes

"Murder?" I said. "Are you sure?"

"You can look it up yourself if you don't believe me."

This didn't seem possible. "But . . . are you sure it was him?"

She hesitated. "Not really. I mean, I Googled 'Roy Hemper' and that's the information that came up. He was in prison in Nevada, near Las Vegas. But there wasn't a picture or anything."

I supposed there was more than one Roy Hemper.

Any further discussion was interrupted when we rounded a bend and saw a sign that read, CAUTION: PATH REROUTED DUE TO SUBSIDING CLIFFS. Beyond it, the trail veered left onto dirt freshly cleared from the surrounding field.

"Not again!" Dave said. "This path is crumbling all over the place!"

"I think it's encouraging," said Roy. "This sign proves that the authorities are clearly marking the places that might be dangerous and have taken measures to keep us away from them."

Brian nodded at him gratefully. "The coastline is always changing. These paths need to be reconfigured all the time. This is nothing unusual."

I traded glances with Billie, whose brow rose skeptically.

We walked along the newly formed path and encountered a man working in a garden beside a large white house. He smiled as we approached. "Good day! Out for a walk, are you?" He introduced himself as Malcolm.

"Good afternoon," said Brian. "I wonder, could you tell me who owns the field that borders this one? The one directly to the west?"

"Why, that would be Jane Berry's land," Malcolm said.

Jane Berry. I remembered her as a member of the antiwalkers cabal that Jessie at the Three Bells mentioned.

"Just as I thought," Brian said. Turning to us, he said, "That makes this much clearer. The authorities already know about Miss Berry and would be very interested to learn she is disregarding the regulations about notifying walkers of the bull in her field."

"You had a run-in with Geoffrey?" Malcolm asked. "He's getting on in years but still is feisty."

Brian explained that the warning sign on the path had been taken down.

"Jane isn't fond of walkers, but I can't see her putting any of them in danger," Malcolm said. "It had to have been just a mishap."

"Whatever it was, we'll report it," Brian said. To the group he added, "The good news is that we'll be well away from Jane's property for the rest of our walk."

We soon arrived at Porthleven, a small coastal village where the van was waiting to transport us back to St.

Mawes. Everyone was silent during the short drive. When we reached the hotel, Brian told us to regroup in the lobby at six o'clock for dinner, which he said was going to be a surprise. He advised us to be sure to dress warmly. As he walked off, Rachel said she was going to hit the hotel gym to work off some of her frustration before dinner.

"Mind if I join you?" Dave asked. "Walking is great exercise, but I need to work something more than just my legs."

I was going to point out that walking is actually a good full-body workout, but Rachel nodded to Dave and asked her daughter, "You want to come with us, darling?"

"I just spent the day walking," her daughter groaned. "Why would I want to punish my body more?"

Her mother, who no doubt was used to her daughter's outbursts—even if she did little to stop them—shrugged and walked off with Dave.

Ivy simmered as she watched them walk away. "He's going to murder her; I know he is. And she's letting him get under her skin."

"There you go again," I told her. "You have no evidence that Dave is a murderer, for heaven's sake. Just because you can't find him online? There would be a lot of murderers out there if that was the criteria."

I expected a snotty rebuff, but something in her eyes told me that my words had struck home, if only partially. "But some of the stuff I see online is true."

"The problem is, how do you know? When I was a police detective, we needed to have definite proof when we made an accusation. That meant gathering evidence—physical, forensic, documentary, testimonial. If we just started tossing around unfounded accusations, we could have been found guilty of defamation of character, or worse."

Ivy looked sobered, aware of the consequences of her

exaggerations. She twisted her gaze up to me. "But what if I get evidence? What if I prove what I've said?"

"That's fine," I said with caution. "But only if you do it carefully and legally. Do you know what I mean?"

She gave me one of her studied glares. "I'm not a baby, you know. Of course I know what you mean." She walked off, her hands stuffed in her jacket pockets.

"You're good with her."

I hadn't noticed Billie standing nearby.

"You mean Ivy? She's a strange one, isn't she? Not like any teenage girl I've ever met. I feel sorry for her. I don't know how she's been raised, but it sounds like her home life has been less than ideal."

"In most ways, she's a typical girl of her age," Billie said. "They act indifferent and contrary, but what they really want is someone to love them enough to discipline them."

"You don't believe her mother is doing that?"

"I don't know Rachel well enough to say. What I do see is that she is distracted. Maybe it's because of the divorce she's going through."

"It might also be because of Dave Langdon. He seems interested in her." Billie nodded, and I thought of Mike. "It wouldn't be the first time Cupid struck on one of these walks."

She smiled. "I like that you're there for Ivy. It shows that you're just an old softie. Anyway, I need to freshen up. We're supposed to meet back here in an hour or so for dinner, aren't we?"

"That's what Brian said. Apparently, he has a surprise in store for us."

"Yes, he was very coy about that, wasn't he? But some surprises can be nice."

* * *

At six, wearing a dinner jacket, thick cotton shirt, and corduroy pants, I returned to the foyer, where most of our group was gathered. The only one missing was Ben.

"Do you know where your son is, Mrs. Campos?" Brian asked Luella. "We should be on our way soon."

Luella shrugged and gave a dramatic sigh. "Benjamin is not one for punctuality."

"I can go check on him," Jorge offered.

"Let's just leave," Luella said. "He's not very good at focusing, but he'll figure out how to catch up with us somehow."

At that point, Ben arrived—but through the front entrance, not from the direction of his room.

"Where on earth have you been?" his mother asked.

Ben wiped one of his hands on his pants, leaving a trace of what looked to be sand. "I was just walking along the seawall, getting a look at the fishermen. It's not a sight I can enjoy at home, that's for sure."

"Looks like you're turning into an adventurer!" Jorge said, slapping Ben on the back.

Luella executed a weary sigh. "Benjamin, an adventurer? He'll need to learn to tie his shoes first."

Ben walked up to her. "Be careful, Mother, or I'll tie yours—together."

She formed her condescending smile. "Your inheritance is hanging by a slender thread, Benjy. Snip, snip!"

"Please stop the teasing, Lulu," Jorge said. "You love Ben, you know you do."

As if she had just been given a stage cue, Luella smiled and put her arm around Ben. "Of course, I love him! We just can't stop having fun with each other."

Parent-child love can take many forms, I knew, but this version was beyond any I'd ever seen.

"Are we all here?" Brian said. "Good! Tonight's meal is only a short walk away."

"More walking?" Rachel said. "Can't we take a taxi?"

"It's not far, I promise. Follow me!"

He led us out to the main road, which we followed (walking on the pavement alongside it) to the west. Soon a small, yet formidable-looking castle appeared on a small rise beside the sea. A sign proclaimed it to be St. Mawes Castle, built in the sixteenth century and currently managed by English Heritage.

"Magnificent, isn't it?" Brian said as we walked onto the castle grounds. "It was built by Henry the Eighth as one of his artillery installations along the south coast. We can't go inside, but it's best appreciated from the outside anyway."

The structure certainly was a dramatic sight, the stone on its rounded walls reflecting the rays of the setting sun. Brian led us to the broad lawn stretched beside it, with gardens on the other side. Set up before us was a large marquee under which was a long dining table. A catering truck was parked not far away.

"What do you know!" Billie said. "We're eating al fresco."

"I'm glad we dressed appropriately," I said, although the evening air was mild.

As we found places around the table, Brian called our attention to a menu chalkboard in the center showing the evening's meal choices: slow-roasted pork belly, lamb fillet, or stargazy pie.

"Stargazy pie," Roy said. "I've heard of that. It's fish, isn't it?"

"There's a fascinating legend behind it," Brian said. "Back in the sixteenth century, around the time when the castle beside us was built, a terrible storm sank many of the ships in the coastal harbors around here. It was near Christmas, and people were facing starvation because they couldn't get the fish they relied on. A local fisherman, Tom Bawcock, came forward and offered to brave the storm in his own small boat. Everyone thought he had a death wish, but when he returned, they were amazed. His catch was generous enough to feed the entire village. He baked the fish—all kinds and varieties—into a pie with their heads and tails proudly on display. It was December twenty-third, and every year. that date is known as Tom Bawcock's Eve in the man's honor."

"It sounds gross," Ivy said.

"That story sounds as fishy as the pie," Rachel added.

Brian smiled. "It might all be rubbish, but trust me about the pie. It is delicious."

"I'm game," Dave said.

"I'll give it a try also," Rachel agreed.

We ordered, and soon the starter—a small crab salad—was distributed, along with a selection of wines. As the sun began to set, rows of lights on the marquee provided just enough illumination for us to see one another and our meals, while not overpowering the ethereal sight of the castle beside us, silhouetted against the night sky. The stargazy pie was brought out with the fish heads and tails artfully arranged, but they were removed when the individual portions were dished up.

As the evening deepened, the food and wine put us all in a relaxed and convivial mood. Jorge refilled everyone's wineglass and embarked on a long story about the time he worked as a bartender in Singapore. (What professions hadn't he attempted?) This prompted others to share similar jobs they'd held. Dave recalled his college-years stint as a bouncer in a nightclub, Rachel bashfully related her experiences as a cocktail waitress, and Roy described his first job as a dishwasher at a diner.

"One of the cooks could spin a soup spoon in his hands

and then flip it right into his mouth," he said. Leaning toward me, he said in a low voice, "I promised myself I'd learn how to do that one day. Well, I never did, but a waiter at one of my restaurants can actually do that with knives!"

I wanted to hear more, but everyone was discussing the merits of their meal. To my surprise, the dinner turned out to be a success, with no talk of trail sabotage or bickering among the diners. After we finished our dessert—a scoop of Turkish delight ice cream for everyone except Ivy, whose diabetes prohibited rich dairy products—the group started preparing to return to the hotel. Brian reminded us to meet in the lobby the following morning at nine.

I needed to use the loo and didn't want to wait until I got back to my room, even though the hotel wasn't far. A server informed me there wasn't a gent's nearby, but if I needed to relieve myself, I could go behind a tree at the far side of the garden. That seemed a rather crude solution, but I had no choice. As I stood behind the large oak emptying my bladder, a woman's familiar voice came from the other side.

"You can cut that 'journalist' crap with me. I know very well who you are . . . and your salacious background. It's clear you've got eyes for Mrs. Scattergood, so let me warn you. If she or her nasty little daughter continue harassing me, I'll let her know all about your past. She won't like that one bit, I can tell you."

I zipped up and stepped out into the open just as Luella walked off. Dave stood there looking dumbstruck. It took him a moment for my presence to register. His eyes jerked toward me, frightened.

"Are you all right?" I asked.

After a pause, he nodded and walked away.

What had that all been about?

* * *

Back in my room, I placed a call to Mike but got his machine. I left a message and asked him to call me as soon as possible.

Frustrated, I looked around for some way to pass the time. After thumbing through a few pages of real estate ads in an old copy of *Cornwall Life* that I'd found on my bedside table's lower ledge, I spotted the TV remote. Maybe I could find an American sports channel.

I switched on the wall-mounted television opposite my bed and started scrolling through the channels. When I came to one showing a film, I stopped. The scene featured three actors—Ted Danson—yes, that was the guy from *Cheers*!—someone else whose name I couldn't recall, and . . . Tom Wakefield. I remembered seeing this film—*Accidental Fathers*.

The remote wouldn't let me pause, so I tried hard to study Wakefield before the film cut to another scene. Yes, the actor was much younger than Jorge when this film was made in the late 1980s, but there was definitely a resemblance—something in the eyes and the mouth. There was also a similarity in the voice, although Jorge's was deeper and perhaps influenced by the trace of a foreign accent (not Spanish or Mexican, despite his name). Of course, Wakefield was an actor and could assume many personas.

Fortunately, I had an onrush of common sense. Why would a famous Hollywood actor come on an English walk? Why would he claim to be an itinerant former pilot? Why did he marry an older woman—even one with money? Why would he put his acting career on hold? Why—

Enough already! I couldn't believe I was giving Ivy's loony theory any credence.

My phone buzzed, and I was pleased to see the caller's name. "Mike!" I greeted.

"Sorry I couldn't answer before," he said. "I was waiting for your call, but Randall's ex-wife, Eileen, phoned and told me Randall's contacted her, believing they're still married."

"Oh, no."

"Their divorce was an amicable one, and she still cares for him, but she doesn't know how to handle him in his present condition. She gave me a recommendation of a care facility nearby, January House. I'll check it out."

"Do you want me to help? I can quit the walk. It would be no problem."

"Absolutely not! You've been looking forward to this walk for such a long time, and I wouldn't dream of depriving you of it. Randall has someone looking after him. There's time enough to do what needs to be done."

"If you're certain."

"I am. Now, tell me how your walk is going."

I didn't know where to begin. Not wanting to alarm him, I described the day's walk in mostly bucolic terms, not mentioning Luella's nearly fatal fall from the top of St. Michael's Mount nor her near-goring by the bull in the afternoon. I also didn't mention the woman who had fallen to her death when the bluff collapsed.

Mike had become astute enough, however, to discern that I was keeping something from him. "There's a slight hesitancy in your tone," he said. "What are you leaving out?"

I should have known better than to deceive him. Still, I was tired and not prepared to go over all the ugly details. "You know me too well. You're right—there have been some hiccups, but nothing alarming. I'll tell you more tomorrow when I have more energy."

"Now you've got me worried."

It was good to hear him worried. "There's no need, trust me," I said. "Mostly I miss you. It's strange sleeping alone again."

"Same here. But it's only for another few nights."

We bid each other good night, and for the first time in days, I felt reassured. Mike loved me, I knew. And I loved him. And even though we needed to work out our living arrangements, love was all that mattered.

I had one more task to perform before going to bed. I brought up Google on my phone and entered "Roy Hemper." Sure enough, an item appeared about someone of that name serving time for attempted murder in High Desert State Prison outside Las Vegas, seven years earlier. But there was no photograph. I looked for other results bearing Roy's name, but none appeared to be him. That was surprising. These days, if someone has a significant business enterprise—such as a group of restaurants—it is odd not to have an internet presence.

Filing that annoying fact away mentally to think about later, I was about to put my phone aside when another of Ivy's searches tugged at me. I Googled Dave's name and was surprised at the first result.

It was that of a cocktail pianist. The man in the photo, wearing a formal suit and poised at a keyboard, was definitely Dave. I remembered that he'd mention he played the piano.

Then I noticed I hadn't entered Dave's name properly—instead of "Langdon," I'd entered "Landon," which was the name that appeared on the screen.

Why was Dave using a variation of his name? And why did he claim to be a writer? It was like Ivy said. Does everybody have secrets? Or it was like what Sam Dundas, one of the captains I used to report to, often said. "People can change their name too easily these days. Don't assume anyone is who they say they are."

Chapter 11

Wednesday, morning,
The Carne

The next morning, I awoke with mixed emotions. On one hand, given everyone's warm company at dinner the previous evening, I was looking forward to a day of walking for the first time since the trek began. On the other hand, there had been too many near misses to feel completely comfortable.

So it was with a mostly hopeful heart that I showered, dressed, and buoyantly walked down to the breakfast nook overlooking the St. Mawes harbor, where the brightly painted fishing boats were heading out to collect their day's catch. That lifted my spirits instantly. How could anyone not enjoy their morning repast with such a view?

Billie, as usual, was already there, knitting something with an alarming chartreuse-colored yarn. A coffee mug sat before her but no plate.

"You haven't had breakfast?" I asked.

"Take a look behind you, Chase. They haven't set most of it out yet."

No sooner had she spoken than a young lad wheeled in a cart steaming with the morning's warm entrées: bacon, sausage, eggs, and porridge. The cold selections—cereal, breads, fruits, and pastries—had already been laid out.

"Yum, yum!" I said, surprised at how hungry I was, given the previous evening's bountiful meal. I began loading up my plate with eggs, bacon, and tomatoes.

Rachel and Ivy appeared, followed by Dave and Roy.

"Something smells absolutely sinful," Rachel said with a smile, as she picked up a plate.

"I've learned how important the morning meal is on this walk," Dave said. "This grub will really charge my barge!"

"It's only boring breakfast stuff," Ivy said. "Just like yesterday. No waffles or pancakes. And their cereals taste like cardboard."

"That's because they don't coat them with five layers of sugar over here," Rachel said. "Stop complaining, and be sure to eat some fruit. You're undernourished."

Ivy shrugged and began surveying the selections half-heartedly. She did look thin, but whether that was due to puberty not yet fully kicking in or her diabetes, I didn't know.

Roy said, "People always take well-prepared food for granted. They don't understand the skill that goes into its preparation. That's why it's so important that we take time to eat slowly and savor each mouthful. Good food should be a wonderful experience."

"You sound like a restaurant owner, all right," Rachel said.

The Campos clan arrived, each looking at odds with the others. Jorge was smiling and exuberant, attired in a thick walking shirt. Ben looked resigned and withdrawn, lost in a world of his own. Luella appeared sluggish, as if she had been drugged. I knew she wasn't a morning person, but she seemed more out of it than usual. Nevertheless, she followed Jorge and Ben to the buffet and selected a plate.

"You'll have to forgive my darling Lulu," Jorge said to the rest of us as he speared a sausage. "We had a wild night! It's amazing what walking can do to the libido. My darling bride was insatiable!"

Ben said, "Do you have to be so crass, Jorge? Why would any of us care about your sex life with my mother?"

"I'm just being real, Benjamin! Sex is a part of life. You should try it sometime."

Luella didn't appear to have heard Jorge's comment. She stared at her muffin as she spooned jam onto it.

"I agree with Ben, Jorge," Rachel said. "Some topics are best kept private."

"I want to hear about it!" Ivy said. "How else am I going to learn anything?"

"You know far too much as it is," her mother said.

Soon everyone was focused on their food. As Luella began to nibble at her muffin, awareness returned to her eyes. Soon she began to exhibit her usual—if disagreeable—self.

"What are you making me eat, Jorge?" she asked, as if noticing the food on her plate for the first time. She stared at her fork, spearing a bite of egg, half-raised to her mouth.

His head cocked. "I'm not making you eat anything, my love. Poached eggs. Blueberry muffin. You love them!"

"Where did you get that idea? Blueberries give me gas."

"Mother, please . . ." Ben said.

"Be quiet, Benjamin!"

A moment passed before Roy said, "Actually, blueberries are one of nature's miracle foods. They lower your blood pressure, slow the aging process, and increase your supply of antioxidants. They don't cause gas at all."

Luella turned toward him. "Well, they give me gas. Just because you run a restaurant doesn't mean you know everything about food."

Roy visibly wrestled with a response but remained quiet.

"Honestly, Mother," Ben said. "You never know when to keep your trap shut."

Luella raised her fingers to make her cut-her-son-from-the-will motion.

"And knock it off with the 'snip, snip!' stuff," Ben said. "It just makes you look petty and childish."

Looking down at her plate, she said. "Very well. I've decided to 'knock it off,' as you say." She looked up at Ben. "It just so happens I was on the phone last night and instructed my lawyer to amend my will. When he makes the changes I requested, you will not receive a dime of my fortune." She looked at Jorge. "I have someone else to fill that role now."

Jorge didn't look pleased. "Enjoy your breakfast, Lulu, please, so you can replenish your energy." Luella gave him an adoring, obedient smile. He certainly seemed to hold control over her.

Ben threw down his napkin and left the room. Roy also stood, placed his napkin on the table, and walked out as well.

Brian announced that we were to meet him in front by the van in thirty minutes.

"This seems to be another one of those problematic groups we so often find ourselves among," Billie said, after the others finished their breakfast and walked out of the room.

"It depends on how you look at it, dear Billie. In a way, every group is 'problematic,' as you put it—people are always dealing with their own challenges and problems. Those challenges often develop into arguments and heated moments. But we're also all capable of blessings and forgiveness."

She looked at me with a grin. "Sometimes you amaze me, Chase. One minute, you're all pragmatic and ultra-logical and the next, you're as spiritual as a monk."

"Can't you see how the two go hand in hand? Anyway, I'm happy to tell you that my monk days are over. At least as far as carnal relations go."

"And that's all I want to hear about that," she said, standing. With a wink, she added, "You sound as uncomfortably honest as Jorge." She paused. "But, of course, I'm glad to hear it."

We walked outside to the van and were soon joined by the others. Neither Brian nor the driver was there, but thirty minutes hadn't yet passed.

Jorge was chatting with Dave. "You say you covered a story in the Amazon? How fascinating! I spent a good amount of time there teaching the natives modern home-building techniques."

Ivy was standing a few feet away, her ears trained on every word. "How did you get to do all that stuff?"

Jorge gave her a smile that looked a bit condescending. "Ah, the young. So naïve. Yes, flying was my career, but that didn't prevent me from doing other things as well. Life is meant to be lived!"

She formed a slightly evil, knowing grin. "I'm young enough to know a lot of things. Including some you might not want everyone to know about."

Jorge's face darkened. "What is with you, Ivy? Do you dislike me for some reason?"

"No. I just find it interesting when people have secrets."

His eyes narrowed. "Secrets? What secrets?"

"You'd be surprised."

He grabbed her arm. "Are you familiar with the term 'playing with fire'?"

I was about to intervene when she wriggled free. "Are you familiar with the term 'child abuse'?"

Rachel walked up. "Is he bothering you, Ivy?"

Ivy's glare remained focused on Jorge for another beat

before she turned to smile at her mother. “Don’t worry, Mother. I can handle him.”

Rachel looked quizzically at Jorge, who walked off to join Luella and Ben. Brian and the van driver, a middle-aged woman in a blue chamois shirt and jeans, approached. He did a visual check to make sure everyone was present. “Before we start out for the trailhead, let me say a few words. I know the past two days have been stressful—not the kind of holiday you were expecting. I have spoken with Coast Ramblers management, and they have agreed to refund fifteen percent of your booking fee.”

“Fifteen percent!” Luella huffed. “You certainly work for a cheap outfit.”

“They don’t have to do that,” Roy said. “I think it’s very generous.”

Brian gave him a grateful smile. “Again, I’m certain that the . . . incidents we’ve experienced are simple, unrelated coincidences. I don’t believe they are part of any organized campaign to harm people walking on local paths. I sincerely believe we will have no further . . . unpleasantness.”

“That’s not what the café owner said yesterday,” Dave pointed out.

“Everyone’s entitled to their own opinion,” Brian said. “All I ask of you is what I ask of all my groups—stay alert. If you happen to notice anything that looks as if it may prove hazardous, please speak up. Does everyone understand?”

We all nodded.

“Brilliant. Let’s board the van then. Today we will begin our walk at mainland Britain’s southernmost point on the Lizard Peninsula. From here, it’s a drive of twenty minutes or so, and we will be walking about ten miles before finishing up in Coverack. The walk is an easy one, however—mostly flat, as it skirts around the bluffs.”

"Not too close to the edge, I hope," Rachel said.

Brian smiled. "You can relax on that score. That part of the coastline is very solid—it is almost entirely made of serpentine rock. You'll see the great streaks of stone in the green cliffs, which make it look like a lizard's skin. That's what gives the area its name."

"And for lunch?" Ben asked. "Are we planning to stop at Cadgwith Cove?"

"That's correct," Brian said. "I like to stick as close to the published itinerary as possible. There will be lunch available there for us."

We boarded the van and began passing through the gentle, rolling countryside, punctuated with trees, rocky farms, and gorse-strewn meadows. The road narrowed so much at certain points that I was certain it could not possibly allow two automobiles to pass one another—but that wasn't unusual in the British countryside, as I'd seen on previous trips. Amazingly, we didn't encounter any vehicles approaching from the other direction on these stretches.

"It sure is beautiful, isn't it?" Dave said. "I don't know what I was expecting this part of the country to look like, but it sure wasn't this."

"If you didn't know what it looked like, why did you decide to write about it?" Ivy asked. "What kind of 'journalist' does that?" The skeptical quotes around the word "journalist" were apparent in her tone.

"Ivy, knock it off," her mother side. "Why are you drilling Dave like this?"

"You must think it's weird too, don't you, Mother? If he's going to write a magazine article about this walk, why doesn't he ever take notes?" Ivy asked.

"I explained that I'm not that kind of writer," Dave said. "I let myself embrace the full experience, rather than pause every few minutes to haul out a notepad. My memory is good enough to retain the necessary details. It actually helps to let them germinate a bit in my mind. Plus, I make sure to take photos. Those jar my memory."

"Makes sense to me," Rachel said.

"You photograph my mom more than anything else," Ivy said to Dave. "Is she going to be in your article?"

Rachel swung toward her. "Ivy, stop it! What has gotten into you? I've brought you up better than to behave like this. It's none of your business who Dave photographs or how he chooses to write his article."

Ivy stayed silent but aimed a resentful glare at Dave. I was surprised she still was so confrontational after all the warnings. She'd seemed so deferential to me, giving in to my criticisms of her web-based nosiness. Was she being hard on Dave simply because he'd shown an interest in her mother? She was well aware her parents were divorcing, with what sounded like no love lost between them.

Soon the van pulled off the main road onto the lane leading to Lizard Point. After passing thatch-roofed houses and stone walls that enclosed brilliant green pastures in which cows stood (passing the time in a way only cows know how), we came to a stop at the end of the road. The driver got out, pulled open the doors, and we stepped outside.

Not far away before us was a National Trust sign affixed to a rock, announcing that we had arrived at Lizard Point. Beyond was a small pier extending into the blue waters of the bay, circled by rocky shoals. The scene stood out with crystal clarity in the crisp weather, with a salty wind blowing.

"It's so peaceful," Rachel said, with a bracing deep breath.

"That is deceptive." Brian pointed out to the sea. "Just out there, in the Channel, is one of the busiest shipping lanes in the world."

At first look, it appeared as if there was no sea traffic at all; then I began to notice ships in the distance—freighters, oil tankers, cruise ships.

Brian led us up a small hill toward the Lizard Point lighthouse, a squat white building with a pointed dome. A visitors center stood beside it, but we walked past it and continued on the coastal path as it followed the contours of the coastal bluffs. As Brian promised, there were no signs of coastal erosion.

Billie was walking beside me, Rachel and Ivy directly behind. Billie took a deep breath and released it slowly. "I swear, Chase, this sea air makes me feel about twenty years younger."

I inhaled deeply and felt the air infuse my lungs with a bracing tingle. "It certainly feels good. But have you taken a look at the fishermen around here? The air might have rejuvenation properties, but the climate makes them look old before their time."

"They just need to moisturize," Rachel said with a laugh.

Ivy began zigzagging on and off the trail around us. "Why does everyone always walk so slow?" she said.

"We're older," Rachel said. "We don't have your youthful energy."

"I'm going to get to where we're going before everyone else," Ivy said, walking fast ahead of us.

"Be sure to stay in sight of Brian!" her mother called out. As Ivy distanced herself from us, Rachel shook her head. "I swear, sometimes I don't know what I'm going to do with her."

Never having had children, I didn't feel qualified to give parenting advice. Yet I said, "She's certainly a very determined young woman."

"That's the problem," Rachel said with a sigh. "She's determined, all right, but I don't know what she wants. Part of it is that she's at an awkward age, but it doesn't help that her parents are going through a bitter divorce."

"Has she always been this . . . inventive?" I asked with what I hoped was appropriate delicacy.

Rachel barked out a short laugh. "That's a good word for it! When she was little, it was mostly harmless, stuff like claiming her dog could speak to her or that one of her friends was really a space alien. It's only in the past couple of years that it's taken a nasty turn. Her therapist claims it's a normal phase she's passing through, but I'm not so sure."

"Is there any truth to what Ivy told us the other night? About you and her being in danger from your husband?"

Rachel walked a few paces before responding. "She exaggerated as usual, but yes, there is some truth to it. Oh, Craig would never actually harm us, I'm sure of that. But he can make our lives uncomfortable in other ways. To be honest, I'm partly to blame."

"In what way?"

She grunted a bitter laugh. "I'm a divorce attorney. One of the best. To get my clients what they want, I often need to be ruthless. You're not seeing me as I am in the courtroom or in negotiations. That's where my claws really come out. Unfortunately, sometimes I let that part of myself loose at home as well."

And not just at home. I'd seen that side of her when she'd exploded at Luella the day before.

"It's even harder to contain myself when I'm in the middle of my own divorce," she continued. "I find I use some of the dirty tricks I use with my clients."

"Dirty tricks? What kind?"

"I shouldn't have used that term. I'm not talking about doing anything illegal, but maybe stretching the truth in order to score a point. It's not something I'm proud of. Actually, I don't know why I'm telling you all of this. Maybe I feel the need to confess."

Ivy was no dummy; she certainly must be aware of this side of her mother. I wondered how much it influenced her own tendency to invent stories that made others uncomfortable.

"Have you ever been married, Chase?" Rachel asked. "If you have, you know how it can prove that old saying: there's a thin line between love and hate."

My relationship with Doug had never, thank goodness, reached the point of hostility—although at times it had gotten closer than I expected. Every couple has arguments from time to time, and whenever I became too fired up (such as over his habit of constantly misplacing his car keys), I had to remind myself: Is this worth it? To Rachel, I said, "I was never married, but I had a partner for a long time. He passed away a couple of years ago."

"Oh, I'm so sorry to hear that. Craig and I might be at swords' points right now, but there's still love there, believe it or not. I would be destroyed if he were to die." She paused before adding, "I certainly hope he still feels that way about me."

Chapter 12

**Wednesday, midday,
Church Cove, Cornwall**

After two hours of easygoing walking, we reached Church Cove, a picture-perfect seaside village with a broad beach on which colorful boats rested at low tide, fishing nets stacked beside them. Around the harbor, the green strata of the rocks lining the shore testified to the peninsula's reptilian name. I pictured seventeenth-century pirates landing here in the dead of the night, sneaking onto the beach, looking for treasures.

"This morning's walk was a hard one, Chase," Billie said, as we followed Brian to an open-air café where we were to have our midmorning break. There was definitely a lag in her stride. "I was hoping my knee brace would lessen the pain, but it seems to have gotten worse."

I hadn't thought the morning's route had been particularly challenging. "I'm sorry to hear that. Maybe you should forego the rest of the day's walk. The van can take you back to the hotel."

Billie took a moment before responding. "I hate to be a quitter, you know that. Let me think about it. I can hold out until lunch, I think. How are you doing?"

"I'm doing well. I can't believe how much I've missed walking."

"You walk back in California, don't you?"

"Of course I do, but it isn't the same. There's something special about walking in England. You know that as well as I—the varied landscape, the history, the climate, or something else. I often wonder if I lived here in a previous life and that keeps calling me back."

"Anything is possible. As for me, I enjoy seeing things I'd never see at home. Look down there—where would I see water so blue and rocks so vibrant back at home?"

I shot her a raised brow. "The last I heard, Vermont is a landlocked state."

"You know what I mean. The seacoasts in New Hampshire and Maine are beautiful, but nothing like this. Maybe it's the same thing as you. Maybe I'm revisiting a previous life."

I laughed. "In the meantime, let's keep enjoying this one." I spied the van waiting for us up ahead on an access road. "I'm ready for a snack."

The van held its usual array of sugar-rich treats, as well as an assortment of crackers and local cheeses. Everyone began sampling a few and passing on their assessment to the others. Ivy grabbed a handful of yogurt-covered raisins, gulped them down, and ran to an adjoining playground, where she jumped up to some parallel bars, grabbed hold, and started inching herself across.

"She certainly has energy to burn," I said to Rachel.

"You can say that again. If only I could get her to channel it more productively."

Watching Ivy, I saw that she was more than simply energetic—she was very fit. I watched her hoist herself up onto the bars and extend her legs in one direction, then change bars and flip them around.

"Be careful!" Rachel called out.

"Does she do gymnastics?" I asked. "She's got the strength and dexterity."

"Now, there's a thought. Maybe I could get her to train for the Olympics. That would use up some of her excess energy."

Brian called for us to finish up so we could get back on the trail. Dave approached with a camera and took a shot of Rachel and me.

"Wouldn't a photo of us walking be more appropriate for your article?" I asked.

He smiled. "I'm not going to provide photos of you guys for the article; I explained that already. These are for my personal collection."

The group quickly reassembled. As we made our way out of the village, a woman having a smoke at the doorway to the local general store smiled at Jorge. "Back here so soon, handsome?" she said.

Jorge laughed nervously but didn't break a stride.

"What was that all about?" Luella asked him.

"I told you, Lulu. Ben and I came here last week to make sure the trail would be good for you. We stopped at that pub for lunch."

Soon we were out of the village and walking beside the sea. The break snacks had been light enough to provide extra energy without making us feel overwhelmed. I had a decided spring in my step. I looked back to see how Billie was managing. She was walking stiffly, but didn't seem to be in pain.

We passed beside coves, beacons, fields, all festooned with slightly blue serpentine rock. After Brian paused to give us a mini-lecture on the prevalence of this stone along this part of the peninsula, I began to see it everywhere: sometimes on the path and on the slabs used for stiles.

"Because of the stone, this path can get slippery in wet weather," Brian said. "Fortunately, we'll have no such problem today. Consider yourselves lucky."

"Lucky!" Luella said beside me as we started walking. "If I had any luck, I'd be back in Florida, sipping a Tom Collins on my lanai."

"Why didn't you just refuse when Jorge offered to bring you over here?" I asked. I didn't expect Luella to give me a straight answer, but she surprised me.

"Why do you think? More than anything else, I want to please Jorge. I thought my love life was over—I'm on the dark side of fifty, after all—and then he came along like a knight in shining armor. I had my eyes wide open, of course; lots of men are attracted to my money. But Jorge proved irresistible. He's smart, strong, handsome—I always think he looks like that eighties actor Tom Wakefield—and, best of all, he shows no interest in my money."

Ben had told me Jorge was actually broke. Luella seemed to be smarter than she came across at times. How did she not know this?

"It's also sweet that he cares about my health," she continued. "Eat this, don't eat that, do your stretching exercises, go easy on the booze. It's so nice to have someone look after me. He's a pain in the butt about it, but I know he has my best interests at heart. That's another reason why I agreed to come on this walking trip—it might help me shed a few pounds."

"You do seem to be getting into the swing of things," I said.

She eyed me knowingly. "Despite the fact that I'm such a mean old bat? Don't look shocked; I know that's what you meant."

"I wouldn't have phrased it quite like that."

"That's because you're too polite. Here's a piece of advice: don't be too polite. It won't get you anywhere. Always look out for yourself. If that means being direct, so be it."

That sounded eerily like Ivy's philosophy. It certainly wasn't mine, but I said nothing.

"You probably think I'm crazy," Luella said. "What with that little terror of a child accusing me of being a thief and Benjamin and I sniping at each other about my will. You probably wonder why you're cursed to have such a loon in your walking group."

"I would never wonder that," I said, although the thought, of course, had crossed my mind.

"There you go, being polite! I'm no fool. I know what people think of me, but you know what? I stopped caring years ago. Ben and I go at it hammer and tongs, but it's all a game, really. It's because we're too close. I should have pushed him out of the nest years ago, but he's been the only steady male in my life all these years. Now that I have Jorge, though, it would better for Ben to make a break and live his own life."

"Is that why you're not leaving your estate to him?" I said.

She blurted a laugh. "Oh, I said that just for fun. Of course, I won't cut Ben out of my will. But he's terrified of growing up. I had thought marrying Jorge would finally give Ben the push he needs, but none of my other marriages had done that, so why would I expect this one will?"

While I never cease to be amazed at how close family members, especially those who truly love one another, play games and fail to truly communicate with one another, Luella went up a notch or two in my estimation. She was no old, embittered harridan, but she was no fluttery pushover either.

* * *

For the next hour, we followed the coastal path as it gently undulated across farms and bluffs, with the sea far to our right. Occasionally, we had to negotiate stone or wooden stiles to get over the hedges or fences that surrounded the fields. At one point, we descended to a cove that had a natural rock arch at its entrance through which the sea passed to fill a small lagoon.

"That is known as the Devil's Frying Pan," Brian said. "It was formed ages ago from the collapsed roof of a sea cave."

Luella said, "It doesn't look like a frying pan to me."

"You need to wait until the weather gets rough," Brian said. "Then the sea churns up to the point where it appears to be boiling. That's when the central boulder starts to resemble an egg in a frying pan."

"Food, food, food!" Rachel exclaimed. "Everything here is always about food!"

"Speaking of food," Brian said, "we'll have our lunch up ahead in Cadgwith." I'd been enjoying the walk so much that I'd forgotten how hungry I was.

Within minutes, we arrived at a tight cluster of thatched cottages in a shallow river canyon, facing a beautiful shingle beach. Weathered fishing boats, testifying to the town's main source of income, sat on the beach near an outcropping of rocks. Hills rose gradually on both sides.

"Cadgwith is a true fishing village," Brian said as he led us into the town. "For many years, it was known for its pilchards, but overfishing has now turned the catch toward crabs, lobsters, monkfish, and conger eels. It won't surprise you to learn that fish is on the menu for today's lunch."

"Good to hear it!" Jorge said. "Fish is great for the circulatory system."

"It's also loaded with calcium, phosphorus, and all kinds of minerals," Roy added. "Fish is a real wonder food."

"Okay, okay, you can stop with the commercial," Rachel said. "Before this week is over, I'll have grown gills."

I could smell fish cooking on an outdoor grill as we approached a café at the base of a small hill. Brian asked us to select the kind of fish we wanted, and whether we wanted it served as a sandwich or by itself. It would then be cooked up and set out for us on a table in back of the inn, at the bottom of the hill. Salads or crisps were available as sides, as were local beverages doled out in cups.

"Everything sounds heavenly," Billie said as we perused the menu board.

The fish choices were cod, haddock, and plaice, which all tend to taste similar to me when fried up by a fish-and-chips vendor. These, however, all looked different, with wonderful smells tempting us from each one. I chose haddock, and Billie chose plaice. Ben was helping the proprietor, who was busy distributing the sandwiches, by pouring lemonade and fruit cider into cups.

While waiting for my lunch, I spotted a classic British phone booth toward the rear side of the café, painted green rather than the usual red. I walked over to get a closer look. On the side was a plaque identifying the phone inside as a "wind phone."

> Welcome to the Cadgwith Wind Phone. This is a place where those who grieve can continue to deepen their connection to the people they love on the other side. Please use this phone to speak with a departed loved one. The wind will take your words to those you love who have walked ahead.

What a bizarre idea. Yet it made sense. Too often, loved ones die without much-needed closure—an opportunity to resolve differences, address unsolved issues, and even say a final farewell. I wondered how much use this "wind phone" received.

I walked back to get my sandwich and drink. Once everyone got their food, Brian said, "Rather than eat inside on such a beautiful day, let's enjoy our lunch up there," he said, pointing to the hilltop above us. "We'll also be able to get a view of the sea."

We all began following him up the hill, although Billie remained at a small table not far from the café. I walked over to ask if she would join us. "I think I'll eat right here," she said to me. "That hill is one more climb that's only going to irritate my knee."

"Then I'll stay here with you," I said.

"No, Chase, go with the others. I'll be fine. I could use some quiet time."

I tilted my head, trying to discern if she was indeed okay. She smiled and nodded up to the others, prodding me to go with them. I smiled back and joined the others as they walked up to the broad, grassy hillcrest, where rocks and logs provided plenty of places to sit. I sat with Rachel and Dave on weathered wooden chairs.

"This is just what I need," Rachel said as she placed her drink on the arm of the chair and opened the wrapping around her sandwich. "Wonderful food after a bracing walk."

Ivy stood before Dave. "I was going to sit there."

"Sit over here instead, darling," Rachel said, gesturing to a nearby rock. "What difference does it make?"

Ivy glared at Dave and walked off to the far side of the hilltop.

"I don't get why she doesn't like me," he said.

"It's no mystery," Rachel said. "She sees you as competition."

"Competition? For what?"

Rachel smiled and squeezed his arm. "For my affections."

He smiled back. "Then she's right. Would you mind telling me who's winning?"

She laughed. "I have plenty enough for both of you. But let's not talk about Ivy. Right now, I just want to enjoy the view. Look at it! It makes you forget there's another life waiting for us back home." She looked out to the sea with a dreamy expression.

The others found places nearby. Ben, Jorge, and Luella were seated around a small table, Roy perched on a rock facing the sea, Brian on the ground not far from him. We all gazed out at the sea, sunlight sparkling on its surface, broken here and there by the shadows of a few wayward clouds passing overhead. The distant calls of seabirds barely penetrated the faint rush of wind. It was exceedingly tranquil, almost spiritual. It made me wish Mike was with me.

Everyone ate in silence. After a few minutes, Ben rose and walked off. Soon he returned.

"Mother, you'll never believe what I found!" he said to Luella. "There's a statue over there of Frederic!"

"Am I supposed to know who that is?" she asked.

"You know. Frederic! That guy from *The Pirates of Penzance*. The one your character Mabel was in love with."

This prompted her to get to her feet. "Really? This I have to see! I just wish it wasn't so cold up here."

"Here," Rachel said, standing and removing her blue jacket. "I'll switch jackets with you. Mine's thicker."

"Thank you!" Luella said. She put on Rachel's jacket and followed Ben to the far side of the hilltop.

Jorge chuckled as he watched them walk off. "Lulu still thinks she's as beautiful as Mabel, and I don't let her feel any different. But Frederic is the lucky one in that operetta.

He was born on a leap-year day, so he ages more slowly than any of the other characters."

Rachel yawned. "Speaking of aging, I need to rest a bit. All that walking and food has made me drowsy."

"Same here," Dave said, yawning as well. "Hey, Brian! Do we have time for a short nap?"

Brian checked his watch. "Certainly. We don't need to leave for another forty-five minutes."

Ben returned and told us that his mother was so thrilled at seeing the statue of her old boyfriend that she wanted to rest beside it. "It's bringing back memories of her long-distant youth."

"Let her enjoy herself," Jorge said. He stood and said he needed to move around. "Ben, could you come with me for a minute?"

He and Ben walked slowly to the bluff side of the hilltop, engrossed in conversation. I stood as well and found myself walking, almost against my will, down the hill toward the wind phone. I spotted Billie seated at her table, knitting and looking up at the hill and then at the sea. When I reached the phone, I looked around and saw I was alone.

This was crazy. I wasn't the type who did weird things like talking to the dead. Yet I walked into the small booth, sat, and shut the door.

I picked up the receiver. There was no keypad or dial. When I put the receiver to my ear, I could hear no dial tone—but then, it would have been insane if I had. Instead, I heard what sounded like wind.

I waited a few moments before speaking. "Hello, Doug," I began. Suddenly ashamed, I went to place the receiver back on its cradle but stopped myself. Putting it again to my ear, I said, "This is Chase. I . . . I miss you terribly. I hope that, wherever you are, you're at peace. I . . . I'm doing better, although it's taken a long time. One thing that's helped is . . . well, I've met someone. His name is Mike, and he's a Brit, can you beat that? We've been spending a lot of time together, and I think he's wonderful. Of course, he could never replace you; nobody could. But I don't want to be alone. And I don't think you'd want me to be alone either. I guess what I'm asking for . . . this is nuts . . . is your blessing. I know you can't actually speak to me, but . . . well, can you give me a sign of some kind?" I paused and heard the faint sound of wind. Whether it was coming from the phone or from outside the phone booth I couldn't tell.

"I'll let you go now," I said. "I want you to know how grateful I am for our life together. But . . . it's time for us to move on. Goodbye, my love."

Wiping a tear from my eye, I placed the receiver on its cradle and slowly opened the phone booth door. I looked up to see small white clouds drifting in the blue afternoon sky, which brought me back from thoughts of Doug. I walked over to Billie, who had nodded off while knitting, and sat opposite her. I was surprised to discover I was feeling drowsy also. Looking out at the sea, I saw a brilliant rainbow form and then dissolve. I blinked, willing the rainbow to return, but all I could see was the clear blue sky.

My heart filled with warmth and hope as I drifted off to sleep.

Chapter 13

Wednesday, afternoon,
Cadgwith Cove

I was awakened by Billie, shaking my shoulder.

"Chase! Wake up! Someone's in trouble!"

It took me a moment to snap back to reality, but when I did, I heard piercing wails in the distance.

"That's Jorge!" I sprang to my feet and began running up the hillside. At the top, our group had gathered at the far end. Jorge was on the ground beside his wife, his face buried in his hands.

"Lulu! My dear Lulu!" he cried. Atop Luella lay a large gray stone statue, her arms and legs protruding from beneath.

"She's been crushed!" Ben exclaimed.

"Quick!" I commanded. "Help me move the statue."

I might have been contaminating vital evidence, but there was still the chance that Luella was alive. Jorge and Ben got on one side, and with Brian and me opposite, we managed to lift the fallen statue off Luella's body. What was revealed wasn't pretty. Luella's nose was smashed and her face purple from bruising. Rachel screamed and looked away.

I knelt, picked up Luella's arm, and felt for a pulse. Nothing. I lifted one of her eyelids, but her eyes were cold and lifeless.

"She's gone," I said, and reached for my phone to call 999.

Jorge collapsed onto her body and started sobbing. "Lulu! Oh, my Lulu! Who did this to you?"

An operator quickly answered my call. I gave her a brief summary of what had just happened and where we were located.

"They're sending someone right away," I said to the others, all looking wide-eyed and stunned.

I needed to check one thing. Statues didn't just topple by themselves on a windless day. Bending close to the base to which the stone figure had been attached, I saw traces of it having been sawed or chiseled.

I looked up to see Billie staring at me, her eyes wide and fearful.

We were both thinking the unthinkable.

Murder had struck again.

It took a few moments for the weight of the situation to descend on everyone, and then they erupted.

"She's dead?" Ivy asked, her tone in a mixture of shock and delight. "I've never seen a dead person!"

"Luella's dead?" Roy said. "You've got to be kidding!"

"I can't believe this!" Rachel wailed. "It must be one of those trail killers."

"They would never do something like this," Brian said.

"It's just an accident, don't you think?" Dave said. "That statue must have come loose."

"Right at the moment someone was asleep beneath it?" Rachel asked, while shaking her head.

The only ones not speaking were me, Billie (whose mind was working like crazy, I'm sure), and Ben. He was looking down at his mother in numb shock. He then fell to his knees beside Jorge and placed his hands on her chest.

"Please!" I said. "Don't touch her. We need to leave the scene unspoiled until the authorities show up." Ben and Jorge moved away from Luella's body and stood.

"What authorities?" Rachel asked me.

"I dialed 999," I said. "Someone will be here soon."

There was something else that needed to be done. I began searching the ground nearby for a telltale clue. How had the statue been dislodged? Not far from us was a stone wall that surrounded half of the hilltop. Its stones were multicolored, but I didn't see any stone on top that looked out of place.

I began walking along the wall. Several feet away, I found a gap that was easy to overlook; the wall that continued beyond it was positioned two feet farther back, and began before the gap, which from a distance made the wall appear to be continuous. Walking through the gap, I spied an object a few feet off. Approaching it, I knew it was what I was looking for—a small steel crowbar.

Billie appeared at my side. "What are you doing, Chase?"

"Look at that," I said, nodding toward the tool on the ground. "I'll be damned if that wasn't how it was done."

Billie bent down to look closer. "You mean . . . someone had pre-cut the statue so that it would fall, and then dislodged it with this?"

"It sure looks like it. Of course, a forensics team will need to take a close look at both this tool and the statue. I would think there has to be a connection, but I could be wrong. In the meantime, don't touch anything. There may be prints on it. I'll let the police know when they get here. Can you stay here by the crowbar until they come?"

"You bet," she said.

I walked back to the group, still gathered around Luella's body. Roy approached me.

"This is terrible," he said. "I had no idea something like this would happen. I should never have brought my mother here."

"Don't blame yourself," I said. "We might not know who was behind this for some time, but there's nothing you could have done to prevent it."

"So, do you think . . . someone meant this to happen? To my mother?"

I didn't want to start tossing out speculations. But I began processing what I knew. Who would want Luella dead? She and Ben were always harping at one another. She had threatened to reveal something about Dave—some type of secret—the previous night at St. Mawes Castle. Ivy had angered Luella by accusing her of shoplifting the bell at the restaurant, and Luella had accused her of lying.

There were three suspects right there. But I had a hard time envisioning Ivy orchestrating something like this, as clever—and strong—as she seemed to be.

Who among us could have pried the statue with the crowbar? Jorge, certainly. He was always taking pains to demonstrate his strength. But who else?

Rachel was urging Jorge to move away from Luella. Ben remained where he was, looking closely at his mother's blood-drenched face. "I've never seen Mother's face so red," he said in a somber monotone. "Such an unusual shade. I think I would call it . . . darkening dusk."

There was nothing more to be done until the police arrived. I stayed close to Luella's body to make sure no one disturbed the crime scene.

A few minutes later, two vehicles pulled up at the base of the hill beside the café, a police car and a van, no siren announcing their arrival. A uniformed woman stepped from the car, and from the van emerged two men dressed in yellow jumpers, clearly assigned to the removal of the body.

They climbed the hill and walked toward us. I approached the woman, who introduced herself as DS Healey. I told her I was the one who called in the crime. She pulled out a pocket recorder and asked me who I was and what I'd seen.

"My name is Rick Chasen. I'm a member of the same walking group as the . . . deceased, Luella Campos." I figured I might as well get my past history as a police detective out in the open, which I did. This elicited raised eyebrows. Then I detailed the basics of finding Luella's body, the condition it was in, and the presence of the crowbar. I said that it might have been used to topple the statue on top of Luella.

Healey's eyes briefly flared. "Isn't that . . . rather unlikely?"

"Perhaps. But it's the only explanation that fits. Come with me. I'll show you."

She accompanied me over to the fallen statue. I explained that we lifted it off Luella's body to see if she was still alive. She nodded as she examined the statue, seemingly unconcerned about our maneuvering key evidence. She stooped to examine the broken base of the statue. "You're saying that this statue was dislodged by a crowbar of some sort?"

"Over here," I said, leading her through the gap in the wall to where Billie was waiting. Healey looked down at the crowbar and nodded. "I'll bag it up," she said, pulled out gloves and a bag, and went to work. When she was finished, she turned to me and gave me a small smile. "Good work, finding this."

She went back to where the men were securing Luella's body to a stretcher, but I lingered behind, looking again at the stone wall, struck by how easy it would be not to notice the gap if you were standing near the statue. How would the killer have known it was there?

Jorge continued to be out of control with grief, crying and blaming himself for not keeping closer watch on Luella. "Why did I leave her alone? How could I have been so thoughtless! I'll never forgive myself."

Of course, I understood the horror of losing a loved one, but still, I thought he might be overdoing it. "How could you have known someone was going to kill her? Go easy on yourself. None of us expected something like this would happen."

"I did," Ben said.

"What do you mean?" I asked, turning toward him. "Did you hear someone planning to kill your mother?"

"Of course not. But she was such a bitch!"

"Does being a 'bitch,' as you say, deserve a death sentence?"

"It certainly might. I couldn't have done it, of course. She's my mother, for God's sake. Do you think I would kill my own mother?"

"Many people have."

"Well, not me. Besides, I was sleeping, like the rest of you."

"We all were," Dave said. "I think one of the local landowners is to blame, to be honest. One of the bunch who booby-trapped the trail. He probably slinks around behind the trees and wears a black costume. The Cornwall Crusher!"

"Don't make a joke out of this," Rachel said. "Luella is dead all right, and someone killed her. But it was no masked crusader."

"It's as clear as day what happened," Ivy said, walking up to Dave. "One of us killed her! And what does the killer do? He tries to blame someone else. It was you, admit it! Luella found out who you really were and you had to shut her up!"

"And who am I, Miss Smarty Pants?" Dave countered.

"I don't know, but I do know you're no writer. Which means you could be a serial killer. You sure look like one!"

"That's enough, Ivy!" her mother shouted. "I don't know what's come over you, but I've never seen you like this. As your mother, I demand that you knock this off. Don't make up lies about people. I've raised you better than that."

Would these demands be as futile as the others she'd given? Ivy glared at her mother. "Is that what you've done? 'Raised' me?" She turned and ran off.

Rachel began crying, and Dave put his arm around her. "Don't worry about her. She's just going through a hard time."

She looked up at him. "And what about me? My husband has threatened to kill me, and my daughter is becoming some kind of a paranoid avenger."

An avenger? Had Ivy killed Luella? She was a young girl, but she'd shown that she had strength beyond her years. Could she have pried that heavy statue loose so that it bashed in Luella? It strained credulity, but it wasn't impossible.

Ivy's capabilities aside, what would have been her motive? Luella had accused her of lying about the shoplifting accusation, but that hardly seemed like justification for murder. Yet who knows what goes on in the mind of a young girl? Perhaps she was trying to frame Dave.

The police crew were about to take Luella's body down to the van, and asked Jorge, as Luella's husband, to accompany them to the local morgue. As the van pulled away, another police vehicle drove up, and a middle-aged woman stepped out, wearing not a uniform but a tailored suit with a brightly colored cerise-and-magenta scarf. She walked up to DS Healy, who brought her up to date on what had happened, and nodded toward me.

"Detective Inspector Sheila Holt, Cornwall CID," she said. "I understand you discovered the body?"

"Uh . . . not exactly. Her husband, I believe, was the one who first found her. He's in the ambulance." She looked over at the departing vehicle and then back at me. I introduced myself and explained, in as few words as possible, the circumstances of the group.

"You're a walking group?" she asked. "Like the Ramblers?"

"Something like that, yes. You really should be speaking with our guide, Brian."

She formed an unusual smile . . . seductive? Coy? "I'm with *you* now, so I'll speak with you. You sound American."

"Guilty as charged. I'm from California."

"I won't hold that against you. You're a big fella, aren't you?"

"Is that a problem?"

"Not with me, I assure you."

Was that a flirtatious smile? I needed to put a stop to this. "I suppose you'll want to speak to the others. They're all over there."

Her smile faded. "Yes, of course. Lead the way."

The nearest of our group was Roy. She went up to him and said, "Your name, please."

Roy hesitated. Was this a difficult question?

"Burke," he said, with a side look to see who might be overhearing. In a hushed tone, he said, "Roy Burke."

Inspector Holt collected the others' names and told us to wait while she went to confer with Brian. When she left, Ben turned to Roy. "Burke? You told us your name was Hemper!"

Roy looked remorseful. "Whatever I may have said, Burke is my name. It doesn't matter now anyway."

"What do you mean, it doesn't matter?" Ben turned to me. "Do you know who this guy is? He owns the restaurant in New Orleans where my mother was nearly killed! She filed a major lawsuit against him. What's he doing on this walking tour?"

Roy was the last person I'd suspect of harboring such a secret. To him I asked, "Is that right? Have you been disguising your real identity?"

He took a deep breath. "My real name is Roy Burke. I own Ragin' Cajun Restaurants in Memphis as well as in the French Quarter. Luella Dean—that was her name at the time—dined there a couple years back. One of my servers was known for doing the knife trick I mentioned the other night. She decided she could do the trick also. She grabbed his knife and proceeded to fling it right into her shoulder. The paramedics were called, but she was okay; she went into hysterics even though she wasn't seriously injured. Then she started making accusations—against the server, against the restaurant, against me. That we were to blame for her stupidity!"

I put two and two together as fast I could. "So . . . you came on this walk . . . why? To try to convince Luella that she was mistaken? Or . . . to get her out of the way?"

"I'm no murderer!" he exclaimed. "You're right, Chase. I thought if I could speak to her, away from lawyers and everything, she might see reason. Hah! It didn't take me long to see there was no reasoning with that kind of woman."

"I could have told you that," Ben said.

"How did you learn that Mrs. Campos was going on this walk?" I asked.

"It wasn't difficult. I asked my lawyer to arrange a meeting between us. He didn't think it was a good idea and told me that she was unavailable anyway. She'd planned some travel with her new husband."

"How did he know that?"

"She needed to give a deposition on the lawsuit. Her lawyer told him that would have to wait until she returned to the States. He mentioned she was coming on this tour. So I decided to sign up for it. I didn't tell him."

"He would have advised you against it," I said. "It's rarely a good idea for the plaintiff and defendant to try to work things out on their own."

Roy nodded. "Yes, I know all of that. But I grew up in a small town in northern Mississippi. When folks there had differences, we didn't get the law involved unless it was absolutely necessary. Most of the time we were able to resolve our disputes among ourselves. I know it's unrealistic, but I thought it could happen here."

"That's why you've been trying to sit near Luella at all the meals."

He raised an eyebrow. "You noticed? Then you saw what happened—she always found some excuse to get rid of me. I try not to be a guy who sees racism behind every slight, but it's pretty clear that's what's going on."

I remembered Luella mistaking Roy for a hotel bellman the day we arrived. She didn't make that mistake with any of the others. I couldn't blame him for making such a connection.

"If she were to have won her lawsuit, that would have been bad news for you, wouldn't it?" Dave asked Roy.

"Her lawyers are top-tier. Even though Luella's claim was bogus, I could have very likely lost my shirt, as well my restaurants."

Dave cocked his head. "Wow. As motives for murder go, that one's a doozy."

"There's one more thing I don't understand," I said to Roy. "Ivy did a Google search for your assumed name and came up with the name of a convicted murderer in Nevada. Doesn't that seem a weird coincidence?"

"Are you kidding me? No way did I know that. I pulled the name Hemper out of thin air."

I was contemplating the likelihood of such a coincidence when DI Holt worked her way through the members of the group, coming up to me. "I've spoken briefly with all the others," she said, "but I'll need to get more complete accounts. Rather than take everyone to the station, which is several miles away in Penzance, I can set up shop at your hotel. You lot are staying at The Carne, is that correct?" When I nodded in agreement, she smiled. "Must be a luxury walking tour company to afford digs like that. Anyway, thanks for your help. I'll see you in a couple of hours." I watched her walk away.

"So it's happened again."

I turned to find Billie by my side. "Don't say it. You think we're jinxed. That we invite murder wherever we go."

"You can't blame me for thinking so."

I placed my hands on her shoulders. "There's another way of looking at it. Like we speculated the other day. Perhaps we're confronted with crime because we're so good at sniffing out the culprit."

"You mean you are."

"Nonsense. You've been essential to the solution of every one of our cases."

" 'Cases'!" she said. "You make us sound like Sherlock Holmes and Dr. Watson."

I looked her in the eye. "Isn't that precisely who we are?"

Chapter 14

**Wednesday, late afternoon,
St. Mawes, Cornwall**

We were a far more morose group on the ride back to the hotel. Because the murder victim was Ben's mother and Jorge's wife, none of us knew what to say in Ben's presence.

Ivy, of course, was the first to attempt it. "So who's going to confess?" she asked Ben.

"Ivy!" her mother said. "What a thing to say. It's horrible what happened to that old woman. How can you think one of us did it?"

"My mother was not an old woman," Ben said. "And, of course, none of us did it! Someone else was walking around up there, probably some deranged local person. Maybe one of the anti-walking-path people."

"There wasn't anyone else up there," Ivy said. "I would have noticed."

I began searching my memory, looking for that temporal toehold that would give me access to my recall, but I couldn't find it. The only recollection I had was of everyone enjoying their lunch on the hilltop and then dozing off. After I finished my sandwich, I'd walked down to the wind phone, and after that I fell asleep as well, beside Billie at her table.

"I don't remember anyone else there either," Rachel said. "But then I fell asleep for a while. Most of us did."

"There was definitely a stranger up there," Ben insisted. "He was tall, wearing a gray jacket and a dark cap."

"It was probably Jorge," Dave said. "He was wearing a gray jacket today, wasn't he?"

"It was a light gray, not dark gray," Ben replied. "I would call it burnished pewter or maybe dusty ash. Anyway, I would recognize Jorge, for Pete's sake, and he wasn't wearing a cap."

Dave sighed. "Let's not quibble over shades of gray. I didn't see anyone else up there besides us."

Ivy formed a self-satisfied grin. "That's just what I said."

"Weren't most us asleep?" Rachel asked. "I saw all of you drift off. Even Brian! We wouldn't have noticed if someone else had come into the field."

"Jorge didn't sleep," Ivy said. "He was walking around before I fell asleep and was still prowling around after I woke up."

"He's strong enough to shove that statue over onto Luella," Rachel said.

"How many times do I have to tell you?" Ben said, his voice rising. "It wasn't Jorge! He adored my mother, for heaven's sake. There was someone else up there."

Everyone was going around in circles, and I certainly wasn't going to add fuel to the fire by adding my own theories—which were only half-formed at that point anyway.

Looking at the passing scenery wasn't much of a diversion. The afternoon had turned cloudy and damp, a fitting turn for this day. We soon arrived at The Carne, where Chief Inspector Holt's car was already parked near the entrance.

As we got out of the van, I saw Rachel give a shiver. "Luella was still wearing my jacket when they hauled her off," she said. "Good thing I've got another in my room."

At the front desk, we were directed to a cozy, firelit nook down the hallway where Holt was awaiting us. Seated with her was a timid-looking, dark-haired Middle Eastern woman.

"Ah! There you are," Holt said as she saw the group. She held up her cell phone. "I made a note of all your names and shared them with DC Kahlil here. She'll be assisting me in my interviews. But, first, let me ask: Was everyone in your walking group on that hilltop today?"

"As far as we can tell, yes," said Brian. "Many of us dozed off after eating our lunch, so it's impossible to tell who may have walked off, but, to my knowledge, none of us did."

"Let me be the judge of what is 'impossible' or not," Inspector Holt said. She paused to let that demand sink in. "So . . . the constable and I want to speak to each of you individually about what you recall—or don't—about what happened to Mrs. Campos today. Our first victim will be"—she checked her phone—"Mr. Teague?"

"That's me," Brian said.

"Quite so. Why don't the rest of you wait somewhere nearby, either here or at the bar. I shan't be long with Mr. Teague, and I will send him to fetch the next victim when we're finished."

"The bar is just a few steps away," Roy said. "That sounds good to me."

"I need to get some air," Rachel said. "Ivy, why don't we wait outside on the terrace? It's turned gloomy, but there's still a pretty view."

"Just boats and seaweed," Ivy grumbled as she went off with her mother, who excused herself to go to her room for her spare jacket.

The rest of us headed for the bar.

"I wish the inspector wouldn't refer to us as 'victims,' " Roy said.

"It's her pale attempt at humor," I commented, thinking that calling us "suspects" would still be unsettling. So far, Inspector Holt hadn't impressed me greatly. I would have expected her to request a thorough search of the murder scene and to question the café staff. Perhaps she had and I hadn't noticed. I wondered if Mike knew her and figured that he must. The county was right beside his own, after all.

When we entered the bar, where Jorge was seated by himself at a far table, looking down woefully at a tankard of ale clutched in his hands. He didn't look up at us.

The man behind the small bar asked us what drinks we wanted.

"Under the circumstances, beer doesn't sound very good to me," Billie said.

"There's no such thing as a bad time for beer," Dave said and ordered a pint of local ale. Ben followed suit.

When I ordered my beer, Billie gave in and did as well. We carried our drinks over to a table beside Jorge, who looked up at us, his expression vacant.

"How did things go at the morgue?" I asked.

"They need to perform an autopsy on Luella," he said. "But it's clear what killed her."

"That cop lady will be speaking with each of us," Ben told him. "She's with Brian right now."

Jorge's face tightened. "They'd better catch the monster who did this! And when they do, they'll need to hold him back from me or I'll tear him apart."

"I don't think that would be a good idea," I said. "You'd better let the authorities over here handle it."

"It has to be one of those locals who want to scare the

walkers off the paths," Dave said. "What better way to do that than to show that a killer is loose?"

I remembered Ben's comment about seeing a stranger shortly before Luella was killed. I asked Jorge, "Did you see anyone up on the hilltop earlier you didn't recognize?"

"You mean . . . someone other than our group?"

I nodded.

He looked over at Ben, who was waiting for his answer. "Well, yes . . . there was someone, I think. It was a short guy . . . that is, I think it was a guy. He was wearing a jacket and had a hat pulled down over his face, so it was hard to tell."

I was about to press him for details, but Ben jumped in. "He was wearing a gray jacket, right? And the guy wasn't short, was he? I saw him too, and he was pretty tall."

Jorge stared defiantly at Ben. "No, he was short." Looking at the rest of us, he added, "But it was hard to tell. He might have been standing on the downside of the hill."

"You didn't fall asleep like the rest of us, did you?" I asked.

He shook his head. "I don't get tired in the middle of the day."

"But . . ." Billie began. "If you weren't asleep, why didn't you notice that someone was . . . attacking your wife?"

Jorge's face twisted with anguish. "I don't know! I can't understand it. I was walking around and wasn't near her, but I should have been paying attention. I could have saved her!"

His pain seemed real, and very affecting. This was a man in torment. Yet his story didn't completely ring true. He had echoed Ben's recollection of another man up on the hill with us, yet nobody else had seen this person. Also, it seemed curious that Jorge heard no sounds of the attack on Luella. Surely chipping away at the base of the statue would have made noise.

"The police will follow up with all the local trouble-makers; I'm sure of it," Dave said.

"I wish I could be as sure of that," Roy said. "I hadn't counted on anything like this happening."

"You must have counted on the possibility that Mrs. Campos would find out who you really are," Dave said. "What would you have done then?"

"What do you mean?" Jorge asked, and turned to Roy. "Who are you?"

"His real name is Burke," Ben said. "He's the guy Mom was suing after getting knifed in one of his restaurants."

"She did that to herself!" Roy shouted at Ben.

"Well, this explains everything!" Jorge said. "Now we have someone with a clear motive."

Roy looked at Jorge face-to-face. "Do you really want to start talking about motives? A younger man who just married an older, wealthier woman?"

"That's ridiculous," Ben said.

Roy swung to him. "And what about you? You and your mother argued like hellcats, and she was just about to cut you out of her will."

Ben stood. "I don't have to listen to this B.S."

Roy had made some good points, but it was time to intervene. "Please, everyone, calm down," I said. "It's easy to get carried away after what we've just been through. I implore everyone to think before they speak."

Dave was about to respond, but he closed his mouth. The talk about motives reminded me of Luella's threat to him the night before. *I'll let Rachel know of your past. She won't like that one bit.*

Brian returned and was assaulted with questions. What did the inspector want to know? Did she have her mind made up about who killed Luella? Were there any other suspects?

"Hold on!" Brian said. "All she asked for were details

about this afternoon up on the hill. I'm ashamed to admit I fell asleep along with the rest of you lot. It was my responsibility to look after you and protect you from danger, and I was derelict in my duty."

"That's nonsense," Billie said. "How were you to know there was a killer nearby?"

Brian hung his head. "Nevertheless, that's how I feel, and I will have to make my peace with it. Oh, I almost forgot. Inspector Holt wants to speak with Mr. Purdue next."

Ben rose and walked off. I figured I had time to go outside and see how Rachel and Ivy were doing. The woman seemed particularly spooked by Luella's death, and I suspected it had something to do with concerns about her daughter.

On the hotel terrace, a sidewalk artist was working on a pastel portrait of Ivy, seated on the terrace wall, the harbor still reflecting the late-afternoon vibrant blue sky. It seemed an odd time for such an artist to be working—there were no tourists about—yet his work was surprisingly good: he'd captured Ivy's odd combination of youthful exuberance and precocious cynicism.

"Take a look at this, Chase," said Rachel, nodding to the portrait. She was wearing her other jacket, a blue weatherproof. "What do you think?"

I took another look at the work in progress. "It's a keeper."

"Are we almost through?" Ivy asked impatiently.

"Just another minute or two, lass," the artist replied, a hollow-faced, sixtyish man speaking in a thick Cornwall accent.

Rachel turned toward the sea, where a stunning sunset was forming. She took a deep breath. "This all seems so unreal, doesn't it? Here we are, in a beautiful corner of the world, and yet ugliness has intruded. Just as it has back home. It seems I can't escape it."

"This has nothing to do with you," I said. "You were just in the wrong place at the wrong time."

"You mean the killer might have pushed that statue on me instead of Luella?"

That wasn't what I'd meant at all. But her comment made me think. "It's possible," I said. "You gave Luella your coat, didn't you?"

"Do you mean the killer thought it was me lying there beside the statue? If that's true, then I was the intended victim. That means they'll try again!"

"Luella may have been wearing your coat, but her face was in clear view," I pointed out. "It's unlikely a killer would make that kind of mistake." I said this to reassure Rachel, although who knows what a killer would think when they were racing against the clock. "I'm sure you weren't the target."

"But why should any of us have been a target in the first place? I came halfway around the world to protect myself, only to place Ivy and myself in harm's way? What a joke!"

It was time to get hold of some facts. "Did you come over here because you felt your husband was a direct threat to you back home?"

Rachel looked up at me. "Absolutely. Despite what I told you before, he can be dangerous when he's cornered, and he hates losing. I know he'd hired people to spy on me and inform him of my whereabouts. I didn't believe he would hurt us, but now I'm not so sure. Why would he hire a detective if he wasn't planning something?"

"Is your husband a man capable of . . . murder?"

She sighed. "He's very possessive, and he sees me as one of his possessions. As I said, he doesn't like to lose his possessions."

"But you and Ivy can't stay here forever. At some point, you'll have to go back home."

"The final hearing for the divorce is in two weeks. Once that's over, I'll be free. In the legal sense, at any rate."

I wondered if her husband was the type to hold a grudge. "Has your husband ever been guilty of a violent crime before?"

"He's too slick for that. He has flunkies who do his dirty work for him."

"How dirty?"

She thought a moment. "You're talking about murder? You know, it's frightening to admit . . . I don't know."

The artist pushed back his chair and held up the drawing of Ivy he'd just completed. "A masterpiece!" he said.

"Let me see," Ivy said and rushed over to look. She was clearly disappointed. "Yuck!"

Unlike her, I was surprised at how artful it was. It showed Ivy a touch beyond her years, with a mature look in her eyes, accentuated by the slight tilt of her head, revealing a jeweled earring that offset her brash adolescent demeanor. I looked toward her and saw that the earring was purely the artist's invention.

"What do you mean 'yuck'?" her mother said. "He made you look better than you really are."

"I know," Ivy said. "That's the problem. I'll never be that beautiful."

I placed my hand on her shoulders and turned her toward me. "Don't say things like that about yourself. You're a pretty young girl, and you're smart and clever. You shouldn't put yourself down."

She hung her head. "I don't know if I'm pretty or smart. But I know other things."

Rachel pulled her close. "You know lots of things, darling. You're a regular treasure trove of knowledge."

Ivy pulled away. "There you go, treating me like a baby again! When I say I know things, I mean . . . I know who killed that old lady."

"Don't be ridiculous," Rachel said.

Was it ridiculous? Ivy was prone to inventing tall stories, but what if she told one that might be correct?

"So, who do you think killed Mrs. Campos?" I asked Ivy.

"Um . . . hello?" she said. "It's obvious."

"It isn't obvious to me," I said.

"It's Jorge! Or that man who calls himself Jorge. He's an actor who was using her to research a role he's going to play. She found out his secret and threatened to expose him."

"Nonsense," Rachel said. "All along you've been accusing Dave of being a killer, and now you say it's Jorge!"

I knelt in front of the girl and looked her in the eye. "Enough of your fantasies, Ivy. If this is true, I have to ask: What proof do you have?"

She lifted her chin in defiance. "I heard the two of them talking—Mrs. Campos and Jorge—this morning, as we were leaving the breakfast room. She accused him of not being honest with her. He swore that he was, and she said he wasn't as good an actor as he thought. See? She knew!"

That didn't exactly sound like proof to me. "Was that all you heard?"

She smiled. "He said one more thing."

"What was it?"

"He was surprised to see me there. He looked at me and said, 'If you tell anyone about this, it will be the last thing you'll ever say.' "

Chapter 15

Wednesday, late afternoon,
St. Mawes, Cornwall

"What?" Rachel said. "If Jorge said that to you, why didn't you tell anyone?"

Ivy's smile faded. "Because nobody would believe me!" She looked up at me. "He would deny it and everyone would believe him. They think I just make stuff up."

I directed my gaze into her eyes. "This isn't a game, young lady. You're talking about people whose lives are at stake. If you swear that was precisely what you heard, I'll believe you. But if it turns out you're wrong, I'll never believe anything you say."

She looked chastened. "Well . . . I heard *something*. Maybe it wasn't exactly like I said. But Mrs. Campos was angry at Jorge and said something about him keeping something from her. And he definitely warned me against spreading it around."

I looked at my watch. "We'd better get back inside. Holt will be wanting to interview us soon."

We arrived back inside the bar just as Ben returned and told Roy he was next on the inspector's list of interviewees. He walked off.

Ben turned to everyone. "Roy Burke! Doesn't his change of name tell you enough? He pretended he was someone else and traveled across the Atlantic to confront the woman who was suing him for everything he's worth. If that isn't a motive for murder, what is?"

I recalled juries who had weighed far more convincing evidence than this and rendered a "not guilty" verdict. "Why would Roy have repeatedly tried to speak with your mother—to reason with her—if his goal was to kill her?" I asked.

"Reason with my mother?" Ben said. "Are you serious? That never happens! Roy learned that and knew that the only way to deal with her was to shut her up . . . permanently."

I studied his frenzied expression. Was it anguish over the death of his mother? Or guilt?

"This is so maddening!" Rachel exclaimed. "Why would any of us have wanted to kill her? Yes, she was a royal pain, but is that enough to want her dead? To kill, someone has to feel threatened."

"Didn't you feel threatened when she went after your daughter?" I asked.

Rachel was taken aback. "Yes, I suppose I did. But that woman was harmless. What could she do to actually hurt us?"

Roy returned, looking none the worse for wear.

"Did you tell them everything?" Dave asked.

Roy didn't respond. Instead, he looked at Jorge and said, "The inspector wants to speak with you next."

It took a while for this request to register with Jorge, but after a few moments, he stood up. Ben directed him toward the room where the inspector was conducting the interviews, and Jorge walked off.

"I feel sorry for him," Billie said. "He got more on this walk than he bargained for."

I squeezed her arm. "We've all got more than we bargained for."

Roy called over to the bartender and ordered a double-strength Manhattan. Turning to us, he said, "There's something about pure Kentucky bourbon and sweet vermouth that soothes the soul as nothing else can. Except Otis Redding singing 'Try a Little Tenderness.' "

Rachel said, "Well, your legal troubles are over now at any rate. There's no lawsuit if the plaintiff dies."

"Her estate could still go forward with it," Roy said.

"That would be unlikely, given how unfounded the accusation seems to be," she replied.

After a few minutes, Jorge returned, looking much the same—deflated. He sat before his half-finished beer and resumed studying it as if it were an existential problem.

"Did you learn anything from the inspector?" Dave asked.

It took a moment for Dave's question to register. Instead of responding to it directly, Jorge looked up at Dave. "She wants to see you next."

Dave girded himself and left the room. I thought again about the accusation Luella had thrown at him the previous night. What was he hiding?

Ivy approached Jorge. "Did you tell that policewoman who you really are?"

"Ivy!" her mother reproached.

Jorge looked up at Ivy. "Why don't you think I am who I say I am?"

"You're Tom Wakefield, aren't you? Come on, it's obvious! How dumb do you think we are?"

Jorge wiped his hands over his face as he digested Ivy's accusation. "Tom Wakefield? You mean that TV star from many years ago? Why would you think I was him?"

Rachel took a closer look at him. "You do look like him. When he was younger, that is."

"All I know is that Mrs. Campos was sure Jorge was keeping something from her," Ivy said.

Jorge lasered his eyes into hers. "Listen, kid, I don't know what you may have heard, but it's not nice to stick your nose into other people's business."

"Even if the 'business' is murder?"

"Why, you—"

"Ivy, ease up," I said sharply.

She was fighting to continue with her accusations, but remained silent. Could she finally be learning to control herself?

Jorge stood and looked at Rachel. "You need to keep your daughter under control. My precious wife was just murdered, for God's sake." He walked off.

"I know what I heard," Ivy said. "He's hiding something."

Rachel was about to respond when Dave returned. He was not his usual pleasant, life-is-a-dream self. His eyes looked haunted, and he avoided her glance.

"What's wrong?" she asked. "You look as if you've seen a ghost."

Dave looked at her but didn't respond.

Rachel came up to him and took his hand. "Come on, now. What did the inspector ask you?"

He shook off her hand. "Just the usual. What I saw, etcetera, etcetera. What could I say? I was snoozing like the rest of us. I didn't see anything!"

His denial rang false, as if he was trying to avoid telling her what really happened.

Rachel noticed it too. "Did the inspector imply that you *did* see something?"

"Of course not. Where's Billie? She's up next."

I motioned to Billie, knitting at a corner table. She nodded, put her knitting in her bag, and passed us on her way out of the room. I caught up to her and said, "Ask the inspector when she wants to speak with me. Maybe I fell off her list."

She gave me a wry smile. "I doubt you'd fall off anyone's list, Chase. But I'll ask."

Dave sat beside Rachel on a barstool, but they didn't speak. Something was clearly on his mind. Usually, the two fell into an easy repartee, and that wasn't happening.

After a few minutes, Billie returned and told Rachel she was next.

"Oh," she said. "All right. Come on, Ivy."

"No," Billie said. "She wants to speak with you alone. Ivy will come after."

"Very well." Before walking off, she turned to Ivy. "I'll be right back. Don't cause any trouble when I'm gone."

"What, you think I'm going to burn the place down?" Ivy asked.

"It's crossed my mind," Rachel said and walked away.

I asked Billie why the inspector hadn't yet called on me.

"She's saving you for last."

Uh-oh. "Why? Does she think I'm the killer?"

"Don't be ridiculous. She knows about your law-enforcement background. I think maybe she wants to have a longer chat with you than with the others." She smiled and went back to the table to resume her knitting.

Now that her mother was gone, Ivy went over to Dave. "I . . . I don't think you're a killer anymore."

"Um . . . gee, thanks."

"But you're hiding something too." She said this without her usual bravado.

"Like what?"

"That inspector lady found out that you aren't who you say you are."

"Ivy," I said. "Remember what I just told you? Don't accuse someone without proof!"

"But I have proof."

"Just because someone doesn't come up in a Google search does not automatically mean they're hiding something. And, more than anything, you're not a law-enforcement official. It's not up to you to accuse anyone." I hoped I sounded convincing. I didn't mention that I'd Googled Dave and found him listed as a professional pianist with a slightly different name.

"I Googled Dave Langdon in New York," Ivy said. "Shouldn't there be at least one person with that name?"

"Stop!" Dave shouted, raising his hands in surrender. "You're right. I'm not a journalist."

Ivy turned to me and beamed. "See?"

He swung toward her. "But I'm not a serial killer or whatever you think I am either. I had a good reason to hide my identity from Mrs. Scattergood. Or at least I thought I did. Now I'm not so sure. In fact, now I think I made the biggest mistake of my life." Dave's eyes were hollowed with regret.

A voice came from the doorway. "I can tell you exactly who he is!"

Rachel came forward, her face twisted with anger. "He's a private investigator! Sent by my husband to spy on me!" She grabbed Ivy and was about to lead her off when Dave placed himself in front of her.

"Give me a chance to explain!" he pleaded.

"What possible explanation can there be?" she shot back. "You deceived me!"

"Yes, I did. But I was just about to come clean with you. Truly I was."

Rachel remained stern-faced but hesitated.

"It's true that Craig hired me to keep tabs on you," Dave continued. "That's what I do for a living. But then something happened that's never happened to me in my whole career."

Rachel looked up at him. "What was that?"

"I started to fall in love with my mark." He paused. "Um . . . that means you."

Rachel's angered expression faded momentarily, then sprang back. "And I'm supposed to believe you now?"

Ivy rolled her eyes. "Oh, brother. He'll say anything! If you'll excuse me, I'm going to go speak with the inspector. I've got lots to tell her." She began walking away.

"Ivy," I called out. She stopped and looked at me. "Whatever you tell her, it had better be the truth."

She gave me a nod before heading off.

Rachel continued to regard Dave coldly. "I can't believe Craig would hire a detective to follow me around! I know he's a lousy jerk, but even this seems beneath him."

"My instructions were to find out anything I can to help his case against you," Dave said. "It's not unusual in divorce cases."

"What kind of things was he looking for? Craig knows everything about me."

"He was convinced you were coming over here to meet someone, a man you'd been seeing for some time. He believed you'd been cheating on him for years."

"Are you serious? Does this mystery man have a name?"

"He believes it's someone called Leon Schneider."

"Leon? This is getting crazier and crazier! Leon's my yoga instructor. He's as gay as gay can be. And I don't think he's ever been to England."

Dave smiled. "Yes, I discovered that pretty early on, but Craig thought it was all a clever bluff. Still, I agreed to come over here and report back what you and Ivy were up to. But I have kept one piece of information to myself."

Rachel's eyes tightened. "What is that?"

Dave placed his hands on Rachel's shoulders. "That Craig has superb taste in women."

This earned Dave an appreciative smile. "Unfortunately, Craig likes to taste a lot of women," Rachel added.

"So I understand. He's a real skirt chaser, all right. Believe me, your case against Craig is much stronger than his against you."

"But . . . what will you do now? Once he finds out your cover has been blown, he may refuse to pay you."

Dave smiled wickedly. "Yes, but Craig doesn't have to know that, does he? I won't tell him if you won't."

"Isn't that unethical?"

"Probably."

Rachel let out a long sigh. "I'm going to get myself a nice strong cocktail."

As she walked off to the bar, I approached Dave. "I need to ask you something."

He turned to me. "Shoot."

"From what I've learned, Craig Scattergood is a well-known lawyer. Are most of your clients that high-profile?"

Dave nodded. "These days, mostly, yes. I've earned my reputation working for famous people who want to be discreet."

"But, in doing that, haven't you become somewhat famous yourself? That can't be good for a man in your line of work."

I could see my comment struck home. "Yes, that . . . is a problem sometimes."

"Has it been a problem very recently?"

His face tensed. "What do you mean?"

I told him the previous night I'd overheard Luella threatening to expose him.

He knew it would be pointless to deny it. "Yes, she knew me as an investigator for hire because I'd helped out one of her society friends. And I know what you're thinking. That exchange gave me a very good reason to shut the old girl up . . . permanently. But I meant what I told Rachel just now. I wasn't planning on keeping up this charade much longer anyway."

He sounded sincere enough, but his explanation didn't fit what I'd heard. "Luella said she would tell Rachel about your past. If the secret was your job as a private detective, how could that be in your past?"

This jolted him. "I . . . I don't know. I guess she got it wrong." He looked over at Rachel. "Excuse me." He went and joined her at the bar.

"She wants to see you next," came a voice beside me. It was Ivy.

"How did your interview with the inspector go?"

"Okay, I guess. I stuck to what I can prove, in case you're worried. I didn't mention anything I'd seen online."

"Good girl."

"Still, she seemed very interested in what I had to say. But I get the feeling that she isn't very smart."

"Why do you say that?"

"She didn't ask many questions. Not like what the detectives do on all the TV shows. Even you ask more questions."

"Don't be too hard on her. Maybe she needs time to process everything. And don't think this is the last you've seen of her. She might cycle back to you with more questions." What I didn't say was that Holt might have underestimated Ivy, thinking her to be more of a child than the frighteningly bright young woman she actually was. I shuddered as I realized that some of the others might be underestimating her too. Including the murderer.

Chapter 16

Wednesday, late afternoon,
The Carne Bar

I left Ivy—eyeing her mother and Dave, chatting together at the bar, without the usual disapproving scowl on her face—and went to find the inspector. In the parlor, she was seated in a comfortable chair by the fire, with Detective Constable Khalil seated on a similar chair on the other side of a small table.

"Ahh, Mr. Chasen," Holt said when she saw me. She nodded to a chair opposite. "Please have a seat. I've been looking forward to speaking with you."

I sat. "I was wondering why you saved me for last. I hope that's not a bad sign."

She chuckled. "Not at all. When I started interviewing your group, all I heard was how lucky we are to have a famous lawman in our midst. Miss Mondreau told me you have assisted investigations on our turf before. You should have mentioned that earlier."

"I didn't see the point, at least not at the time. I'm not one for blowing my own horn."

"So I've learned," she said and looked down at a tablet on her lap. "But now that we have that out in the open, I'd like to see if your recollection about what happened this afternoon matches what I've heard from the others."

I took a deep breath. "Well, let me see what I can do. We reached Cadgwith Cove after our morning walk, arriving at around eleven-thirty. We ordered our lunches from the café, and once they were ready, we went up the hill to eat, as Brian suggested."

"Brian suggested that?"

"Yes, but it was an obvious decision. There were tables and chairs around the café, but there was no view from there. It was a beautiful day today, and the hilltop was a perfect place to sit down and look out at the sea."

"Did Brian instruct everyone where to sit?" Holt asked.

"No, nothing like that. We all found places to sit on chairs or rocks, or on the ground. Oh, I forgot to mention—not all of us went up there. Billie's knee was bothering her, so she remained down at the café."

"Yes, she mentioned that to me."

"Good." I was about to continue my explanation of what happened before Luella's body was discovered, but paused. How much did I want to reveal to Holt? I figured if Dave and Roy could come clean, so could I. "After I finished eating my sandwich, I decided to go back down to the café. I'd discovered . . . an unusual phone there. It's called a wind phone."

"Wind phone?" Holt looked puzzled, but her face melted into realization. "Oh yes. I've heard of those. People use them to speak with the dead."

I didn't go into any further details about who I wanted to converse with. "Anyway, after my 'call,' I sat beside Billie at the nearby table. She'd fallen asleep, and pretty soon I did too."

DC Kahlil leaned forward. "Do you mind if I ask about that? It appears that almost all of your group dozed off. Is that typical? Or do you think you'd been drugged?"

"It's not typical, no. I thought the same thing myself. Except, how would that drug have been administered? We all got our drinks from the selection at the lunch grill." I struggled to remember the scene, which was chaotic. Except . . .

"I do recall Ben was helping distribute the drinks. I suppose it would have been possible for him to have slipped something into each one."

Holt wrote this down in her notepad. "Very good. We'll need to speak with him about that. Please go on."

"Well . . . as I said, I fell asleep. The next thing I knew, Billie was shaking me. We both heard screams and commotion coming from above. I don't know how I got my energy back, but I raced up the hill and found everyone standing by Luella's body at the edge of the hilltop. She lay beneath the statue that had fallen on her."

Holt nodded. "Her son told me that when he mentioned the statue to her, she wanted to rest beside it."

"That's right. Apparently, she was in a production of *Penzance* many years ago."

"Correct. So she lay down and fell asleep, like all the others. What I'm trying to determine is where everyone was between the time Ben left his mother at the statue and the time Jorge found her."

I sighed. "I'm afraid I can't be much help to you there. I went down to the wind phone after I ate, and everyone was still awake then. I assume Mrs. Campos's body will be checked for intoxicants or substances that may have put her to sleep?"

"Of course. But tell me what you saw when you joined the others at the statue."

"Everyone looked like they were in shock, as you'd expect. Jorge was crying his head off. As far as I could tell, it seemed genuine. But then . . ."

My pause made Holt look up. "But then what?"

I gave small laugh. "You interviewed Ivy, the youngest member of our group."

Holt formed a wry smile. "Yes. She's quite the young woman. Too smart for her own good, I'd say. She's convinced that Mr. Campos murdered his wife. Ivy claims she overheard Mrs. Campos accusing Mr. Campos of keeping something from her. I'll need to have a further discussion with him."

"I would advise you to take everything Ivy says with a grain of salt. She's been telling tall tales ever since we began this walk. For a while, she was certain that Mr. Campos was an actor. Not just an actor, but a famous television and movie star from thirty or forty years ago. Tom Wakefield. Have you heard of him?"

Holt shook her head. "Can't say that I have."

"Jorge bears a resemblance to the man, but of course he isn't him. Ivy likes to make provocative accusations. Still, it makes you wonder. I believe I've shaken her to the point where she thinks twice before making unfounded accusations. Yet her contention that Jorge is a professional actor isn't outside the realm of possibility. He's had a lot of diverse experiences. And a professional actor would be able to fake emotions very well."

Holt made a note on her notepad. "That also would apply to Mr. Langdon and Mr. Burke. Both of them are someone other than what they originally told everyone. If this a group of imposters, Mr. Campos might be one too. Anyway, let me ask you to think back to the scene of the crime. I understand you suggested moving the statue off of Mrs. Campos?"

"That's right. I realize we risked contaminating evidence, but there was still the chance that Luella could be alive."

"No, you did the right thing. But Mrs. Campos showed no signs of life, is that correct?"

"I know how to check for the basics. She was gone. I pulled out my phone and dialed 999."

"And then?"

"I'd already looked around, to see if there was anyone else besides our group on the hilltop, and saw no one. Then I checked the base of the statue, which appeared to have been cut in some fashion. That's when I did a quick reconnoiter of the immediate area and discovered the crowbar. Shortly after that your detective sergeant arrived."

"Well done." Holt's gaze rose from her notepad to me. "And there's nothing else you noticed? Either before or after?"

"If you mean about what happened up there on the hilltop, no, I don't think so. But I've certainly noticed a lot of things over the past few days. Some of it might have a bearing on what just happened, but I'll need to sort it out first."

Holt smiled. "Brilliant. That would be extremely helpful."

I wondered how much she really considered us partners in this investigation. "Would you mind if I asked how much my account matched what the others told you?"

"I don't mind at all. For the most part, your recollection matches the others. With a couple of noticeable differences."

I nodded. "Yes, I know what some of those might be. Both Jorge and Ben claim they saw someone else on the hill—someone outside of our group. Jorge never fell asleep like the rest of us, or so he claims, and Ben claims he only dozed off for a minute or two."

"Yes, that is what they say. But their descriptions vary. Ben said this stranger was tall, wearing a gray jacket and a dark cap. Jorge said the person was short, wearing a light jacket, and was most likely a woman."

"Excuse me, Inspector," DC Kahlil said. "The husband wasn't definite about that point, remember? When you pressed him, he became confused. He said that the person could have been a man—he hadn't really taken a close enough look."

"Yes, thank you, Constable, you're correct," Holt said. Looking down at her notepad, she added, "Those two accounts were the only ones that differed from yours, Mr. Chasen. Oh—there was one more observation. From Miss Mondreau."

"Billie? What did she say?"

"She told us that, from her viewpoint at the bottom of the hill, she couldn't see what was going on at the top. But, at one point, she did see Ben and Jorge walk together along the edge of the hilltop. And Mr. Burke appeared in her view as well."

"Burke? Oh, you mean Roy. But . . . he says he fell asleep along with the others."

"Yes, he did. So I'll need to question him further as well."

The whole sleeping business was nagging at me. "It's not unusual for someone on a walking tour to nod off after eating, but not the whole bunch of us. That's what makes me wonder if we'd been drugged."

"It's a possibility to pursue, definitely. You remember Ben serving up the drinks?"

"It might not have been only him, but he's the one I remember. The rest were staff of the café."

"Did everyone drink those beverages? Nobody opted for beer or canned sodas?"

"Not that I could tell."

"We'll have to wait and see what the toxicity report on Mrs. Campos reveals," Holt said resignedly. "Other than that, there's not much to go on. Most everyone in your group was sleeping, and the two who weren't both claim to have seen someone else in the field. Yet their descriptions are so vague, it might as well be anyone. Still, we will make enquiries."

"How closely have you been monitoring the local landowners group protesting the incursion of the coastal path into their properties?"

She smiled. "You mean LUAU? What a ridiculous name! Yes, we keep our eyes on them, but they're a bunch of paper tigers, really. There's little they can do except make a lot of noise. They know they haven't got a legal leg on which to stand. The government is entirely within its rights to make whatever changes it wants to the coastal path. At any rate, those malcontents haven't yet come anywhere close to actually killing someone."

I mentioned the incidents that occurred on our walk over the previous days.

"Yes, some of the others in your group brought those up as well. Were they suspicious? Perhaps. An indication of homicidal intent? Doubtful. There's a far more troublesome aspect to this whole business besides the LUAU bunch—the question of faked identities."

"You're right. Two of our group have been using assumed names. Roy has been revealed to own a chain of restaurants and was being sued by Mrs. Campos, and Dave is actually a private investigator sent by Mrs. Scattergood's husband to track her activities."

"That's correct. Mrs. Campos's lawsuit against Mr. Burke certainly gives him a motive to silence her permanently. However, I can't see how Mr. Langdon's deception gives him a motive."

That was my cue to tell Holt about my eavesdropping on Luella when she threatened Dave with exposure. "He was concerned about Rachel learning about his being hired by her husband. She was furious when she found out, but he said that he was planning to come clean with her anyway."

"That speaks well for him," DC Kahlil noted. "He could have tried to continue the charade until we did a thorough check."

"And yet . . . when I overheard Luella threaten Dave, she said she knew a secret from his past. His job as a detective is in the present."

Holt made another note. "One more thing for us to follow up on."

"There were other flare-ups with Luella as well," I said, mentioning the frequent bickering between Luella and Ben over her will, and Ivy's accusation of Luella stealing the café bell, which prompted Rachel's outburst at Luella afterward.

Holt let loose a breath. "Whew! That is a lot of animosity and friction for a group of people who only met one another three days ago."

"Well, to be honest, Luella was an abrasive sort. She wasn't the type to turn on the charm to impress people. Some might admire that quality, though it mostly rubbed the others the wrong way. Of course, that shouldn't automatically set her up as a murder victim."

"Unless we're dealing with someone who is far more deranged than they appear."

"That's always possible," I conceded.

"Very well, then," she said, as she stood and stretched her arms. "I believe that's enough for now. DC Kahlil and I must see what the forensic chaps can tell us about the evidence collected at the crime scene and the state of Mrs. Campos's body. We'll be back tomorrow morning. Thank you for your time, Mr. Chasen."

"Please call me Chase. I don't do well with the 'mister.' "

"Chase it is!" She gave me a pleasant nod, turned to leave, and turned back. "However, please don't call me 'Sheila.' It will remain 'Inspector'—just so we know who's in charge."

As she and the DC walked off, I reflected on her comment, and why she felt the need to make it. It seemed she was another woman who spoke her mind.

Chapter 17

Wednesday, evening,
The Carne

I couldn't let another moment pass without bringing Mike up to speed on what had happened. I pulled out my phone, called him, and he answered immediately. But he didn't sound as pleased to hear from me as I'd expected.

"It's been a hard day," he said. "Mostly paperwork, but sometimes that's more stressful than all the dead bodies. Plus, Randall has been acting up more than usual."

"In what way?"

"He phones me nearly every hour, Chase! He's forgetful and doesn't realize it. I understand he hasn't seen me for months, but it's been a challenge dealing with him and getting my work done as well. Also, I just can't help but think I should be the one taking care of him, not some paid caregiver."

Mike and I had been through many discussions about Randall, and they always boiled down to a simple fact: his brother's condition required constant supervision, something Mike didn't have the time—or training—to provide.

"Not to add to your worries, but my day hasn't been a bouquet of roses either," I said.

"You didn't fall and break anything, did you?" He was always concerned about my injuring myself on my walks.

"I wish that's what it was. There's been another death. And it looks like murder."

The silence that followed was so long I feared we'd lost our connection. "Are you serious? Another? Who is it this time?" Mike sometimes jokes that I see more dead bodies than he does.

"A woman in our group. She was killed while napping during our lunch break. A large stone statue fell on her and crushed her head in."

"Good Lord! Was it windy? Some of those old statues are so weather-beaten a strong breeze will topple them over."

"I don't believe that was the case this time. It looked like the base of the statue had been tampered with."

"That's incredible. Let me think. Mark Jessup is the medical examiner in that area, so he's probably the one who responded. I can check with him to see what he's learned. Do you have any idea who might be responsible?"

I explained that I'd just met with Inspector Holt—Mike knew her well, calling her a "good but sometimes overly enthusiastic investigator," whatever that meant—and said that I'd told her everything I'd observed. Which didn't amount to much, mostly.

"Anyone could have pushed over that statue," I said. "It was heavy, but it looked like it had been prepped to fall over with a strong shove. The real question is, who did it? Most of us were asleep or groggy. The killer would have avoided that, but who was it?"

"Now I'm worried about you," Mike said. "Would you like me to come down and help?"

"Of course, I'd love to see you. But . . . you've got enough on your plate. If the authorities here are as good as you say, we'll be fine. We'll have plenty of time to be together once this is all sorted."

Another pause. "I don't like this. You're sniffing around—and the murderer won't like that. You can only be lucky for so long."

There was more than an ounce of truth in what he said. "I appreciate your concern. Still, I can take care of myself."

"There's always a second murder with these people, Chase. And even a third. I don't want either of them to be you."

"But if you come down here, you're putting yourself in danger as well."

"Still, I'd feel better if I were with you there."

Of course, I wanted to be with him, but the circumstances were not ideal. Above all, I wanted Mike to be safe. "This will all be over soon," I assured Mike, although I was far from sure. "If there are any unexpected complications, I'll let you know, and you can come right over."

He sighed. "What a week. I'm tempted to come down just so I can hold you and do naughty things."

That sounded perfect to me as well. But it was not the time.

"Tell you what," I said. "Let's see how things go tomorrow. My experience has been that these investigations move ahead pretty quickly."

"Is that a promise? Apart from everything else, I'm sorry you won't be doing any more walking."

He was right, but I couldn't feel too sorry for myself. Luella wouldn't be doing any more walking—ever.

That night's dinner was a somber affair. Given the circumstances, I didn't expect it to be a normal group dinner, with Brian outlining the following day's itinerary. Yet it turned out he'd arranged a table for us in The Carne's restaurant, alongside one of the view windows, and nearly everyone showed up on time and took their seats without complaints. Brian calmly explained what all of us expected, that the walk was officially over. As a courtesy, he'd extended our stay at The Carne, at least through the next few days. I'm certain I wasn't alone in hoping that finding the killer wouldn't take anywhere near that long.

Instead of socializing and reflecting on the day's walk, as we normally would have, we sat with quiet reverence, as if someone had just died—which, of course, is exactly what had happened.

For me, it was an opportunity to observe at close range my fellow walkers, one of whom could very well be a killer, and most likely a first-time killer. Amateur murderers often make mistakes.

Not everyone was there, however.

"Where's Jorge?" I asked.

"I haven't heard a word from him since . . . since we met with that inspector woman," Ben said. "Do you think one of us should check on him?"

"Somebody needs to," Rachel said. "Given what he's been through, there's no telling what his frame of mind might be."

Ben stood up just as Jorge appeared, looking morose but not particularly suicidal. He took the remaining seat at the end of the table. We waited for someone to break the silence. Finally, Roy said, "You were the last one to speak with the inspector, Chase. Did she let on who she thinks did this?"

I was about to respond when the server came to take our drink orders. I was glad for the reprieve—it gave me time to formulate my response. When she left, I said, "It's much too early for speculation. Not that Inspector Holt had any obligation to tell me anything—I'm as much a suspect as the rest of you."

"That's not true," Rachel said. "You're a cop, just like she is."

"I'm an ex-cop. And cops have certainly been known to be criminals."

"Criminals!" Ben snorted. "Is that what that inspector thinks we are? The killer is obviously one of those LUAU people."

"I wish you had gotten a better look at the guy," Dave said.

Ben paused, trading nervous glances with Jorge. "How were we supposed to know he was a murderer?" Ben said. "The inspector asked me to describe him the best I could, but I'd only seen him from a distance. All I remember is he was tall, broad-shouldered, wearing a gray jacket and a black cap."

To me that sounded like a fairly good description of Jorge, minus the cap.

"I didn't see anyone but us up there," Ivy said, with a sharp nod. "I'm positive."

"But you were asleep some of the time, remember?" Rachel said. "So how can you be sure?"

Ivy turned and gave her mother a withering look. "I was only pretending to sleep, Mother. How else would I know what was going on?"

"You weren't pretending," Ben said. "You were definitely asleep."

"I'm a good pretender," she shot back.

"If you were awake, you might have seen who killed Mrs. Campos," Roy said.

Ivy hesitated. "Well . . . she was way off on the other side of the hill. I could see that statue, but not anyone around it. Anyway, I didn't know she was going to be murdered. All I know is that . . . one of us here did it."

"That's absurd!" Dave said. "Most of us were not pretending to be asleep—we actually *were* asleep."

Ivy faced him. "Then you don't remember waking up and walking away? I saw you do that."

Dave's mouth dropped before he caught himself. "I had to go relieve myself. All that beer I'd been drinking. But I came right back and lay down again."

Ivy swung toward Roy. "And I saw you get up too! You were digging around in your backpack."

"My backpack? Oh . . . right. I wanted to take a photo of the sea. It only took me a few seconds to do that, and then I felt the urge to sleep like everyone else."

"Do you have that shot on your phone?" I asked. "It might include the mystery man that Jorge and Ben saw."

"My phone's up in my room. I'll take a look after dinner."

Billie cleared her throat and looked at Roy. "I saw you too. Just before I fell asleep. You were standing, looking out across the hilltop to the sea. But I didn't see a phone in your hand."

"It was in my pocket."

Billie turned to Ben. "Roy must have seen you two. He was looking in your direction. It looked to me like you and Jorge were having a heated argument."

Ben and Jorge traded glances. "We weren't arguing," Ben said. "We were talking about whether to continue on the walk. I could see my mother wasn't into it. Anyway, what difference does it make?"

"Everything can make a difference where murder is concerned," I said.

"He's lying, can't you tell?" Ivy said. "Both of them told us they were asleep!"

"I never said that!" Jorge said. "After our discussion, I asked Ben to keep an eye on my wife and then went to sit down. I wasn't in the mood to nap like everyone else."

"Did you go check on your mother?" I said to Ben.

Ben's eyes darted between me and Jorge. "I did, and she was resting fine. Then I started feeling drowsy also. I saw Jorge sit down and knew I'd have to rest also."

"Yeah, right," Ivy said, with obvious disbelief.

"No, he's telling the truth," Rachel said. "I remember when Ben and Jorge walked off, but a short time later Jorge was back on our side of the field. I must have awakened for a moment and saw him."

"I never saw him walk back there," Ivy said.

"I saw what I saw," her mother countered.

Jorge stood, his face twisting with anger. "My wife was killed, and all this kid can do"—he pointed at Ivy—"is throw out baseless accusations! What about her? What if she's the killer?"

"My daughter?" Rachel said. "Now who's throwing out accusations? You think she can push over a two-ton statue?"

Ivy's dexterity that morning on the playground parallel bars came to mind. I had a feeling she was a lot stronger than her mother believed.

Jorge's anger began to melt. "I wouldn't put anything past her."

Ivy glared at him. "I could have done it, but I didn't. As you know."

"You little—"

"Don't encourage her!" Ben said. "Can't you see what she's doing? She's trying to pit us against one another. To her, this is all a game."

"Stop haranguing my daughter!" Rachel shouted, her lioness nature coming to the surface. "You told us what you saw today, and she's simply doing the same thing. Why is it okay for you and not her?"

"Because I'm telling the truth!" Ben said.

Rachel stood and threw down her napkin. "I'm not listening to any more of this." She glared at Ben. "God help you if you ever have to be on the witness stand. I'd tear you apart." She took Ivy's arm and started to walked away, then paused and turned. "I'll tell you what I remember. I saw Ben go over to the statue, and I waited to see him return. But he didn't."

"Of course I did," Ben said.

"You did, but not from the direction of the statue. I looked and saw you behind me."

Ben huffed out a laugh. "You were groggy from sleep. If you saw me behind you, I obviously must have walked back. How else would I have done that? Fly?"

"That's weird," Dave said. "I noticed the same thing."

"You saw me appear out of nowhere?"

"No. It was Roy. I saw him get up and walk away, and the next thing I know he was just a few feet away."

Roy shook his head. "It's like Ben said. You were sleepy, like everyone else. I can't fly either."

"That's another thing," Rachel said. "Doesn't anyone think it's weird that we were all so wiped out? It wasn't that way yesterday, or the day before. Do you think someone drugged us?"

I knew the police would be exploring that possibility, but I didn't want to be the one putting it forward.

"Not all of us fell asleep," Dave said. "Ben and Jorge didn't."

"That's weird, too," Ivy said.

Rachel led Ivy away, and the server returned to take our meal orders. None of us had even thought to look at the evening's selections. Billie leaned close to me and whispered, "I'm not really hungry, are you? Let's go somewhere and talk on our own."

That sounded good. We stood, excused ourselves, and made a quick exit.

* * *

Outside, the night air was crisp but not oppressive. A thin cloud layer barely masked a haloed moon. Lights from the town reflected on the still waters of the bay. Billie and I walked along the cobbled pavement ringing the harbor.

"Curiouser and curiouser!" Billie said. "How were we to know there was such a beehive of activity on that hilltop today?"

"It's puzzling, that's for sure," I said. "Everyone claimed to be asleep, but it turns out the only ones not seen walking around were Rachel and Brian. I began to wonder whether I had woken up and walked around."

"If our drinks were spiked with something, perhaps it had a delayed effect."

I looked at her. "How long were Jorge and Ben talking when you saw them?"

"I don't know. But they were really getting into it—shouting at each other, even though I couldn't make out the words from that distance."

"Was Roy close enough to hear them?"

She thought a moment. "Probably not. He was quite a ways away. I'm sorry, but that's all I remember before I conked out."

"No need to be sorry. What you saw could be important."

"I hate to admit it, but I think Ivy might be onto something. Jorge's an odd duck. How much do you think Ivy is making up about him?"

I pondered the question. "With Ivy, it's always a mix of fact and fantasy. I'm not sure where it comes from, but she has this need to prove to everyone how smart and observant she is. She's learned how to take something crazy and weave it together with a smattering of truth. It's really kind of awe-inspiring."

Billie contemplated this. "She did get others to admit they hadn't been asleep the whole time. How long would it take someone to walk over to Luella, dislodge that statue, do her in, and come back before anyone noticed?"

"That depends, I think, on whether it was planned or improvised. If our killer had somehow prepped the statue beforehand, the whole operation might have taken less than a couple minutes."

"Prepped in what way?"

"Chiseled the base to make it easier to break when prodded by a crowbar."

"That seems risky."

"I'm no engineer, but if I were to do it, I'd fashion a beveled chunk of granite holding the statue up, then knock it out with that crowbar we found."

"Where is that chunk of granite, then?"

"I didn't see it when we were at the statue, but it might have been pretty small."

"And where did the crowbar come from?"

I shrugged. "The killer could have been carrying it in their backpack. Or they had placed it in the field behind the wall beforehand."

"Ben and Jorge had visited some of the stops on this tour a couple weeks ago," Billie noted.

"I know. I'll need to remind Inspector Holt of that."

"There are motives there. Ben and his mother bickered all the time. And Jorge could be a gold-digger, marrying a wealthy woman for her money. They could have been planning something together."

"But others have motives also," I reminded her. "Luella was suing Roy. She'd accused Ivy of lying about stealing that bell from the café. And she'd threatened Dave with exposure of his secret."

"Those don't sound like very strong motives. Besides,

Dave came clean with the Inspector about really being a detective."

"If that was the secret Luella was talking about. I have a feeling he's carrying around another secret."

"We need one of those incident boards that police detectives use, Chase. There are too many suspects and motives."

An Adele song emanated from the jukebox of a tavern we were passing. "There's still that mystery person that Ben and Jorge claim to have seen," I said. "Strange that nobody else saw him."

"They could have invented him to disguise their own guilt."

"But why disagree on the person's appearance? If they were planning Luella's murder, wouldn't they have agreed on that important detail?"

Billie let out a sigh. "This is all so crazy. Why couldn't someone have killed Luella the usual way, with a gun or a knife? Why set it up to happen with a statue?"

I laughed. "Poetic justice perhaps. Luella gets done in by one of her former loves."

We'd reached the other side of the harbor, where a stone wall kept us from walking farther. I asked Billie if she'd like to return to the tavern we'd passed and have a late-night drink, or perhaps a snack since we'd missed dinner, but she said she only wanted to go back to the hotel and get into bed.

"Your knee doesn't seem to be bothering you," I said as we began heading back.

"I put some ointment on it before going down to dinner. It's still painful, but not as bad as it was earlier. Maybe I'll make a complete comeback like that Dan Barter fellow you mentioned from the Red Sox."

"Daniel Bard," I corrected. "And I'm certain you will."

When we reached the hotel, we bid each other good night and went to our rooms.

Before turning in, I sat at the small desk with my journal and wrote down as much as I could recall of the day's events. It took me longer than I expected; I didn't want to leave out anything. Unfortunately, no blinding insights revealed themselves. I also detailed my "conversation" with Doug at the wind phone. I struggled to remember how it had concluded. When I glanced at the bedside clock and saw it was nearly eleven, I gave up my struggle.

Instead of calling, I texted Mike and wished him a loving good night. He responded in kind, adding, **Fingers crossed for a less eventful day tomorrow.**

Turning off the light, I closed my eyes and remembered the rainbow I'd seen just before I fell asleep at lunch. Was that what I'd been trying to recall after using the wind phone?

I'm not prone to fanciful thinking. But that brief and improbable rainbow was again filling me with the confidence to anticipate a bright future.

Chapter 18

Thursday, morning,
The Carne

My good mood continued through the night; even my dreams were pleasant, mostly involving Mike. I was whistling "Jambalaya," one of Hank Williams's more upbeat numbers, when I made my way to the breakfast room the next morning. The sun outside was shining, and I could detect the crisp morning air even inside the hotel. The bubble burst, however, when I found Ben and Jorge squabbling when I entered the breakfast room.

"Hell no!" Ben exclaimed. "Why would I want an 'impromptu' memorial service for my mother? Why would *any* of us want that?"

"Your mother was a beautiful person," Jorge replied. "She deserves a remembrance."

"Man, I don't know what happened, but she sure had you fooled," Ben said, storming off to the buffet, where he angrily speared a chunk of melon from the fruit tray.

Jorge looked at me with his hands held up in defeat. "I'm going to plan a small service anyway. It's the least I can do . . . I feel so helpless."

"It's a good idea," said Billie, seated nearby with her knitting and a cup of coffee.

"I'll go speak with the manager," he said and walked off, passing Rachel and Ivy as they came in. Rachel's face was wet with tears and strained with anguish. Dave immediately went up to her.

"What's wrong?" he asked. "Has something happened?"

She took a breath. "I called Craig and told him I discovered who you were."

"I wish you'd have let me do that. I was just about to."

She managed a weak smile. "No, I needed to do it myself. But it turned ugly right away. He accused me of seducing you! After all the affairs he's had! Then he threatened to take Ivy away from me permanently."

"He can't do that," Dave said.

"Don't underestimate Craig. You should know what he's like—he doesn't like to lose. And he can afford the very best legal defense there is."

Dave placed his hands on her shoulders. "Yes, I know what Craig is like, but I also know what you're like. You're every bit as good as any lawyer he can come up with."

"I won't go live with Dad, no matter what kind of lawyer he has," Ivy said.

"You might not have a choice," her mother said.

Ivy flashed one of her confident smirks. "Just let me speak to the judge. I could tell him stories about Dad that would make his eyes bug out."

Rachel's face tightened. "What kind of stories? I don't want you to make anything up."

Ivy smirked. "Make anything up? Come on, Mom. Who needs to do that with Dad?" She grabbed a plate and started her journey through the buffet.

Roy appeared, looking more relaxed and calmer than the day before—perhaps because the threat of a crippling lawsuit had been lifted. He greeted us with a nod and proceeded to the buffet.

I hadn't yet gotten my breakfast, and I was hungrier than usual, having skipped dinner last night. I joined the line and soon was piling my plate with bacon, tomatoes, beans, and eggs. I sat with Billie. She told me she'd already eaten, but went back to the buffet to get a scone.

When she returned, I held up the garment she'd been knitting. "What is that going to be?"

"It's a sweater, silly. Or at least I think it is. Maybe it will end up a bed throw."

I savored my first bite of bacon. Say what you will, but it tasted immensely more restorative than any healthful swallow of porridge or granola. Ben sat next to us.

"Sorry about the scene just now," he said.

"Why are you so dead set against a Jorge arranging a service for your mother?" Billie asked. "It would help cheer him up."

Ben gave one of his bitter laughs. "Jorge is such a drama queen. He's always been like that. Does things more for show than for what they really mean. Yes, he cared for my mother, but he knew as well as me how frustrating she could be. Any 'memorial service' will seem hypocritical."

"Still," Billie said, "you must have had some affection for your mother. After all, you agreed to accompany her and Jorge over here to England."

Ben took a sip of coffee. "Of course, I loved her, but I hated her as well. That can happen, can't it? Relationships are complicated. And I knew better than to let her out of my sight, especially with a new husband. She had a history of letting her heart get the better of her. Someone had to look out for her interests."

I figured Luella was pretty adept at looking out for her interests. "Are you certain Jorge had designs on her money?" I asked.

Ben gave a half smile. "What do you think? He's broke, and she was loaded. It doesn't take much to put two and two together."

"As her husband, he should get most of her estate," Billie said.

"Not everything. Mother joked about cutting me out of her will, but she never did it and never would have. I don't know exactly how much of her estate Jorge will get, but he might be in for a disappointment."

"You're right about your mother," I said. "She confided to me that she had no intention of cutting you out of her will. But neither did she mention that she knew Jorge was broke." After a pause, I asked, "Do you think Jorge killed your mother?"

Ben looked away and seemed to seriously consider the question. He looked back at me and said, "Definitely not."

"How can you be so sure?" I asked.

"Because I know him, and I'm a good judge of character. Jorge could never bring himself to kill anyone. It was that other guy we saw on the hilltop, I'm positive."

I consider myself a good judge of character as well, and yet many times I've nearly been bamboozled by a cunning murderer, whose pathology often included the art of expert deception.

"Here's one thing I don't get," Billie said. "We know that our drinks that day were probably spiked, and nearly all of us slept during our lunch break. But it also looks like almost everybody was up and around at some point. So why did nobody else see this guy you're talking about?"

Ben waved the question away with his fork. "How would I know? All I know is what I saw."

Billie and I traded looks that said the same thing: this line of discussion was over. We dutifully finished our meals and made our exit. As we walked through the bar, we passed Ivy, standing still with her eyes focused, a dart in hand, aiming it at the dartboard. She flung it out, and it struck the edge of the board, falling to the floor.

"How do people do this?" she asked, picking up the dart.

"Practice," Billie said. "It's a hard thing to learn when you're young, but as you get older, you'll learn."

"I wish everyone would stop talking about how 'young' I am," she said. "I'm not a little girl anymore. I'm a lot more mature than people think. I know a lot."

"Knowledge isn't just stuff you see on the internet," I said.

She tossed the darts on a table. "Yeah, yeah, I know. Okay, so Jorge isn't Tom Wakefield. I was wrong about that. But he wasn't any airline pilot either. Whenever I ask him about that, he always finds a way to change the subject. Very suspicious. Did that ever happen when you interviewed suspects?"

"Of course. But it doesn't always mean what you think it does."

"It means they have something to hide."

"Not necessarily. It could be that the subject makes them nervous for another reason."

"All I know is he's creepy. A person doesn't act like that unless they have something they're covering up. If I—"

At that moment, Jorge strode in, but he stopped in his tracks to stare at Ivy. The two remained locked on each other, their eyes transfixed.

"Where have you been?" I asked Jorge in as non-threatening manner as I could manage.

My comment broke the standoff. Looking up at me, he said, "I was trying to find the manager so I could arrange a service for Luella. But he's nowhere to be found."

Ivy held her contemptible glare at Jorge for a moment more and then walked off.

After she left, he said, "What is it with that kid? She doesn't like me, but I'll be damned if I know why."

"Don't try to figure out twelve-year-olds," Billie said. "My years as a librarian taught me that."

He digested this tidbit of information with puzzled indifference.

I was heading back to my room when I heard a voice call out. "Chase!"

It was Inspector Holt. She was outfitted more resplendently than the previous day—in a becoming ultra-feminine, lemon-yellow blouse with contrasting navy-blue slacks. She looked as if she was off to view the finals at Wimbledon rather than pursue a murder investigation. "I need to speak with you."

"By all means. Have you learned anything new?"

She smiled demurely. "I was going to ask you the same question. You're my eyes and ears on the scene, after all."

"Am I? I thought I was just another suspect, although one perhaps not on the top of your list."

She maintained her smile as I followed her into the parlor. "You're on top of my list, but not the list of suspects."

Did that mean what I feared? We entered the parlor, and she proceeded to the sofa, where she sat and patted the seat beside her. I was uncomfortable sitting so close to her, but I did.

"Now then," she said. "I think we got off on the wrong foot yesterday. I appreciate your powers of observation, if I didn't make that clear. And I must admit, this is the oddest case I've ever come across. An American lady killed on one of our coastal paths? And with a statue, no less? It's a far cry from our usual homicides, which mostly involve the usual inbred group of locals with lifelong animosities toward one another. Or violent gang tussles. You can see why I can appreciate your perspective, particularly with your impressive background."

This was a distinct about-face from her demeanor the previous day. She hadn't been obnoxiously officious, but there was a definite drawing of boundaries between her role as the officer in charge and mine as a possible, if unlikely, suspect.

"Let me ask you this," I said. "Do you think there is any possibility that one of the local agitators—that LUAU bunch—is behind this?"

She formed a smile and shook her head. "No joy there, I'm afraid. They're not homicidal. They make a lot of noise, but they're harmless really."

"I have found that, when you dismiss someone's power, it only makes them more resolute to exercise it," I said.

"That is possible, certainly. But I'm familiar with this lot; I've known many of them all my life. Granted, there can be the odds and sods who come along. But, given the law of averages, I would have to say the chances of any of that bunch being a killer is a . . . what is it you Americans say? A long shot? No, our murderer in this case is someone else."

I nodded. "So what we're talking about is one of the walking group being the murderer."

"Don't you agree? From what we've learned, nearly every one of them has a motive."

"They have motives for revenge perhaps. But murder? That suggests something else entirely."

She lowered her eyes, fluttered them a bit, and smiled. "I believe we can work this all out if we combine forces. What do you say to talking it out over dinner? They have a marvelous salt pollock here that is the envy of the culinary world."

There was no question: she was suggesting something beyond just an innocent dinner between interested parties.

It was time to nip this in the bud. "I would like nothing better than to discuss this case with you, Inspector. But first I'll need to check in with my fiancé. He's due to join me here this evening."

She couldn't have registered more shock if I'd blasted her with a taser. "Fiancé? He?"

"Perhaps you know him. Mike Tibbets? Devon County coroner?"

The sequence of expressions that crossed her face were a wonder to behold. "Mike Tibbets? The corpse grinder . . . um, that is, the medical examiner over in Exeter? Why . . . yes, indeed, of course, I know him! Wonderful chap. How on earth did you two pair up?"

I gave forth a laugh and explained how we met when murder struck a previous walk. "I know this is a lot to spring on you, but I thought it would be best if you knew where things stand. The fact is, I'm not available . . . at least not in any romantic way."

Holt sat back and did her best to assume a professional façade. "Absolutely, of course, of course. Please don't assume I meant anything of the sort. It's only that you . . . what I mean is that you don't look . . . oh dear, I'm really digging a deeper hole for myself, aren't I?"

I laughed and reached out to pat her knee. "Don't feel bad. To be honest, if you had wanted to pursue a deeper relationship with me, I'd feel flattered. Although . . ."—I thought of how best to phrase this—"it wouldn't have been terribly professional, would it?"

She took a breath, looked down, and managed a small laugh herself. "I feel such a fool. Perhaps I've been single too long. I divorced three years ago, and let me tell you . . . the dating waters around these parts are dreadfully understocked. All the decent blokes are either married, or they're complete wankers, or . . ."

"Or they're gay?"

She formed a bittersweet smile. "Exactly. Sad state of affairs, is it not?"

"I've been in the same place myself. Here's what I can tell you. Just when you give up hope, that's when the world can shift beneath you. What I'm saying is . . . never give up hope."

She nodded. "At this moment, my hope is that we find who it is who killed Mrs. Campos."

Her mobile phone buzzed. She pulled it from her bag and viewed a text that had just come in. "Here's news," she said. "The toxicology report has just come in on Mrs. Campos. Traces of benzodiazepine were found in her system."

"That's some kind of sleeping medication, isn't it?"

"Yes. It's fairly common, and forms of it are sold over the counter here in the UK."

"Well, that explains a lot."

Holt shut her phone off. "We checked with other diners at the Cadgwith café that day. No one outside of your group complained of being drowsy."

"That doesn't surprise me. Someone spiked our drinks. Ben Purdue was helping serve the drinks, so that makes him the likeliest suspect, but it wouldn't have been difficult for someone else to slip in a pill or tablet or whatever other form this drug takes."

"And it possibly limits the number of people who could have had the remaining strength to push over that statue. I'm going to have to consult the toxicologist, but the drug doesn't work the same way on everyone."

The inspector's phone buzzed again.

"Oh, dear," she said as she checked it.

"What is it?"

"A walker on the coastal path has been attacked. Quite seriously, it seems."

"Attacked? Do you know by whom?"

Inspector Holt looked up at me. "Lawrence Hancock."

Chapter 19

Thursday, late morning,
The Carne

"Hancock?" I said. "That's the guy who threatened us at a rest stop. What did he do?"

Holt studied her phone. "Seems he was caught on CCTV releasing two adders onto the coastal path, just before a group of walkers from Japan were approaching. Here, let me show you." She handed me the phone, and I looked at the video clip of a man kneeling beside the path, opening a small crate out of which two alarmingly large snakes emerged.

"Adders are deadly, aren't they?" I asked, handing back the phone.

"They can be, but most of the time their bites just cause inflammation. Those bites can be quite painful, though—enough to ruin a walking holiday."

"And discourage walkers," I added. This was a strong indication that the LUAU bunch—or Hancock, at any rate—was behind booby-trapping the trail to scare off walkers. The big question, of course, was: Would they resort to murder? Bashing in Luella's head was very different from unleashing marginally dangerous snakes.

"Hancock also has no reliable alibi for the time that Mrs. Campos was killed," Holt added. "He's in custody, so that's good. But I'm not sure how probable a suspect he is for our murder."

"I'm not either. There's quite a gap between scaring people and killing them."

"Yet we can't rule out the connection entirely." She sighed and stood. "I must get back to the station. Please keep your eyes open, won't you, Chase? Contact me if you see anything unusual in your group."

My group was the very definition of "unusual." And here I was, being regarded again as "Keep Your Eyes Open" Chase. Yet what else would I expect, not being employed in an official detective capacity anymore?

I simply said, "I certainly will. And cheer up. You're an attractive lady, and there still are men around who appreciate that."

After Holt left, I went into the hotel lobby, looking for some peace and calm, yet found Ivy and Rachel at swords' points with one another.

"You don't know anything about that man!" Ivy shouted at her mother. "He's our killer. I know he is!"

Rachel grabbed hold of her daughter's shoulders. "I want you to knock off these delusions, you hear? First you think Dave is a serial killer, then it's Jorge, and now it's Roy! Where did you dig up that one? The same place where you were sure my chiropractor was a terrorist?"

For once, Ivy looked slightly chastened. "Your chiropractor was Iranian, and he was in the country on a forged visa."

"So that makes him a terrorist? You're going to have to stop imagining the worst of everyone. It will only make you look foolish, which you already do, if I must say. I don't know what's happened to you, Ivy. I really don't."

So thinks every parent of a twelve-year-old, I imagined.

"Then leave me alone!" Ivy screamed and ran off.

Rachel looked defeated. I approached her cautiously.

"I couldn't help but overhear," I said.

It took her a moment, but she looked up at me. "Well, of course you did. The people in the next town must have overheard."

"Can we talk?" I suggested.

She took a breath and nodded. I led her over to the lobby sofa, and we sat.

"I know that Ivy can be difficult," I said. "But I sense she's a good girl at the heart of it all. It's just that she's troubled. She's rebelling against something more than the usual teenage angst."

Rachel teared up and bowed her head. "You're right. Ivy's a smart girl, but frankly I haven't been the best mother to her. I've fought tooth and nail with her father in this divorce battle, and that's taken me away from paying attention to her. I think all her fabrications are an effort to get my attention."

I'm no child psychologist, and Ivy was still—technically, anyway—a child. "You could be onto something there. Yet there might be something more going on. Don't get me wrong—I don't have children and can't pretend to know what's best for them—but is there anything that could be plaguing Ivy other than your issues with her father?"

Rachel remained silent a moment. "Very possibly. It happened a couple of years back. Ivy became good friends with boy at school. I hesitate to say it—they were only ten—but I think she fell in love with him. He was just a kid too, of course, and at first, it looked like he was returning her affection. He spent a lot of time with her, and she was on cloud nine."

"But something happened?"

Rachel sighed. "It sure did. One day he completely became someone else—vindictive, bullying, teasing. He told all her friends that he didn't care about her at all. He just wanted to show what a romantic sap she was. She thought she had found love, and all she got was humiliation."

"How terrible for her." Not uncommon, I thought, unfortunately, remembering the vicious teasing and bullying I received in school, over suspicions that I might be gay (prompted mostly by my aversion to, and inability to properly play, contact sports like football and hockey).

"I did the best I could to put it all in perspective for her, and she seemed to get over it, but she asked a lot of questions. About why someone would be so mean as to do something like that. She pointed out that her father had a lot of business associates who seemed to be good men, but who turned out to be criminals who fed on other people's weakness. It's hard to explain to a child that dark side of human nature."

"Has she developed an attraction to anyone else since?"

"No. In a way, it's a relief; kids grow up too quickly anyway. But I want some boy to restore her faith in love and in people in general. She's always trying to find the worst in everyone."

"I suggest you go easy on yourself. There's not a parent in the world who doesn't wonder if they're doing the best job of raising their child." I reached over to hold her hand. "You're a good mother, that I can tell. You and Ivy will get through this, I promise."

She blinked back a tear. "I can't tell you how good it makes me feel to hear you say that."

"Do you know why Roy is now her number one suspect?"

She laughed. "Ivy claims he was wiping off his hands when she saw him up on the hillside right before Luella's body was discovered."

"You mean possibly wiping off bits of the statue he had just pushed over?"

"Something like that. But honestly. People wipe their hands for all sorts of reasons. You'd better watch out. You'll be Suspect Number One next."

"I can handle Ivy's suspicions. I'm more concerned about Inspector Holt's."

"What about your own?" Rachel asked. "It sounds like you've got more experience in this kind of thing than Holt does."

"Don't underestimate her."

"Believe me, I don't underestimate women in traditional male roles. They've got to be good to get where they are." She stood and stretched. "I'd better see what Ivy's up to. Thanks for talking to me, Chase. Right now, I'm going to find Ivy and try to reason with her."

Lunchtime was approaching, and though I had stuffed myself at breakfast, my body clock was sending me "Eat now!" signals. I walked toward the hotel café and came upon Dave and Roy, poised threateningly before one another.

"Are you accusing me?" Dave said. "You had the strongest motive to kill Luella of any of us! She was going to sue your pants off!"

"Not everyone being sued kills the person doing it," Roy said. "But you were walking back to the group right before Luella's body was discovered."

"I was just about to say the same thing about you!"

It looked as if the two might come to blows. Against my better judgment, I felt the need to step in.

"What's going on here?" I asked.

The two men stared at each other before Roy turned to me. "I'm tired of living with all this uncertainty. Whoever killed Luella is not some local running around killing walkers on the trails. It has to be one of us. And I saw Dave yesterday on the hilltop, walking back to the group right after Luella's body was discovered. He was wiping his hands on his pants, as if to get something off of them. It might have been ground residue from the statue."

That's the same accusation Ivy was making about Roy. Was he indulging in one of the oldest criminal tricks in the book—projection—in order to deflect his own guilt?

"Why would I have killed her?" Dave yelled.

Turning to Dave, I said, "You wouldn't have killed her because she discovered you were a private detective. But did she know something else about you?"

I wasn't expecting this question to have the impact it did. Dave looked like he'd been found out. But his words didn't match his expression. "What makes you say that?"

I told him about overhearing Luella's threat the night we had dinner by the castle.

Dave didn't deny it. "She'd heard one of her high-crust friends talk about hiring me to trail their wife. Small world. But that's not a motive for murder."

"So you say," Roy said.

"Let's calm down, okay?" I said. "If you look hard enough, nearly everyone in our group has a motive for killing Mrs. Campos. We're all being detained, and tempers wear thin. Let me give you two some advice. It's easy to let your mind go wild when something like this happens, but ninety-nine times out of a hundred, you'll be wrong. It happened to me all the time in my career. You need to weigh evidence, cold hard facts, not just hunches and suppositions. If you know something—anything that is concrete, something real—then you need to tell the police."

I was expecting more fireworks, but the two men calmed down.

"He's right," Roy conceded. "It might have been someone else I saw. Maybe that guy Ben and Jorge are talking about. The sun was in my eyes."

Dave nodded. "That's probably the case with me too."

"I'm glad you've come to your senses," I said, although I'd made a note of their accusations. As the two men walked off, something remained alarmingly clear. Anyone in our group could have killed Luella Campos.

The only one in the restaurant from our group was Ben, morosely eating a sandwich. I'd looked around for Billie but didn't spot her. I was just about to sit with Ben when Rachel came in and walked over.

"I'm worried about Ivy," she said. "I thought she went back to our room, but I just checked, and she isn't there."

"She probably just went for a walk."

"Running off isn't like her. She's the kind who likes to sit and brood and plan a cunning countermove. I'm afraid something's happened to her."

"Have you tried reaching her on your phone?"

"That's the first thing I tried. But no answer."

Normally, I would have reassured Rachel, but given the fact that a murderer was on the loose—and he or she might think Ivy knew something that she actually didn't—I thought again.

"This town isn't big," I said. "There aren't many places where she could hide out. She couldn't have gotten very far."

"Will you help me look for her?"

"Sure thing." We went out the hotel's side entrance, which presented us with two alternative routes: going to the south, along the harbor, or to the north, around the hotel and up the hill to the castle. I offered to explore the harbor, and Rachel agreed to look near the castle.

Even though it was a pleasant, clear day, not many people were out and about—mostly locals getting on with their business. That was good for my search, as Ivy would certainly stand out, with her pre-punk wardrobe and long black hair. Yet I didn't spot her.

Like most Cornish coastal villages, St. Mawes is situated in a small river cove with hills that rise on either side. The harbor was actually the mouth of the Percuil River, with the harborside walkway ending where the inlet narrows. I remembered it from the walk Billie and I had taken the previous evening.

Ivy wasn't visible, but I decided to explore the harbor front anyway. The walkway passed in front of the Idle Rocks, the town's most prominent inn (with a popular pub and café), and continued past other establishments before going up a short grassy slope and proceeding into a more residential section before it terminated.

Along the way, I looked for anyplace into which Ivy might have gone. She could have spotted a stray cat, grabbed a bite to eat, or found a private spot where she could explore the internet without her mother hovering over her. I didn't want to think the worst, and it would seem highly risky for her to be attacked in broad daylight, but I surveyed the waters beyond the shore to see if could spot a body floating. Fortunately, there was nothing like that to be seen.

Along the town's strand of sand was a brief row of colorful beach huts, still closed up until the summer arrived. I went down and eyed the small enclosures, some of which command prices rivaling those for full-scale homes. I called out Ivy's name and received no response.

Going back to the promenade, I soon arrived at the north section of town, an area of mostly separate residences, many bearing signs announcing their availability as holiday rentals. Beyond them lay muddy cow pastures.

There was not much to do but turn back. Ivy had most likely returned to The Carne, but I felt uneasy. She was unpredictable. Might she have taken the ferry across the river? I certainly could picture her getting a thrill from making everyone worry about her.

When I arrived back at the hotel, Rachel was inside the parlor off the lobby, out of her mind with worry. That wasn't helped when I revealed my search had been fruitless as well.

"Ivy is nothing if not resourceful," I said, in as reassuring a voice as I could manage. "She maybe just wanted some alone time. She knows how to take care of herself."

Rachel's face twisted with anguish. "You don't understand. Ivy's diabetic. She needs insulin every few hours. It gets even worse if she's scared or excited. If she doesn't get it soon, she'll die!"

Chapter 20

**Thursday, afternoon,
St. Mawes, Cornwall**

"Doesn't she have insulin with her?" I asked.

"No. Back home she wears an insulin pump that will mete out the dosage she needs. But she hates wearing it, especially if she's active, like we've been on this walk. So I've been handling her regular injections with an injection pen. Those usually are good for around four to six hours, and it's been almost five since the last one."

Ivy must have known this. She wouldn't go off for hours if that would put her life in danger. Rachel must have known she knows too, so I didn't say it aloud.

"We'll need to alert the authorities," I said, pulling out my phone. "We'll get quicker action if I contact Inspector Holt directly."

I'd entered Holt's number on my phone directory, and she answered my call immediately. I quickly explained that Ivy had been missing for more than an hour and told her about the insulin situation. I gave the phone to Rachel to describe what Ivy was wearing. She passed the phone back to me. I said thanks to Holt and pocketed my phone.

Rachel sat on a divan, completely drained. "I may never

see my daughter again," she murmured weakly. "I shouldn't have let her go off on her own with a murderer on the loose. I'm the worst mother ever."

I sat beside her. "Nonsense. You're a good mom, and Ivy's a resourceful girl. She won't let anyone get the better of her."

Rachel gripped my arm. "I hope you're right. I don't know what I'd do without her."

I looked up as Roy entered the room. "Is everything all right?" he asked when he saw the concern on our faces.

"No, it isn't," I said. "Ivy's missing. When was the last time you saw her?"

"Ivy? Um . . . I don't know. At lunch maybe?"

"Where have you been since then?"

"Well, you saw me. I was talking with Dave. Then I went back to my room. What else is there to do in this town?"

Ben came in, looking worn out, dour and sagging. His eyebrows rose when he saw us. "What are you all doing here?"

"My daughter is missing!" Rachel exclaimed. "When did you see her last?"

"Ivy?" Ben searched his memory. "I don't know. She's always running here and there. Maybe she's out on the terrace?"

Jorge emerged from a side room. He held a small book in his hand. He looked up, surprised, when he saw everyone looking at him.

"What are you reading?" Ben asked.

It took a moment for this question to register. "*The Idylls of the King*. Tennyson."

"Tennyson?" Dave asked. "Where in God's name did you get that?"

"In the hotel library. I've always loved tales of King Arthur."

Billie chose that moment to make her entrance. "Did I hear someone mention King Arthur?" She began humming the theme song to *Camelot*.

"Stop!" Rachel shouted. "Who cares about King Arthur? Ivy's gone missing! She's in danger!"

"In what way?" Dave asked.

She gripped his arms. "She's diabetic. Didn't I tell you? If she doesn't get her insulin shot, she'll die!"

"Insulin?" Dave asked. "You mean insulin detemir? Or insulin glargine?"

Rachel did a double take. "How do you know about insulin?"

Dave paused. "I . . . know a lot about drugs. I studied pharmacology in college."

"Okay. But I don't know the answer to your question. The doctors told me about the different types of insulin, but I don't have a head for that. All I know is that Ivy needs to get it now!"

My phone buzzed, and I pulled it from my pocket. The display showed it was Inspector Holt.

"Chase? I just received word that a body has been seen floating in the harbor."

My stomach sank. "Whose?" I could barely get the word out.

"I don't know. Just received word. I'll let you know when I hear more." She signed off.

I didn't share Holt's news with the others. But they were, of course, curious about the call.

"Who was that?" Rachel asked.

I tried my hardest not to show my anxiety. "That was Inspector Holt. They haven't found Ivy yet. But all their people are out on the search."

My response wasn't very reassuring, I realized. Taking action is always my go-to solution when things look bleak. What could I do?

"We all need keep looking for Ivy as well," I said. "The more eyes out there, the better. I scoured the harbor area, but I've got a feeling I may have missed something. I'll retrace my steps. It would help if each of you could explore other parts of the town."

Dave stiffened. "I'll look up the hillsides to the north."

"I'll search the hotel," Roy said. "There are a lot of nooks and crannies in this place."

Ben looked at me. "Are you going to the east?" I nodded. "Then I'll look to the west."

"I'll check all the cafés," Billie said. "Ivy might have been tempted by a chocolate soda."

"I'm coming with you," Rachel said and followed Billie out the door.

Jorge looked stranded, holding his book. "What can I do?"

"Stay right here," I said. "If Ivy returns, you have my phone number, right?"

"I think so."

"Good." I headed outside, overcome by the feeling that I'd overlooked something. When I emerged onto the terrace, the sky was beginning to darken, and the fishing boats were returning with their day's catch. What had I overlooked? I'd covered the harborside, keeping my eyes and ears open. I'd detected nothing. And yet . . .

I began walking again to the east on the harbor ledge, the fishermen passing before me, carrying baskets of their catch. The sweet and salty scent of the bay's brine tickled my senses. I spotted a police boat at the far reaches of the harbor. Perhaps that's where the body Holt mentioned had been spotted. Two fishermen were walking up the small, rocky beach toward me, laughing as they talked.

"Excuse me," I said. "Have you seen a young girl around here? Long black hair, eyeglasses?"

They shook their heads as they passed.

I looked around the small beach, noticing a pile of large rocks nearby. Approaching them, I noticed a ragged, blue, weather-worn scarf sandwiched between two. Had Ivy worn a scarf like that? I reached down to examine it further. It showed the wear of several months' exposure to the sea air, not just a few hours.

I straightened up and surveyed the beach again. Even in the late-afternoon sun, the row of beach huts looked out of place without tourists and sunbathers around. I walked toward them, my eyes peeled for anything unusual. A young couple, laughing as they held each other, passed before me, making the huts look even more desolate. Beach huts aren't designed for prolonged habitation; they're used to store beach gear and provide a spot to relax from the rays of the sun for a few hours.

As I neared them, I heard the faint notes and rhythms of a pop song. They sounded familiar: notes being picked out on a guitar, backed with a bass rhythm. They stopped and repeated. I remembered where'd I heard the music before—on Ivy's cell phone. Some Taylor Swift song.

The ringtone ceased playing, but it was coming from second hut on the north end. I approached the door, pulled my sleeve down over my hand, and yanked its handle. The door didn't budge, but it was most likely locked.

"Ivy?" I called out. There was no response from within.

I pulled more forcefully on the door, this time feeling it give a little. Looking down, I saw a white stone wedged in the small space beneath it. I grabbed it with my hand and tried to move it, but it was lodged in tight. I was wearing my walking boots and gave the rock a firm kick. Two more kicks dislodged it. I yanked on the door handle again. Without the stone wedged against it, the door pulled away from its hinges, allowing me to get inside.

My heart stopped when I saw Ivy crumpled on the floor.

There was a severe bruise on the back of her neck. I crouched down. "Ivy? Ivy, answer me!"

My heart regained its rhythm as her eyes briefly fluttered open. She was too weak to speak. I pulled out my phone and called Holt.

"Sheila? It's Chase. Get some medics to the beach huts by the hotel! I've found Ivy, but she needs immediate attention."

Chapter 21

Thursday, late afternoon,
St. Mawes Harbor

I carried Ivy outside and carefully laid her down on the sand. She moved slightly as she felt the sun on her face, and her eyes slowly opened. She didn't appear to have any broken bones, but I needed to keep her still until the medics arrived.

"You'll be okay," I told her as she looked up at me, confused and frightened. Knowing that her mother was going wild with worry, I called Billie, who answered immediately.

"I found Ivy," I said. "Please tell her mother that she's okay. A medical team is on its way to take her to the local hospital so she can get her insulin."

"Thank God!" Billie said.

The police medical van soon arrived. A man and a woman got out, and as they prepared to load Ivy onto a stretcher, I explained what had happened, and that she was in need of insulin.

The crew gently lifted her up and told me they were taking her to the local hospital, a couple of miles away. My phone buzzed with a call from Rachel.

"Chase!" she said. "Is it true? You found Ivy?"

"She's fine, and the medical crew will give her insulin. I'll go with them to the hospital."

Rachel said she would be on her way as well. I climbed into the van and sat beside Ivy as we sped off.

She looked up at me. "You saved me," she said weakly.

I squeezed her hand. "Are you strong enough to tell me what happened?"

She took a deep breath. "I went out for a walk. Mom and I just had a fight. I was mad, so . . . I wasn't watching where I was going. Then someone grabbed me, dragged me to one of those little buildings, and I blacked out. That's the last thing I remember."

"You don't remember being hit?"

She shook her head.

"And you didn't see who attacked you?"

She looked down. "No. But it must have been a man. He was real strong."

Of course, women can be strong as well, but I said nothing. Whoever it was, luck had been on their side—they'd found a beach hut that wasn't locked.

The female EMT gave Ivy a cup of water. After she took a drink, she said, "I'm scared. Someone tried to kill me!"

"But they didn't succeed," I said.

We soon arrived at the emergency entrance of the small local hospital. As Ivy was being taken inside, a local taxi drove up. Rachel quickly emerged and rushed up to me. "Is she here? Is she okay?"

I led her inside, where an orderly took Rachel to see her daughter. My phone buzzed, and I answered a call from Inspector Holt.

"Finding the girl was a stroke of good fortune," she said. "Did you get any information from her?"

"She's very weak. She's been through a lot. She believes a man attacked her, but I'm sure we'll get more out of her later. The main thing is she was found in time and will be all right."

"What you mean is, *you* found her in time. Good work, Chase. By the way, that body sighted floating in the harbor wasn't a human body at all. Only a large deceased otter."

Perhaps Ivy would get a kick out of being mistaken for an otter. Or perhaps not.

"We also need to check out that beach hut in which you found her," Holt continued. "I'm sending our forensics team to have a look around."

"You might also check to see what other strangers the fishermen or locals may have seen walking around at the time," I suggested, although the one they'd probably mention was me.

Holt signed off just as Rachel returned. She was smiling.

"Thank the Lord this turned out all right," she said. "Ivy's stabilized, but they want to keep her here for a while. She shouldn't have any long-term injuries from her attack. Chase, I can't thank you enough for finding her. I'll stay here until they say it's okay for her to go. You can leave if you'd like. My taxi should still be outside."

I gave her a hug and placed my hand on her shoulders. "I can understand if you don't want to take Ivy back to The Carne. One of our group could have been the one who abducted her. But please do. I assure you that I'll keep her safe."

"Do you think her reappearance might lead that person to confess?"

"Hardly that. But . . . I might notice something less obvious."

She nodded, and I went outside, where Rachel's taxi was waiting. On the ride back to the hotel, I reviewed the day's events. Someone had tried to shut up Ivy for good, which meant they thought she might know something that would lead to identifying them as Luella's killer. I shuddered to think of what would have happened had the charge on Ivy's phone run out—or had the killer noticed it and snatched it away before sealing her up in a would-be tomb.

But who did this all point to? Ivy had accused nearly everyone in our group of murder at one time or another.

When I reached the hotel, I found Billie in the parlor, her yarn and knitting needles on a chair beside her. She was too agitated to actually knit, however. Her eyes lit up when she saw me. I told her of what happened to Ivy.

"That's horrible! The killer must have wanted to keep her from talking."

"My thoughts exactly."

"It had to have been a man who attacked her," Billie said. "Ivy's a strong girl, and I'm sure she must have put up quite a fight."

The only female suspect was Rachel, and although she was strong, I couldn't imagine her harming her own daughter.

"There's that Jane Berry woman," Billie said. "Remember? The one whose field had the bull in it? I've never seen what she looks like, so I don't know how strong she might be. She seems a long shot to be Ivy's assailant anyway—her farm is quite a distance away, and this attack certainly was not intended to scare someone off the trail." Billie thought a moment. "Unless she thought Ivy had incriminating evidence about her."

"How would she even know about Ivy? Or what she looks like, and where to find her?"

"Yes, that's true. What a mess."

I looked around. "Where's Jorge? I asked him to stay here."

"He's around somewhere. I think he went to the men's

room. We need to tell the others that Ivy's been found. Have you seen any of them?"

I was about to respond when Jorge approached. I leaned close to Billie and whispered, "Don't say anything about Ivy being found. Don't tell Roy, Ben, or Dave either!"

"Any luck in finding the girl, Chase?" Jorge asked, hope in his voice.

"Afraid not," I said. "Have you seen any of the others?"

He shook his head. It wasn't long, however, before Roy walked in. I shared with him the same report I gave Jorge.

"She can't have gone far," Roy said. "This town isn't that big, and I doubt she would venture too far outside it."

"Even though it's a small town, its layout is confusing, just like a lot of these old villages," Jorge said. "She probably got lost, that's all."

Dave and Ben were the next to walk in. "So here's where you all are," Ben said. "But I don't see Ivy or Rachel."

"Rachel's still out looking," I said.

"I should have gone with her," Dave said. "She shouldn't be alone at a time like this."

"The police have been notified," I said, "so there's nothing more we can do at this point."

Dave collapsed on a stuffed chair. "We need to get our minds off this. Anyone up for a couple hands of poker?"

"Board games are more my style," said Ben.

"A game of Clue might be appropriate," Billie suggested dryly.

"When Ivy gets back, someone needs to give her a good talking-to for all the trouble she's caused," Jorge said.

"Ivy's not such a bad little thing," Roy said. "Kids start getting rebellious at that age, and seeing what her parents are going through can't exactly be fun for her."

"I could give her lessons about living with difficult parents," Ben said. He stood by the window and examined the sea view outside.

"Difficult children sometimes make difficult parents," Jorge commented, earning a glare from Ben.

While they continued talking, I discreetly sent off a text to Rachel. She quickly responded that she and Ivy were on their way back.

"Speaking of missing, has anyone seen Brian?" Roy asked. "I know he's not staying at this hotel, but he said he'd check in with us later."

"Here he comes now," I said, seeing our walk leader come in through the front door.

When he joined us, he said, "Good to see you all here. I'm hoping you can update me on the investigation. If the authorities have found the culprit, we can resurrect some of our itinerary."

"You seriously believe we want to go back on the walk after all of this?" Ben asked incredulously.

"It might do everyone some good," he said, although I agreed that his proposal made little sense. He looked around. "Wait—you're not all here, are you? Where is Mrs. Scattergood and her daughter?"

"Here we are," came a voice from behind him.

As Rachel appeared with Ivy (wearing a neck brace), I scanned the faces around me, quickly assessing their reactions. Ben looked surprised, but pleased. Roy looked confused. Jorge was stone-faced. Only one of us expressed what could seem to be shock.

Dave.

Chapter 22

Thursday, early evening,
The Carne

But Dave's eyes weren't on Ivy. They were focused on Rachel. "What the hell happened to you?"

Rachel recoiled in surprise. "Me? What do you mean?"

He approached and placed his hand on her face. "You look awful!"

"Wow," she said, backing up. "You really know how to sweet-talk a girl, don't you? I've been worried to death over my daughter, in case you've forgotten."

Dave then noticed Ivy, but the others beat him to it. Ben, Jorge, and Roy gathered around her. "Where have you been?" Ben asked. "Everyone's been worried sick! We've been searching all over for you!"

Rachel pulled Ivy to her side. "Go easy on her, will you? She's been through a lot."

"What happened?" Jorge asked.

I quickly explained that someone had attacked Ivy and barricaded her in a beach hut. This set off a buzz of speculation about the LUAU people striking again.

"Stop!" Ivy exclaimed as forcefully as she could. Summoning some inner resolve, she glared at the others and announced, "Someone tried to kill me today. And it was one of you!"

This set off a round of denials that merged into one meaningless buzz of voices.

"Listen up!" I announced. "This isn't the way to go about this. There are a lot of unanswered questions about what happened to Ivy this afternoon, and it's up to the police to sort them out. Inspector Holt is working on it. In the meantime, calm down. Ivy was hurt but is okay now. Nobody is being accused of anything."

"You don't seriously think one of us would attack Ivy," Jorge said to Rachel.

"I didn't seriously think anyone would kill your wife," she countered.

"We were all here at the hotel this afternoon," Ben said.

"How do we know that?" Rachel asked. "Were all of you within sight of one another the whole time?" I could definitely picture her in a courtroom, giving the other side hell.

"I wasn't out of anyone's sight for very long," Roy said.

"You stepped out at some point," Ben said to Roy. "I saw you coming back in from the harbor entrance."

"I was bored, so I went out to get collect a stone or two from the harbor," Roy said. "I thought I might catch a glimpse of Ivy. Instead, I saw him out there." He nodded toward Dave.

"Me?" Dave countered. "I was sitting at one of those tables outside the bar!"

I stepped between them and waved my hands. "What did I tell you guys about throwing accusations at each other? That's not getting us anywhere."

"I need to get Ivy up to our room," Rachel said. "She needs rest. With our door firmly locked."

After they walked off, Jorge approached Dave and looked him in the eye. "I'll say one thing and then hold my peace. Ivy's got something on you. I don't know what it is, but each time she mentions it, you look like somebody knows a deep, dark secret."

Dave laughed. "That's funny. I could say the same thing about you, Jorge. Or even Roy. Ivy claims to know dirty secrets about all of us."

"What do you say we form a brotherhood?" Roy said with a half smile. "The Ivy Scattergood Blackmail Crew."

Roy's joke appeared to have diffused the tension among the men; they began to laugh. This situation was too dark for me to join in their laughter, however. Someone had tried to keep Ivy quiet, for keeps. That wouldn't have happened over a harmless white lie or an exaggeration. Whether unknowingly or knowingly, she might have said something incriminating.

"There's too much tension down here," Billie said. "I'm going to my room for a nap." She gave me a wink goodbye as she walked out.

Immediately after she left, a loud crash came from the foyer. Afraid that something might have happened to Billie, I rushed out and saw that a grandfather clock had fallen over. Behind it, a young man was perched atop a short ladder, a framed painting in his hand.

"I barely touched it!" he said. "I was hanging this painting and only rested my hand on the clock for a second."

The clock was blocking the entrance to the hallway leading to the rooms. The desk manager knelt beside it, surveying the damage. "Thank goodness this wasn't a valuable antique," she said. "We'll see if it's worth repairing, but in the meantime, we need to get it out of the way."

The men had now joined us. Roy stepped over. "Here,

let me." He crouched, put his hands under the clock, and began to lift it.

"Let me help," Dave said, going over to him. "That thing must weigh a ton."

"No, no," Roy grunted as he lifted the clock. "I can do it."

He was wearing a polo shirt that clung to his upper body, his chest and arms bulging with the effort. I was surprised to see what a muscular build Roy had—almost rivalling Jorge's, although he wasn't nearly as tall or bulky. For the past few days, it had been hidden beneath his walking jacket. Soon he had the clock standing erect again, but he leaned it against the wall and placed a heavy side table in front of it to keep it from toppling again. Roy let out a breath and said, "This thing is too top-heavy." He turned to the desk clerk. "Weigh the bottom down if you plan to keep it."

She thanked him and offered to buy him a beer, but he declined. On the wall clock behind her, I saw it was dinnertime. With Luella's murder and Ivy's attack hanging over everybody like ominous clouds, a group dinner was probably not going to happen.

So what were my options? I could order room service, but that sounded dismal. Sequestered in my room, eating before the television? No, thanks. Eating in the hotel dining room might bring me into proximity with the others, and although that would be an opportunity to gather more information, I needed a break. Maybe a solo dinner at the Idle Rocks was the answer.

I went to my room, changed clothes, and was planning a subtle exit from the hotel when Billie walked toward me.

"I thought you were taking a nap," I said. "Have plans for dinner?"

She looked a bit defeated. "I couldn't get to sleep. Too

much on my mind. Maybe some food will perk me up. Frankly, I'm in a bit of a muddle. I should be helping you ferret out the murderer, as I usually do, but in this one I'm all at sea."

"That makes two of us."

"I don't believe that, Chase. You'll figure this one out, I know it."

"But not without your help. Why not join me at the Idle Rocks? We can compare notes and might come up with the solution."

The invitation brightened her up. "Lead the way!"

The restaurant offered both outdoor and indoor dining, both with impressive harbor views. Given the warmth of the evening and the fresh breeze blowing in from the sea, we opted for outdoors. Once seated beneath a large umbrella, with a view of the boats in the harbor and the beginnings of a glorious sunset over the English Channel, I knew we'd made the right choice.

Billie looked out and couldn't help noticing the beach huts, inside one of which Ivy had been imprisoned. "Why is it every time we come to England the beautiful surroundings are always tainted by murder?"

"That hasn't happened every time," I reminded.

"True," she conceded. "Just almost every time."

The server appeared, and we gave her our drink orders. She left us with the menu, a printed sheet with the day's seafood catch. We gave it a quick study and decided upon the lobster (for me) and spider crabs (for Billie). After our drinks had been delivered and we placed our dinner orders, I said, "So who looks the likeliest to be our killer?" I tried to convey a light tone, despite the seriousness of the question.

"You want me to be honest?" Billie asked.

"Of course."

"I think it's Dave. We know he's not a writer, which is what he told us at first. Then we discover he's a private detective hired by Rachel's husband, which he tried to make light of. You heard Luella threaten him that night at the castle."

"Don't forget I found that photo of him online, advertising his services as a cocktail pianist, under his real name."

"See what I mean? Too many identities. I'll bet there's one we haven't yet learned that's a real doozy."

I spun a swizzle stick in my G&T and took a sip. Divine. "Those are good points. But there have been other deceptions also. Roy hadn't told us his real name either, because he didn't want Luella to know he was the man she was suing."

"So you think Roy is our man?"

I let out a sigh of frustration. "I'm not sure. It could be Jorge or Ben also. They might be deceiving us as well, especially Jorge."

"You're forgetting Rachel."

"Oh, come on, Billie. She's a devoted mother to Ivy. Can you picture her imprisoning her own daughter?"

"But what if she didn't do that, yet she still killed Luella?"

"That doesn't make sense. Why would someone try to shut up Ivy if they weren't the killer? And is Rachel strong enough to have pushed over that statue?"

"I don't know! I'm just trying not to rule anyone out."

"You're ruling me and you out, I hope."

She smiled. "You know what I mean."

"What are you two up to?" a voice intruded.

We looked up to see Jorge looking down at us.

"We're about to have our dinner," I said. "Have you eaten?"

He sat. "Not hungry," he said, the scent of alcohol distinct on his breath. "I'm too riled up. This whole trip has been a nightmare."

"A hearty dinner might make you feel better," Billie said.

As much as I wished to be alone with Billie so we could compare notes, the opportunity to speak with Jorge without the influence of the others was too good to pass up. "Yes, please do," I said.

He hesitated a moment and picked up a menu. We motioned the server over, and Jorge ordered another cocktail and a meat pie.

"You must be at a complete loss," Billie said to Jorge when the server departed. "But I know how good the British police are. They'll find the person who killed your wife."

I studied Jorge's reaction. There again was that mixture of macho bravado and childish weakness. "How could anyone have expected something like this to happen?" he said. "It's like something out of a horror film."

"Do you have any idea who could have killed Luella?" I asked.

He shook his head. "If we were back in Florida, maybe I would have an idea. Luella had enemies—she wasn't afraid to speak her mind. But how would any of them manage to kill her over here? It's crazy!"

"She made enemies here too," I noted. "We learned that she's suing Roy. She was belligerent to Ivy. She made threats against Rachel. And we've discovered that she was threatening to expose Dave about some secret in his past."

"What?" Jorge said. "My Luella doing things like that? I don't believe it!"

Again I was faced with a suspect I could either take at face value—believing in their statements one hundred percent—or parse the guile behind them.

Regardless, this was my chance to resolve a question that was at the top of my mind. "Speaking of things that are hard to believe, you say you worked most of your career as an airline pilot. But you bring up all these other jobs you've had—race-car driver, physical therapist, bullfighter even! Seriously, now. How is all of that possible?"

The server appeared to deliver Jorge's daiquiri. He took a sip and said, "Yes. I see why you're confused. But I've always been a driven person. One occupation has never been enough for me. I became proficient in one and then wanted to tackle another. So, yes, I was an airline pilot for a while. But I was also many other things—race-car driver, therapist, actor."

"Actor?" I said.

He took another sip of his daiquiri. "Not a movie star or anything like that. But I did quite well in college and community theater. I even won an award for playing George Gibbs in *Our Town*."

George Gibbs. The class president and all-American boy. I could picture Jorge in the role. But how all-American was Jorge, really? His name was Hispanic, and there was a slight southern European tint to his complexion.

"Your having that role is quite a coincidence," I said. "Ben told us he also played a small role in *Our Town*."

"Is that so?" he said. "Well, that play is such a classic. Even grade schools put it on."

"The character of George is fascinating," Billie says. "He gives up his plans to go to agriculture school so he can marry Emily. When Emily dies, Thornton Wilder means for the audience to pity George, not only because he's lost his sweetheart, but because he's caring too much about things that cannot change. Except George doesn't feel he's cared enough. That's a problem we all have."

Jorge dropped his drink, causing it to fall over and spill

its contents, and started emitting short sobs. "I didn't mean to fall in love with her . . ." More sobs. "It just happened. Poor, dear Lulu . . ."

Billie looked pleadingly at me, regretting her commentary on *Our Town*. She began sopping up his daiquiri with her napkin. "Forgive me. Sometimes I get started before I know what I'm saying."

The server arrived with our food, which snapped Jorge out of his reverie. Soon the conversation veered toward our meals, which were uniformly excellent. That, together with the effects of our drinks and the harbor view, created a mellow vibe in which the specter of murder receded.

Nevertheless, I explained that Lawrence Hancock had been seen (and photographed) releasing poisonous snakes on the trail.

Billie gave a shiver. "I hate snakes. That's why I always wear high-topped boots when I'm out walking."

"This Hancock guy could be the one who killed my wife," Jorge said.

I remembered Hancock as a tall, angular fellow, possibly the man seen by Ben but not the short man recalled by Jorge. "I'm sure Holt and her team will explore his alibi," I said. "At any rate, the trails around here are safer now."

"Let's hope," Billie said.

Jorge began yawning, and Billie and I followed suit. "You need to get some sleep," Billie said to Jorge. "Let's walk you back to The Carne."

"No, I think I'll stay here a while. Don't worry. I'm through drinking. I'll be okay."

I was concerned, but he seemed sincere.

Billie and I headed outside. "What do you think?" Billie asked. "Was Jorge acting especially weird tonight or what?"

It had been a long day. Multiple thoughts were swarming in my mind. I was trying, as always, to sort them out. I felt like a third baseman with players on first and second and the other team at bat with the score tied at the bottom of the ninth. There was pressure, but of a good kind.

"Let me think on it," was all I said.

Chapter 23

Thursday, late evening,
The Carne

The hotel seemed quiet when we arrived, but when we passed the parlor, someone called out, "Chase!"

Roy, Dave, and Ben were seated at a game table. We walked over and saw a familiar game board.

"You're playing Clue!" Billie noted. "How appropriate."

"Except over here they call it Cluedo," Ben said. "Wonder why?"

I knew the answer to that one. "It's a nod to the Latin word 'ludo,' which means, 'I play.' " I looked down at the iconic board, showing different rooms in a stately old mansion. "Who's winning?" I asked.

"We just started," Dave said.

"I forgot how lame this game is," Ben said. "We have to find the murder weapon, the room where the murder happened, and the murderer, right? But we don't have to find the most important thing of all!"

"Motive," I said.

"See what I mean?" Ben said. "How do you solve a murder if you don't know why it was done?"

"Are any murders committed without a motive?" Roy asked.

"It would be hard to think of one," I said.

"Oh, that's not true," Dave said. "What about serial killers? Or some maniac shooting off strangers from a rooftop?"

"Even then there's a motive," Billie said. "Serial killers usually have some deranged reason for killing, and the maniac's motive is buried in his or her mania."

Dave turned toward me. "I'm sure you and that inspector lady have looked at each of us to see what motive we may have had for killing Mrs. Campos."

I nodded. "Of course we have. And you all have one, as you well know."

"But you need opportunity, too, don't you?" Ben asked. "Motive and opportunity."

"We all had an opportunity as well as a motive," Dave said. "One of us—or one of the LUAU people—waited until everyone was either asleep or doing something else at lunch that day, and killed Mrs. Campos."

"You could be right," I said. "Yet how could someone manage to do that without clearly being seen? We've learned that, despite drifting off to sleep for a bit, all of you were awake at least part of that time, and Luella wasn't that far away. It's a miracle nobody saw it happen."

"Maybe it was just blind luck," Roy said.

Billie said, "That's an awfully big chance for the murderer to take."

"Unless he or she felt that it couldn't wait," I said. "There was some reason that Luella needed to killed at that moment."

Everyone looked at each other, waiting for some revelation, but all appeared stumped.

Dave sighed and picked up his playing piece. "Too bad in real life murder isn't as simple as a board game."

I studied the board again. "Maybe it is . . . in a way. Hand me that pad on which you've been writing the scores, will you?"

Roy pushed it over. I picked up a pencil and began drawing an irregular shape.

"What are you doing?" Dave asked. "What's that supposed to be?"

I finished drawing and let everyone look. "I may not have got it exactly right, but this is roughly the shape of the field where we had lunch when Luella was killed."

"I see what you're doing," said Billie. "You're recreating the crime scene."

"Yes, something like that," I replied, and continued drawing. "Now, let's see. Here are those big rocks near the center, and the trees behind them, off to the west. Here's the statue. Now maybe we can all remember where we were."

Dave pointed to one of the rocks. "Rachel was there the whole time, either seated on the rock or leaning against it." I marked down RS. "She walked around a little before Luella was found, but I'm not sure where. And I was not far away." I marked DL. "To my other side was Brian." For him, I marked BT.

"Did you see any of the others?" I asked.

Dave said he'd spotted Ben near the statue where Luella was found, Roy not far away, and Jorge on the other side of the field.

Dave claimed that he too saw Ben, but it was Roy at the far end of the field, not Jorge. "I walked around a little too, I think, but more toward the north."

Roy pointed to a nearby spot. "Well, I'll tell you exactly where I was. I was asleep over here, but I got up and walked around a bit to stretch my legs."

"Here?" I asked, pointing to the west.

He nodded. "Maybe a dozen feet or so. Not where the others say I was." I noted RB and drew a dotted line to indicate the path he may have taken.

"What about you, Ben?" Billie asked.

"After I left Mother, I came back to the group. Jorge wanted to speak with me, and after we talked, I'm not sure where Jorge went. I think I saw Roy where Dave said he was. Then I saw that other guy who wasn't with the group, over here." He pointed to another position on my diagram.

By pooling our recollections, we determined that Jorge, Roy, and Ben all had been more active than we thought. We were in agreement as to where they sat or lay down to rest and eat their lunch, but after that our memories diverged.

"This is nuts," Dave said. "From what everyone says, it's like Jorge, Roy, and Ben were all over the place, appearing at one end of the field and then the other, with nobody noticing them walking from one point to another. That can't possibly be right."

I marked Jorge's and Ben's sightings with a JC and a BP.

We all took a look at what I'd drawn. I realized that, while I placed the members of our group, there were other items, such as trees and large rocks, that could have obscured our view.

"According to your map, Chase, most of us were all over the field," Dave said. "But nobody could have see all of it from any one place."

I studied my map. "I realize it's difficult to remember precisely what happened two days ago, especially with the chaos that followed. But it could also be that somebody isn't telling the truth."

"Are you accusing one of us of lying?" Roy asked. "You don't trust us?"

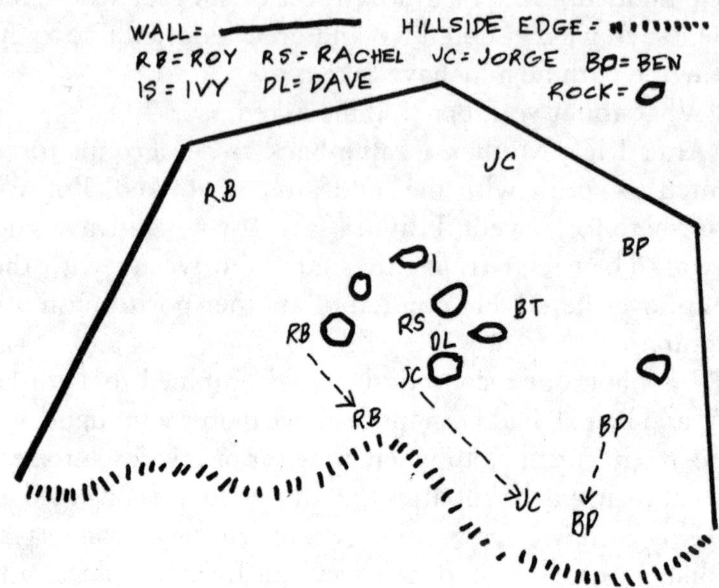

I looked at him. "Luella trusted all of you. Look where that got her."

My statement was perhaps a bit strong, but it was the truth. Someone was lying to me. Billie sensed my discomfort. "Listen. It's late, and we're all tired. What do you say we revisit this tomorrow morning?"

"What is this, game night?" a voice asked from the entrance to the room. I looked up and saw the most welcome sight I'd ever seen. It was Mike, carrying a small overnight case. After overcoming my shock, I went over to him and, not caring what the others would think, gave him a long and tender welcoming kiss.

I introduced Mike to the others as my "friend," without going into detail about our relationship or his occupation. That kiss probably told them all they needed to know about the former. I was pleased when they welcomed him warmly. He looked over at the Cluedo board.

"That's one my favorite games!" he said. "Except I rarely win. I never figure out those secret passages."

"Want to join us?" Ben asked.

Mike eyed me quickly, and said, "Perhaps tomorrow. I'm a bit worn from the drive." Translation: he wanted to be alone with me. Judging from the knowing expressions on their faces, the others understood perfectly.

In my room, Mike and I spent several minutes showing how glad we were to see each other. When he pulled away from me, he said, "Wow! What is it with you and murder investigations? They fire you up!"

"No, you fire me up. But why did you decide to come here? Don't you have work to do?"

He ran his fingers through my beard. "I couldn't bear the thought of you being embroiled in a murder investigation when all you wanted was a relaxing and invigorating walk. Do you think I could leave you alone at such a time?"

I kissed him and said, "Thanks. This means more than I can say."

He stretched out on the bed. "So tell me where things stand."

I lay beside him. "It's been quite a day," I said, and told him about Ivy's disappearance, my search to find her, and the close call with her insulin injection.

Mike was shocked, and concerned. "Someone's not playing around, Chase. I don't like it. Leave the sleuthing to the professionals, will you? I don't want to lose you."

I curled my arm around his head and gave him a kiss. "You're not going to lose me. Inspector Holt and her team are doing all the dirty work." I explained about the man from LUAU being arrested for releasing snakes onto the trail.

"No doubt that's who's behind your murder," Mike said.

I shook my head. "He's been in custody all day. He couldn't have been the one who shut Ivy inside that beach hut."

He grimly accepted my reasoning. I could tell something else was gnawing at him—and I knew what it was.

"You went to see Randall today?" I asked.

A pause. "This afternoon. He's not doing well. One minute he is fine, and then he becomes sullen and resentful, begging to come live with the two of us. It's so sad, Chase. I don't know how much more I can take it. He's always been a handful, but nothing like this."

This is what I'd feared. Randall might not have been what is considered "normal," but he knew precisely how to pull Mike's strings and get him to do what he wanted. He wouldn't let up until Mike gave in and took him in.

"What about that place his ex-wife told you about? January something?"

"January House. I have an appointment there the day after tomorrow. I checked them out online, and they seem like a good option. Except . . ."

"Except?"

"They cost the earth, Chase. I have money saved, but it won't cover the expense for more than a year or two. And Randall's mostly bust as well. He's never been good at saving or investing. His house will bring some money, though. Perhaps that will be enough."

I traced his chin with my finger. "I have money too, you know."

"I couldn't ask you to pay for this."

"You're not asking. I'm offering."

After a lengthy kiss, Mike smiled and said, "I wish our situations were as easy to solve as that Cluedo game. Perhaps I can be Professor Plum."

"Who am I, then? Miss Scarlet?"

He laughed. "You're a Colonel Mustard if I've ever seen one. Now all we need to do is discover the secret passageway between the rooms."

I froze. *Secret passageway*. Of course. Why hadn't I thought of that?

"Is something wrong?" Mike asked.

"There's nothing wrong at all," I said, followed by a kiss. "You've given me an important new clue."

Chapter 24

Friday, morning,
The Carne

It took me longer to fall asleep that night with Mike's clue careening around my brain. After a while, though, fatigue took its toll, and my thoughts incomplete, I drifted off.

The alarm clock rang at six a.m., and it took me a few minutes to awaken. The first thing that came to mind was the clue I'd been pondering the night before. The second was in bed beside me. I smiled at Mike sleeping peacefully. I gently stepped out of bed so I wouldn't disturb him, rinsed off my face in the bath, and put a coffee pod in the room's percolator.

After a bracing cup of coffee, I dressed and checked my cell phone. There was a message from Holt, informing me that Hancock might have an alibi after all for the time period in which Luella was killed. She said she'd be stopping by at ten o'clock to question Ivy.

I left a note for Mike explaining that I'd be down in the hotel café for breakfast. To my surprise, Rachel and Ivy were there, eating bowls of granola. The girl was still wearing her neck brace.

"How are you feeling this morning?" I asked Ivy, before I perused the breakfast bar.

"Fine," she answered, her mouth full.

"She's made an amazing turnaround," Rachel said. "Her neck will be sore for a while, but other than that, she's her old self."

That was good news, but I was hoping that Ivy would morph into a new self—one who didn't put forth unfounded allegations. I told them that the inspector would be there soon to interview Ivy.

"I don't remember much, you know," Ivy said. "I already told you everything I know."

"That's fine. But you need to tell the inspector. Don't make up things just to impress her."

"I'm not doing that stuff anymore," she said, surprising me. Maybe her new self was emerging after all.

Billie soon joined us, but we saw none of the others. Shortly before ten o'clock, Inspector Holt and DC Kahlil appeared at the doorway. They greeted us and asked Rachel and Ivy if they would be okay with my sitting in on their interview.

"Sure!" Ivy replied. Billie said she'd be knitting at one of the tables on the terrace.

Once the five of us were situated in the corner of the main parlor that Holt had reserved for her interviews, DC Kahlil turned on her phone recorder and stated the date, time, and names of the persons being interviewed.

"Now, Ivy, you know why we're here," Holt said with forced indulgence, as if she were speaking to a much younger girl.

"Of course," Ivy replied. "You want to know what I recollect about being attacked, and whether that has any bearing on your murder investigation." She was visibly surprising Holt with her eloquence.

"Precisely," Holt said. "Do you recall anything—anything at all—about the person who attacked you?"

Ivy thought a moment. "Sorry, I don't. He grabbed me so quick from behind that I didn't have a chance to look at him. But I'm sure it was a man."

"Why are you so certain?"

Ivy shrugged. "He felt like a man."

"He said nothing to you?"

"Nope."

Further questions yielded nothing new. DC Kahlil then asked if Ivy remembered anything else, apart from her attack, that could have a bearing on the case.

"You mean besides everyone lying about who they are?" she countered.

Holt formed an admiring smile. "You mean Mr. Burke and Mr. Langdon."

"And also Jorge. He may not be a famous movie star, but I'll bet he's lying about who he is, too."

"Ivy," I cautioned, "remember what I told you about making accusations without proof?"

She said nothing and looked down.

"It is true that this case has more than its share of hidden identities," Holt said. Turning to me, she asked, "Have you any knowledge of Mr. Campos having a different identity?"

I reflected on her question. *People can change their name too easily these days. Nobody might be who you think they are.* "Nothing verifiable, no," I responded, although I strongly suspected there was some truth to Ivy's statement.

"I can tell you something I heard," Ivy said. She saw my eyebrows raise disapprovingly and said, "No, really. I did hear it! I remembered while I was in the hospital."

"Go on," Holt prodded.

"I was walking away from the others on the hilltop, and

Ben and Jorge walked past me. I don't think they even knew I was there. Ben said to Jorge, 'So we're really going to do it, right?' "

Holt and I exchanged looks.

"They must have been planning to murder Mrs. Campos!" Ivy said. "What else could it be?"

"For heaven's sake, Ivy," Rachel said. "They might have been planning to have lunch. Or see a movie."

"I know they weren't talking about anything like that," Ivy retorted.

I was tempted to lecture her again when Holt said, "Very well. We'll make a note of that. Anything else?"

In a weak voice, Ivy asked, "Do you think someone will try to kill me again?"

Holt raised an eyebrow. "It's possible. That's why you mustn't run off on your own, no matter how angry you are. Stay with your mother until we have Mrs. Campos's killer behind bars."

She nodded. "I will."

Rachel thanked us and led Ivy away.

"She's an imaginative young woman, I'll give her that," Holt said.

I chuckled. "The trick is separating truth from that imagination. Here, let me show you this." I pulled out the diagram I'd made the previous evening.

"What's this?" Holt asked, looking it over. I explained it was a depiction of everyone's positions on the hilltop the day Luella was killed, based on their recollections, including Ivy's.

"We have to allow for these recollections to be imprecise, but they give us a place to start."

The inspector and the constable looked it over intently. "What it looks like is that everyone was everywhere."

"Exactly," I said. "The group had varying opinions about where everyone was. It seems that people appeared one moment, then disappeared the next. That didn't seem possible, of course. But that's when Mike Tibbets noted something about Cluedo."

"Cluedo?" the inspector asked "You mean the mystery game?"

I nodded. "I'm sure you know it. Players sometimes move from some rooms to others by means of a secret passageway. That's what gave me the idea. What if there were secret passages between the hilltop field—the one in which we were gathered—and the ones beside it? There was a long wall, and I recalled that there was a lot of foliage. I'd discovered one break in the wall, through which the killer tossed the crowbar, and figured there may be other places like that. It would be very helpful if we could go back to the scene itself."

"Return to Cadgwith Cove?" Holt asked. She looked at DC Kahlil, who nodded. "Let's go!"

After informing Mike where I was going, I found myself in Holt's police car heading west along the winding B coastal highway, with a frustrating pause at the River Fal to board the King Harry Ferry. Holt knew instinctively how to navigate the myriad connecting roads down to the coast, and we miraculously arrived at the outskirts of Cadgwith Cove before I expected.

She pulled into the small parking area beside the café at which we'd eaten the day of Luella's murder. Stepping out of the car, I surveyed the hilltop rising before us. Had it only been a couple of days since then? The incident seemed to have occurred weeks before, if not months.

"So, what did you need to check, Chase?" Holt asked, as we began walking up to the hilltop. When we got there, I pulled my diagram from my pocket.

"I had something of a brain wave last night," I said. "Let's go over to where Luella was found."

As we walked toward the fallen statue at the east side of the field, Holt said, "The medical examiner and forensics team have already swept the area clean. They weren't able to find fingerprints on the statue or the crowbar we suspect was used to dislodge it. That isn't surprising, of course."

"The killer would have been careful not to leave prints," I said.

We reached the statue, which seemed to be mocking us, even in its prone position, with its defiant, haughty pose. I called Holt and Kahlil's attention to the wall beyond, ringing the field. "When you stand here, the wall looks unbroken, doesn't it?" I asked. "It appears to be a continuous barrier stretching to the other side of the hilltop."

"That's true," Holt said.

"Now, follow me," I said and began walking alongside the wall until I reached the gap through which I discovered the crowbar. It was partially hidden from view by the surrounding greenery, but it was easy to see when you knew what you were looking for. The wall continued, barely perceptibly, beyond the gap, but set back a few millimeters. It overlapped slightly with the first wall. There was little doubt that the wall was intentionally designed to hide the gap. The pattern of its stones easily blended with the continuation of the wall in front of it.

"This is where the killer may have disappeared after he or she killed Luella," I said. "Now, let's continue walking along the wall."

We proceeded for another hundred feet or so, and just when I feared that my theory was wrong, there it was—another gap in the wall, hidden by bushes and branches. It was barely wide enough for a body to squeeze through. As with the previous gap, the wall on one side overlapped the other so that it would be undetectable from a distance.

"Here is where our killer could have returned to the

field," I said. "Perhaps this wall was designed to hide the pirates who plundered ships in this part of the country many years ago."

Holt stepped through the gap, avoiding the nettle bushes, and back again. She looked back to view it with amazement. "So, whoever killed Mrs. Campos could have disappeared through the first gap, tossed aside the crowbar, gone along the wall on the other side, and emerged from this gap."

"It's a strong possibility," I said. "Given the way these walls have been designed, it would seem as if they appeared out of nowhere."

We walked further and discovered one more gap where two walls overlapped. "Or our killer could have gone back into the field right here," I said.

"But . . . who does that implicate?" DC Kahlil asked.

I sighed. "Well, that's where this gets tricky. We have to rely on people's memories, which aren't always reliable. Roy, Jorge, and Ben were all seen by different people at different places on the hilltop, sometimes at different places at the same time." I again showed Holt and the constable my diagram.

"There's still that person whom Ben and Jorge claim was in the field that afternoon," Holt pointed out.

"Except the others don't remember seeing him," I said.

She nodded, lost in thought. "Hold on. What about Mr. Teague?"

"Our guide? Well . . . he was with us at first, but then went back down the hill to the village, I believe."

"Nevertheless, we must consider him a suspect as well." She gave a sigh and looked back at the field. "I appreciate your making this diagram, Chase, but I don't really see what good it does. Yes, we've discovered these secret passages, if that's a good word to describe them, but if your map is anywhere near accurate, our killer should have been in plain view of at least one other person the entire time, even given the holes in the wall."

I didn't think my drawing was as useless as she did. I examined my schematic of the field again and looked back up at the real thing. "Unless . . . they *were* seen."

"If someone was seen toppling the statue on top of Mrs. Campos, why hasn't anyone spoken up?" Holt paused. "Oh, wait. Are you suggesting that they didn't let on because they and the other person were planning the murder together?"

"That's right. We've established that everyone had a motive to want Luella Campos out of the way, although some of those motives might seem like a stretch. What if two of them decided to join forces?"

"Outside of mob hits, I've never known that to happen," Holt said.

"I encountered it once back in California—a woman and her boyfriend teamed up to kill her spouse."

Holt looked back at my drawing. "Any situation like that among this lot?"

"Dave Langdon and Rachel are falling hard for each other," I said. "But she's divorcing her husband, and Dave isn't married."

"Luella appears to have been threatening Dave, and Rachel had a big blowup with Luella," DC Kahlil said. "But is that a reason to jointly agree to kill her?"

"There's Jorge and Ben," I said. "They seemed to always be in sight of each other during the hour in question. Ben certainly had a motive to do his mother in—he was always fighting with her. Jorge, Ben told me, is broke and would inherit Luella's fortune. Yet he seemed devoted to her."

"But there's that comment Ivy heard them make on the trail," Holt noted. "Something about doing something together. What about Mr. Burke and Mr. Langdon? In your drawing, it looks like they might have been near enough to talk."

"That's a possibility, and their motives are strong. Dave was afraid Luella was going to inform Rachel and her husband about his true purpose here, and Roy was facing a potentially crippling lawsuit. Still, I can't quite see it."

"What about the girl?" the constable asked.

"Ivy?"

"There's something not right about that lass. I can picture her bringing up the idea of murdering Luella to one of the others."

It was true that Ivy was often devious to a fault, but was she really the "bad seed" Luella accused her of being? "Ivy can be a handful, but I don't see her as a conspirator," I said. "And don't forget, it appears someone tried to kill *her*."

"That's true," Holt said. "She could hardly have closed herself in that beach hut and barred the door shut. Unless her accomplice staged that to deflect suspicion."

I couldn't think of any additional likely pairings. "There's a fundamental problem when two people agree to commit a serious crime such as murder," I said. "One of them always cracks sooner or later—either by blackmailing the other or confessing themselves when their guilty conscience weighs them down."

Holt shook her head. "We might have to wait awhile for that to happen."

"Perhaps not," I said, taking a look at the hilltop before me. It appeared so pastoral and calm that it was nearly impossible to imagine it the scene of a savage act of murder. I closed my eyes. The ghostly images of our walking group began to appear in a mental image, walking around, appearing and disappearing.

Other recollections began returning. Snippets of conversation. Quick observations. I struggled to connect them.

After a few moments, I heard Holt ask, "Chase? Are you still with us?"

I opened my eyes. "I may have figured something out."

Holt's phone buzzed before she could question me. She looked down at a text message, raised her eyebrows, showed it to DC Kahlil, then passed it to me. "It's from Duncan, one of our desk men. He does good research. There's new information about Mr. Campos, and Mr. Langdon."

As I read the message, it seemed to me that Duncan could show Ivy a thing or two about checking personal history online.

"This lines up with what I've been thinking," I said as I handed Holt's phone back to her. "But it's still not conclusive."

"It looks conclusive to me," Holt said. Turning to DC Kahlil, she said, "Let's go."

Chapter 25

Friday, midmorning,
The Carne

As we sped back toward St. Mawes, I didn't challenge Inspector Holt's certainty that we'd caught our killer. She most likely was correct in her thinking, based on the new facts uncovered by her research specialist. Yet it wasn't enough for me to move entirely into her camp.

Holt pulled up before the whitewashed façade of The Carne, which looked as beguilingly placid as ever, yet again I knew not to be taken in by surface appearances. We walked into the foyer, and the desk clerk in attendance that afternoon, a perky young woman with short dark hair, looked at us with gratitude.

"Thank goodness you're here! Please go into the parlor. One of your walkers has just been attacked."

"Attacked?" Holt said. We rushed into the parlor to find Roy seated on a small divan beside a male attendant, holding a towel over his eye.

"What on earth happened?" I asked.

"It was Ben," Roy said. "I came out here and found him fuming about something that Jorge is planning to do. I went to him to place my hand on his shoulder when he pulled back and punched me in the eye!" He removed the towel, revealing a nasty swollen bruise.

"What was he upset about?"

"Who knows? He's nuts! I was about to deck him myself, but he ran out."

Rachel appeared, frantic. "Has anyone seen Ivy?" she asked.

Dave was right behind her. "Is she missing again?"

She turned toward him. "I turned my back for a second, and she was gone. Just after I told her to stick with me like glue. She saw Ben and Jorge go off, and I'm afraid she's gone out to find them."

"Oh, no," I said. What was wrong with that girl? "Who else is unaccounted for? Where's Billie?"

"Over here, Chase," came a voice from the hallway leading from the dining room. Billie walked in, accompanied by Mike.

"What's going on?" he asked.

"It's vital that we find Mr. Campos and Mr. Purdue," Inspector Holt said. "Does anyone know where they are?"

"I saw Jorge a few minutes ago, lingering over his breakfast," Dave said. "He was looking as low as I'd ever seen him. He walked outside when he finished."

"Did it look like he was going in search of someone?" Holt asked.

Dave shook his head. "It looked more like he was going to find a cliff to jump off."

"Why would he go off wandering with a killer loose?" Roy asked.

"Let's go out and do a search," Dave suggested. Rachel nodded in agreement.

"Not a good idea," I said. "The last thing we need is to put you two in danger as well."

"Chase is right," the inspector said. "You lot stay here. I'll call some of my men in to join the search."

Outside I heard a loud shriek.

"Ivy!" Rachel said.

We raced out of the hotel and onto the harbor walk, where two fishermen were putting away their nets. Another shriek sounded. I looked up at its source: a swooping petrel, preparing to dive-bomb its lunch in the harbor. I asked one of the fishermen if they'd seen someone fitting Ben's or Jorge's description. They shook their heads.

"How about a young teenage girl with black hair?" Rachel asked.

"That we did," the fisherman said. "The young lass went up that way." He pointed toward the castle on the hill up the coast.

I was determined not to be a lone ranger on this hunt. I hurried back inside the hotel, found Holt, and told her that I feared Jorge and Ben had gone up to the castle, with Ivy in pursuit.

"Is that girl determined to do herself in?" Holt said. She told Rachel and the others to wait. "We'll bring her back, don't you worry."

I wished I'd had Holt's confidence. She, DC Kahlil, and I rushed past the boats in the harbor to the north. St. Mawes Castle stood before us on the hill, its domed turret shining in the late-morning sun. A row of cypress trees cast long shadows on the path. We saw no people.

The three of us approached the castle cautiously, listening for movements or sounds. All I could hear was the sea crashing against the rocks on the shore and the occasional wail of a petrel. Once we reached the main entrance to the castle, we began to hear faint voices inside. Halfway up the first flight of stairs, we saw Ivy, crouched behind an opening on the second floor. She saw us and motioned for us to be quiet.

It was then we heard the two men's voices, coming from above.

"We need to come clean, Ben, don't you see that?" Jorge said, his voice breaking. "I can't take this one more day."

"Are you insane?" Ben shouted. "Do you want to spend the rest of your life in prison?"

"I don't care anymore!"

"What about me? Don't you care what happens to me?"

"Wise up, Ben! It's over!"

Holt nodded, and I followed her and the constable as they moved stealthily forward until we could peer into the room. We found Jorge kneeling on the floor, Ben standing over him.

"I don't care about Luella's money anymore," Jorge said, his voice choking. "Can't you see that I'd rather have her back than anything else? How did things get . . . so far out of control . . ." He stood and moved over to an open window.

"*Stop*!" Ben yelled. "You don't know what you're doing!"

Holt stepped forward and grabbed Jorge by the arm. "I'm arresting the two of you for the murder of Luella Campos. You do not have to say anything, but it may harm your defense if you do not mention when questioned something which you later rely on in court. Anything you do say may be given in evidence."

After instructing Ivy to return to the hotel, Holt and Kahlil cuffed Jorge and Ben, and I accompanied them to the St. Mawes police station. We found a small room in which to conduct the interrogation. Kahlil turned on her phone recorder, and Holt faced the two men. She didn't beat around the bush. "How long have you been planning to kill Mrs. Campos?" she asked. "And don't lie. We've already heard from your own mouth that it was you. Tell the truth, and maybe the judge will reduce your sentences."

Ben and Jorge shared guilty, frightened looks. "About a year, I guess," Ben said.

"I can't believe I let you talk me into it," Jorge said, glaring at Ben. "You always knew how to play me like a fiddle."

A grin broke out on Ben's face. "That's because you're a chump, George. Always have been, always will be."

Jorge turned to Holt and me. "I needed money; that's the main reason we planned this."

"We learned that your actual name is George Fields," Holt said to Jorge. "That 'Jorge Campos' alias was a clever twist."

"Changing the name was my idea," Jorge said. "I was an assistant professor in the theater department when Ben was in college. That's when we first met and became friends. I'd encountered Luella a couple of times, but always in a large group. When we cooked up the idea for me to court her and marry her, I didn't think she'd recognize me by sight, but she might have remembered my name. It turns out, when we decided to go ahead with this, she didn't remember me at all."

"So you planned to get her to marry you, then do away with her and inherit her fortune?" I asked.

Jorge nodded. "When you put it that way, it sounds pretty crude, doesn't it? But Ben made her sound like a despicable person who deserved to die."

"She was," Ben said.

"And all our plans seemed to work like a charm," Jorge continued. "Ben knew exactly the kind of men his mother liked, and how she liked to be courted. Sure enough, she fell for the whole shebang."

"And you came to England because you thought it would be easier to kill her over here?" I asked.

Ben and Jorge exchanged glances. "Not really," Ben said. "I'd heard about the incidents of trail sabotage over here and put that together with my mother's love of Cornwall from her *Pirates of Penzance* days. So Jorge and I came over and explored the itinerary of this walk, looking for an appropriate spot to do her in. Seeing that statue at Cadgwith Cove gave us the idea. We bet on the chance that the trail saboteurs would be suspected."

"Let me guess how you set it up," I said. "You managed to saw a bevel in the base of the statue that could be knocked out by a crowbar, which would unbalance the statue so that it fell over. Then you drugged us when we stopped for lunch and Luella and convinced her to rest beside the statue."

Jorge nodded. "I did some calculations to figure out the proper spot to cut the statue base so it would fall directly where we would encourage Luella to rest."

I was pleased he was coming clean. "I noticed the shop owners acknowledge you at St. Michael's Mount and Church Cove. One was a chemist's shop, where I'm guessing you purchased the sleep medication to put in our drinks, and the other a general store, at which you purchased the crowbar and the saw to cut the granite."

"When Chase mentioned those places to us," Holt said, "we checked with the proprietors, and they both clearly remembered you and what you purchased."

"The curse of being tall," Jorge said grimly. "You don't go unnoticed."

"What really perked up my ears was your mention of playing George Gibbs in *Our Town*," I said. "I didn't know your actual name was George at that point, but I remember Ben saying he'd appeared in *Our Town* also."

"George directed me in that production," Ben said.

"The setup of the murder still puzzles me, though," Holt said. "How could you be sure that Luella would comply and lie down directly beside the statue?"

"I can answer that, I think," I said. "She suffered from a

form of narcolepsy, where she would doze off easily at mealtimes. Combined with the sleeping medication in her drink, that made her very compliant."

"That's correct," Ben said with a frown. "I also knew being beside the *Pirates of Penzance* statue would mean something to her."

"So everything went exactly as you planned," Holt said. "Chase also pointed out the gaps in the wall where you could quickly disappear, and reappear somewhere else."

"Well, it didn't go *exactly* as we planned," Ben said, looking at Jorge.

"What do you mean?" asked DC Kahlil. "What went wrong?"

Jorge tilted his head. "Is this for real? You actually think we killed Luella?"

"If you two didn't, who did?" Holt asked.

"I don't know. But it sure as hell wasn't us!"

Chapter 26

Friday, late morning,
St. Mawes Police Station

Holt's eyes widened. "This is absurd! Why did you do all that planning, then, if not to kill her?"

"Jorge got cold feet!" Ben said. "Right at the last minute."

Jorge began tearing up again. "I realized I'd actually fallen in love with the old girl. Can you believe that? Something I was certain would never happen. Yes, everything was in place for us to kill her, just as Ben and I had planned, but . . . I couldn't bring myself to do it."

Ben was fuming, his eyes shooting daggers at Jorge. "When he told me, I couldn't believe it. I explained to him how we had carefully planned the whole setup, piece by piece. I reminded him of all the work that we'd put in—getting the crowbar, giving everyone sleeping medication, preparing the statue. But it didn't make any difference. His mind was made up."

That must have been the argument Billie had seen the men having from her viewpoint at the bottom of the hill.

"When Jorge told me flat out he wasn't going to do it," Ben continued, "I saw all her money flying away. It would be just like her to outlive me so I never saw a cent. It was up to me to kill my mother, even though that wasn't the plan. Jorge begged me not to go through with it, but I didn't have any newfound love for her holding me back. What held me back was lack of strength. I'm not as big and strong as Jorge. I could never have dislodged that bevel and made the statue fall over."

Listening to Ben talk so matter-of-factly about killing his mother made my head swim, but it justified my hesitation at being taken in by Holt's assertion of their guilt. If, that is, what they said was true.

"I walked around the hill, trying to get up the nerve to do it," Ben said, "But I also knew that if I did a half-assed job, my mother might live, and I'd be in hot water. I also suspected the moment had passed; there were too many others walking about. That's when I heard Jorge screaming."

Holt exhaled and shook her head. "So if I'm to believe you, who pushed that statue over? It didn't fall over by itself."

Jorge shrugged. "Someone else must have carried through on the plans we made."

"Someone found the crowbar you'd hidden and knew where to strike the statue?" I asked. "That seems unlikely."

"I don't for the life of me know how, but yeah, someone must have," Jorge replied.

"There was no stranger on the top of the hill, was there?" I asked.

Ben and Jorge looked at each other. "No, that was something we made up to throw you off the scent. Except we didn't coordinate our stories about what the stranger should look like."

A fine pair of would-be murderers these were. Or were they actually would-be? Their story about another killer stepping forward after Jorge grew a conscience sounded preposterous. And yet I strongly suspected it wasn't. It meant that one of the other walkers was the culprit.

"Let me ask this," I said to Jorge. "Did you try to push Luella off the turret that morning at St. Michael's Mount?"

Jorge nodded and hung his head. "That was a spur-of-the-moment thing. We'd seen the castle on our previous visit and discussed it as the spot to kill Luella, but it's always crowded with tourists. We needed someplace more private. And yet . . . I saw my chance that day when I was walking around with Luella. I went to push her, but . . . well, the same thing happened. I pushed her enough to get her to cling to the side of the castle, but not enough to send her over. I just couldn't do it."

Holt shook her head, apparently having difficulty absorbing all this. Two men go to great pains to commit a murder, and yet they apparently didn't go through with it. Or were they just telling us that?

"So what's to become of us?" Jorge asked Holt. "We planned a murder, but we didn't actually commit it. Is that still a crime?"

"We only have your word that you didn't commit murder," Holt replied. "Until we discover who may actually have killed your wife, you're still our primary suspects. We can't leave you two here, though. I'll take you back to the hotel, but you're still in custody. The constable will be there to keep an eye out. Don't you dare try to scarper on me."

As DC Kahlil shepherded the pair back to her car, Holt took me aside.

"What do you think, Chase? Have you ever come across anything like this?"

"No, I can't say that I have. But we have other suspects, you know. Two fairly good ones, if I'm not mistaken."

"Are you thinking of Mr. Langdon and Mr. Burke? How on earth would they have known about the statue? And how to make it fall on Mrs. Campos? No, these chaps are the ones we want. They're doing this little dance to confuse us."

I disagreed. "Let me think about that one. In the meantime, could your research guy check out something else?"

"Absolutely."

"It's about Dave. We know he was masquerading as a journalist, but I suspect he might have other secrets as well. Have your man do research on Dave Landon. That was Dave's name when he was a professional party entertainer, a pianist."

She quickly sent a message from her phone.

On the drive back to the hotel, I kept quiet with my suspicions of other suspects because Jorge and Ben were in the vehicle; I didn't want them to start voicing their own opinions. Once we arrived, DC Kahlil led the two men through a side entrance to reduce the chances of being seen. Holt and I went through the main entrance and found everyone—including Ivy—gathered in the front parlor, awaiting news.

"You're safe!" Ivy shouted when she saw me, and ran to give me a hug. "I knew you'd get the better of those guys."

The others began hammering me and Holt with questions. I gently separated myself from Ivy and held up my hands to calm them down. I told them that Jorge and Ben were being held in suspicion of Luella's murder, but the investigation was continuing.

"The *two* of them killed Luella?" Rachel said.

"As Chase said, the investigation is continuing," Holt replied.

"I've always thought that pair had something to hide," Dave said. "They gave us something to make us sleep that day on the hilltop, didn't they?"

"It appears so, yes," the inspector said.

"What was it? Zolpidem? Zaleplon? Doxylamine?"

I wanted to speak with Holt, but I had something else to take care of.

"Have you seen Mike?" I asked Billie.

"Just a few minutes ago. He had some calls to make regarding work. He's probably up in your room."

I told Holt I'd be right back. Mike was just finishing a phone call when I entered. He smiled at me, but didn't look entirely happy.

"Well, it's done," he said. "I've enrolled Randall at January House. He won't be happy about it, but I've no other choice."

I went to sit beside him on the bed. "When does he need to be there?"

"In two weeks."

"I'll help you get him ready."

He squeezed my arm and gave me a kiss. "It's times like these when it helps to have a partner."

"Everything will turn out fine. You'll see."

"This whole situation is far from what I would call fine." Mike paused to wipe his eyes dry. "How about your murder? Any progress?"

I formed a sly grin. "Perhaps. The police are checking a few things out, but I think I'm onto something. I need to talk further with Inspector Holt. Would you like to join me?"

"I'm not here in an official capacity."

"Neither am I! But that doesn't seem to be an issue for Holt."

Mike laughed. "All the same, I'll let you confer with her alone. But . . . I will be close by. As I've mentioned, I don't like the fact that a killer is still at large. You've told me many times that's when they get the most desperate."

"Holt and her constable will be with me," I said. "I'll be all right."

* * *

Mike accompanied me downstairs, but we parted ways at the bottom, Mike heading off to the bar and me heading left toward the parlor, where Holt was waiting. I started whistling "Move It On Over," buoyed by confidence that the case was near its close.

The inspector was alone when I arrived, making notes on her phone. She looked up as I entered. "What's that song you're whistling?"

I told her. "Hank Williams. American country music legend."

"I love Hank Williams," she said. Remembering our purpose, she looked back down at her phone. "Listen to this." Reading from her phone, she continued, "David Richard Landon, age twenty-two, a police lieutenant in Evansville, Indiana, convicted of selling illegal narcotics, served seven years in an Indiana state penitentiary."

"Was there a photo in that file?" I asked.

"Yes, indeed. It's the same bloke. The one now calling himself Langdon. This file doesn't say what he did after leaving prison, but that was nearly ten years ago."

"I believe he cleaned up his life. Or so it appears. Perhaps that was the dirty secret Luella Campos threatened to reveal to the group. She might have known some of his customers."

"Yet if he cleaned up, as you say, why be ashamed of it? It should be something to be proud of. Do you think he's our man?"

"Well, it's one more secret in a case already teeming with them. Where is he, do you know?"

Holt nodded behind me. "Probably with the others. They're getting stir-crazy, as you can imagine, even in an idyllic place like this. I told them not to wander far off. I expect most are out on the terrace, given that it's such a lovely day."

We walked through the hotel, passing the bar, where Mike was seated at a table and Brian not far away. In the hotel solarium, the small room leading to the terrace, sat Ivy and Rachel, playing cards. Dave was on a lounge chair nearby.

Holt walked over to him and leaned down. "May we have a word, Mr. Langdon?"

All three—Dave, Rachel, and Ivy—looked up at the inspector in surprise. "With me?" he asked.

"Yes, please. Over here." She led him to a table at the far end of the room, beside a potted ficus plant. The three of us sat. Holt pulled out her phone and showed Dave the page detailing his criminal past.

I watched his expression carefully. When criminals are presented with evidence confirming their guilt, they often react in one of several ways—shock, calm indifference, haughty denial, smug gloating, cornered terror, or grim acceptance. Dave was clearly exhibiting the last. "What's that they say?" he said. "You can't escape your past?"

"Your familiarity with medications gave me pause," I said. "So it didn't come as a surprise to learn of your history as a drug dealer."

"I know what you're thinking," he said. "Mrs. Campos discovered my secret, and I killed her to keep her from blabbing it out. Well, you're dead wrong. She recognized me from my piano-playing days, that's all. Hardly a secret to kill someone over. But even if she had found out about my life of crime, so what? That was a long time ago. I'm not proud of what I did, but I've lived a respectable life ever since. I learned to play piano in prison and chose the society circuit as my target market for being a private detective. It was from playing at high-end events that I saw the opportunity to put some of the detection skills I picked up as a policeman to use. Rachel knows all of this. I've come clean with her about who I am."

Holt looked at me, curious as to whether I was buying Dave's story. For the most part, I was, but my mind was thinking fast.

"Besides, how would I have managed to push over that statue?" Dave continued. "If I was going to kill Mrs. Campos, I'd never have thought of something so wild."

Holt paused and gave a sigh. "Very well, Mr. Langdon, or whatever your name is. I'll let you know if we need you again."

He gave a nod and went back to Rachel and Ivy.

The screeches of seabirds outside directed my attention out to the late-morning sky, thin clouds peppering the horizon. Roy walked in, carrying the bag in which he collected his rocks from the sea. He set it down by the door. "Chase!" he said. "We were wondering where you've been. Have they locked up Jorge and Ben?"

"Not yet," I said. "Been out looking for rocks again?"

He sat on the chair vacated by Dave and stretched his feet. "That's right. On the beach down there. I hope that's not farther than we're supposed to go. I didn't find anything, anyway."

I walked over to Roy's bag and picked it up.

He shot up. "Hey! Put that down!"

I peered inside the bag and saw what I was looking for. I reached in, grabbed the item, and held it up.

Holt rushed over. "Why, that's . . ."

I handed the small wedge of white granite to her. "This must be the bevel that Jorge cut from the base of the statue. I was wondering why we couldn't find it." I looked at Roy, standing a few feet away. "It helps that some people like collecting souvenirs."

Roy's expression fell into the "cornered terror" category of reactions. He looked around, as if hoping for a quick escape route. He stood, darted over to Ivy, yanked her from her chair, and wrapped his arm around her neck. He began dragging her backward, toward the entrance to the hotel.

Rachel screamed, and Dave began rushing toward Roy.

"Stop!" Roy yelled. "If anyone comes near, I'll strangle her, I swear I will!"

Ivy struggled in his grasp, but as she'd suffered a neck injury only the day before, there wasn't much fight left in her. I looked toward Holt, who was in the same state of paralysis as I was. And yet . . . was she? I saw that her fingers were manipulating the keys on her phone.

Roy managed to maneuver Ivy through the door into the main hallway of the hotel. He was acting out of sheer panic, without any predetermined plan of action. He tried to look behind him, to ensure he was moving toward the front door, but he needed to keep his eyes on us as well. When he looked our way, a figure approached behind him. Instantly, he froze and quickly released Ivy, who hurried back to Rachel.

Holt and I rushed through the doorway to see DC Kahlil pressing a gun against Roy's back. Roy's face had gone limp in defeat.

The inspector confronted Roy and arrested him for the murder of Luella Campos. Without a word of denial, he let himself be cuffed and taken outside to the police vehicle.

Chapter 27

Friday, evening,
The Idle Rocks

"That's precisely what I was afraid of!" Mike exclaimed when I filled him in a few minutes later in our room. "What if that man had taken *you* hostage? Chase, you need to be more careful."

"I don't think I would have made as desirable a hostage as Ivy," I said with a grin. "In all seriousness, though. Holt and her constable were there. Roy wasn't going to get far."

Mike smiled too as he put his arms around me. "I'm glad it's all over. But what a wild story." The kiss that followed made it all worthwhile.

We went down to join the others, who were gathered for a short walk to the Idle Rocks for dinner. Rachel, Dave, and Ivy were clustered together and chatting pleasantly, looking more like a newly formed family than ever. Brian was chatting with Billie, who was wearing a sweater I hadn't yet seen. The blue-green pattern contained intricate overlapping images I couldn't immediately make out. I peered closer.

"They're whales," she said.

"Whales? That doesn't seem particularly Cornish to me."

"It's rare, but they're occasionally spotted in the Channel."

"If you say so, my friend."

On the walk to the restaurant, I learned from Inspector Holt on my phone that Roy had been charged with murder, while Jorge and Ben were charged as accessories. I shared this information with the others, whose reaction was a mixture of shock, relief, and curiosity. They began peppering me with questions. How did I know Roy was the killer? Especially since all clues had been pointing to Jorge and Ben? I told them all would be revealed once we were seated and were served drinks.

Our server had no sooner set down the final pint glass of ale than Rachel said, "Come on, Chase. Spill the beans. You know the whole story, I'm sure."

"We know Roy wanted to get Luella out of the way, but how on earth did he know about Ben and Jorge's plan with the statue?" Dave asked.

I took a long sip of my beer, holding everyone in suspense. Just before they were about to scream in frustration, I said, "They told him."

"That's crazy!" Brian said. "Why would they do that?"

I pointed to my mouth. "Read my lips. Ben and Jorge told him all about it."

"But . . ." Ivy said, trying to understand. "Jorge had second thoughts about killing Mrs. Campos. You told us so yourself. So why would he ask Roy to do it?"

I caught Billie smiling and knew she'd figured it out. "No, that's not what Chase is saying. He's telling you to *read his lips* because that's how Roy got all the details."

"He read their lips?" Rachel asked.

"Remember when I asked all of you the other night to remember where everyone was standing during that hour we were up on the hill?" I asked.

"Sure," Dave said. "You created a diagram of it."

"At one point, Billie saw Jorge and Ben together, having a heated argument. They admitted it themselves. Jorge had just told Ben he couldn't bring himself to murder Luella, and Ben was furious. But what Billie also noticed was Roy, standing at a distance from them, watching them."

"He was about as far from them on the hilltop as I was at the bottom of the hill," Billie continued, "so he couldn't have heard what they were saying. But he was watching them, intently."

"I didn't think anything about that at the time," I said. "But then I remembered, on the first day of our walk, Roy told me he was deaf as a child. His hearing had been restored when he was a teenager. So he was taught how to read lips. He couldn't hear Jorge and Ben from where he was standing the other day, but it didn't matter—he could see their lips moving. Ben was reminding Jorge of the whole setup, detail by detail, and Roy was taking in every word. Before that, I don't think he had any intention of doing Luella harm, but the situation presented itself. He simply couldn't resist."

Brian shook his head, amazed. "So . . . he knew where to find the crowbar, and knew where to strike the statue so that it would fall onto Mrs. Campos."

"Exactly," I said. "He also knew about the gaps in the wall, so he could return to the group without anyone suspecting he'd been near Luella. But he made one mistake. When I searched the ground around the statue afterward, I couldn't find the piece of granite he'd dislodged to make it collapse. That seemed odd. Why would he keep it? Today, I remembered Roy's penchant for collecting small rocks from the places he visits. What if he put that chunk of the statue in with those?"

"And that's what he did!" Ivy said. "What a dumb move that was. I knew there was something sneaky about him."

"Darling, you've been suspicious of everyone," her mother reminded.

"I have not!"

"Let me remind you," I said. "First you accused Dave of being a serial killer. Then it was Jorge who had a dark secret. And then Roy."

She looked a bit chastened. "Well, he did have the same name as a guy who'd been convicted of attempted murder."

"But Hemper wasn't Roy's real name. That was his alias."

Rachel looked puzzled. "If you're going to choose an alias, why pick the name of a convicted criminal? Was that just a weird coincidence?"

"Chase doesn't believe in coincidences," Billie said.

"It's not that I don't believe they happen," I said. "But when they do, they're a reminder to explore all other connections." Turning to Ivy, I said, "Just like the connection of you disappearing right after you stated clearly that you were certain Roy was the killer."

"He heard me?" she asked, surprised.

"It's very likely. He probably felt fairly certain Jorge and Ben would be charged with Luella's murder, as he knew how carefully they'd set it all up. But killers get desperate. If he thought there was a chance you may have seen him, he needed to shut you up. I saw how strong he was when he lifted that grandfather clock. He was not only strong enough to abduct you—you're pretty strong yourself, you know—but strong enough to dislodge that bevel so the statue would fall over."

"When you first explained all of this to me," Mike said,

"I couldn't understand how the son and the new husband had so quickly planned it all. Then you said they knew each other at university. But how did you know that?"

"Early on, I started to get the sense that Ben hadn't just met Jorge recently. At least twice, he accused Jorge of doing something he 'always' did. If the man had just entered his life a few months before, how would he know what he always did?"

"That could have just been a figure of speech," said Brian. " 'Always' can mean different things to different people."

"I didn't trust him from the start," Ivy said. "It was obvious he was pretending to be someone else. So I Googled him. 'Jorge Campos' brought up some results, but none seemed like this guy. None had been an airline pilot, for one thing. I'd just seen an old movie on TV and Jorge looked a lot like one of the stars—Tom Wakefield. So I Googled 'Tom Wakefield' and found that he was 'preparing for a new role' somewhere. His current photo really looks a lot like Jorge. So, I thought, that makes sense. He's come over here to get into his character."

"Well, he was no movie star," Rachel said. "But he was still acting."

"Roy called out to Jorge at the café on the second day," I said, "and even though he was just a few feet away, he didn't respond. He said his name again. Nothing. Finally, Roy asked if he'd heard you, and he said, 'Were you speaking to me?' He'd clearly heard Roy, but he didn't think he was talking to him. Why, I thought? What I came to see was a man who was not only pretending to be someone else, he was not very good at it. He hadn't gotten fully used to his new alias. As it turns out, Jorge's real name is George Fields."

Billie chuckled. "Pretty clever. Jorge Campos is 'George Fields' in Spanish."

"There were other slips also," I continued. "Ben and I were chatting about Jorge on the trail, and he was very clear that Jorge was broke and married his mother for her money. If he knew they were planning together to kill her, why provide me with a motive? Especially a motive that no one might ever discover?"

"Didn't all these slips make you realize Luella was in danger?" Brian said.

"I can't read lips like Roy," I joked. "And I'm not going to beat myself up over not figuring it out. That's a lot easier to do after the fact. Most people can't even do it then."

"So . . . Jorge wasn't who he said he was," Dave said. "And Roy wasn't who he said he was. It makes you not want to believe anything."

"You weren't who you said you were either," Rachel said, although with a tender gleam in her eye.

He smiled back. "Yes, but I didn't change my name. Well, only a little."

Our meals arrived, and we spent the next hour or so chatting about more mundane things like favorite films and home do-it-yourself projects. Mike shocked me by revealing he was about to install solar panels on the roof of his house and do the work himself.

Rachel laughed. "You're still at that phase of your relationship when you can surprise one another. That's nice. Don't let that pass."

It was still midevening, but the events of the day had taken their toll on everyone's energy. Brian stood and said, "I've certainly learned something from you lot. I'm going to make damn certain my next walking group tells me their real names as well as their aliases. Good night, all!"

That was the cue for the rest of us to say good night as well. As we headed outside, Mike took my arm and guided me away from the others. "Are you up for a short walk around the harbor?" he asked, trying to frame the question as a lighthearted suggestion but unable to disguise the discomfort beneath.

How could I refuse?

Chapter 28

Friday, evening,
St. Mawes Harbor

For a minute or so, Mike and I walked slowly, in silence, holding hands, looking out at the fishing boats bobbing in the water, the lights from the town dancing around them. It was romantic, certainly, but I felt uneasy. Something was definitely on Mike's mind.

"It's nice out here, isn't it?" he said.

I squeezed his hand with mine. "Very nice. But you seem preoccupied."

"I'm sorry it's so obvious."

"Are you concerned about Randall?"

He stopped walking to look at me. "Of course I am. But I'm also concerned about you."

I laughed. "Me? I'm fine. I didn't get murdered."

"No, but I've seen how energized you've been over these past two days. You come alive when you have a puzzle to solve. I'm afraid life with me won't provide that kind of spark."

I grazed the side of his face with my palm. "There are other kinds of sparks, you know."

He didn't look convinced. "You know what I mean.

Outside of work, my life is rather boring, Chase. I sit at home, listen to jazz with the Aga providing barely enough heat from the next room. I might watch a mystery show on television and then go to bed. Exciting stuff, right? I'm afraid it won't be enough for you."

I placed my hands on his shoulders. "Enough of this nonsense. We've just spent three months back at my home, where we mostly stayed inside and did exactly the things you just described. I never felt bored for a second! Why would it be any different here?"

Mike looked down. "I don't know. Our relationship is still new. The excitement wears off eventually. You know that as well as I do."

"You know what I think? I think you're scared, and you're dreaming up all the worst-case scenarios that can happen."

He looked up at me, his eyes dewy. "You're right, Chase. I am afraid. I've been so happy with you, happy that I've found someone long after I ever thought it was possible, and I'm worried it won't last. I'm getting older, and I dread the prospect of being alone again."

I wrapped my arm around him. "It's normal to feel that way. I do sometimes also. After Doug passed, I didn't know how I'd go on without him. I felt too old to start over with anyone else. But when you and I met, it was as if all my prayers had been answered. Then I became terrified that I was being unrealistically hopeful. You see? We both do it."

This got a chuckle out of Mike. "I suppose you're right. We should just take things one day at a time. Isn't that what they say?"

I held up his chin with my finger. "I prefer to take a longer view than that. One bad day isn't going to end things between us. Nor will two or three bad days. I'm in this for the long haul, Mike. Are you?"

He looked up at me. "You know I am, Chase."

Our ensuing kiss was passionate, loving, and comforting at the same time. A half-moon shone down on us, reminding me of the rainbow I spotted after visiting the wind phone. As we held each other, I marveled at the odds of two people from such different parts of the world finding happiness in one another.

We started strolling back to the hotel, holding each other's hand and not saying a word. It was as if we had just passed some important juncture in our relationship, like a walker passing a way marker on the trail that reminds him he is, indeed, going in the right direction.

An hour or so later, I stepped out of bed and went over to the small desk in our room. Mike was sound asleep. Trying to be quiet, I switched on the desk lamp, pulled out my journal, and began writing down the events of the day, not wanting to leave out any of the details leading up to Roy's apprehension. When I finished, I was surprised to see that it had taken me the better part of an hour to get down all my thoughts.

I turned off the light and crept back into bed. Mike murmured contentedly and curled his body against mine. That was exactly the comfort I needed to quickly fall asleep.

Chapter 29

Saturday, morning,
The Carne

The following morning, I awoke at six-thirty as usual, dressed quickly, and tried not to awaken Mike, who liked to sleep in later. On my way down to breakfast, I realized this was the day when the walk was scheduled to end, at Looe, a town up the coast.

Because of the early hour, the breakfast selections had not been brought out, but coffee was available. I sat, took a bracing sip from my cup, and scanned news headlines on my cell phone. The Red Sox had lost to the Yankees . . . again.

"Good news, Chase?"

I looked up to see Billie, clad in a blue-and-gold sweater with no discernible animals or plants in the pattern. "No, just the usual. How are you this morning?"

She sat opposite and curled her fingers around her coffee mug. "Whatever ointment that local doctor gave me seemed to do the trick," she said. "My knee still gives me a little trouble, but nothing like the other day."

"Glad to hear it."

"So . . . things seem to be going well in the romance department for you, from what it appears."

I smiled. "I'd say so, yes. Mike and I are determined to make this thing work. It's all gone smoothly so far, even with the challenges of distance and time zones. But I'll be on Mike's turf now, and he's facing some challenges." I filled her in on Randall's situation.

"Challenges are part of the equation. Try reading *Revolutionary Road* by Richard Yates. It's one of the best books I've ever read about the challenges of marriage. It might not brighten your day, but it will show you what to avoid. I wish I had read it when I was married."

"That's right," I said. "I'd forgotten you were married once."

"For two and a half miserable years. But you know what? I wouldn't have traded it for the world. I learned a lot about myself."

"Doug and I were never married legally, but we had the same kind of bond. So I know a thing or two about what to expect. However, I hope my relationship with Mike is more than a learning experience. Neither of us are young men anymore. We're looking for stability, love, and companionship. But we still need to work out the living arrangements."

Billie tilted her head. "Why is that a problem? You're crazy about this country. Would living in England be such a sacrifice?"

"I honestly don't know." I'd lived my entire life in a small radius of my hometown, Oceanside. I got my education at San Diego State, and although I considered venturing to other parts of the country for employment, I ended up working with the San Diego Police Department for my entire career. I met Doug at a Human Rights Campaign mixer in La Jolla.

Somewhere along the line, I developed a passion for England. Why, I never could explain. My mother's side of the family had come from Britain, but how much of that would have permeated into my consciousness? She rarely spoke of her childhood. I often thought it was my love for the British pop music of the sixties, yet millions of Americans were bitten by that bug, and they didn't all become anglophiles.

No, there was more to it than that. I love England's quirky pageantry, loony pop culture, mindless devotion to royalty, and also its dazzling countryside, gut-wrenching history, and mind-boggling literary, artistic, and musical heritage. Is there any place on earth like it?

Yet I also loved the good old USA. It certainly had its flaws, but it had been my home for more than sixty years.

"I honestly don't know," I repeated. "Moving here would be such a big step."

Billie reached out to hold my hand. "You wouldn't be moving to Jupiter, you know. You can still go back from time to time to see your beloved Red Sox."

I was about to respond when a familiar voice called out, "Good morning!" Mike was walking toward us, freshly shaven and carrying the morning newspaper.

"I was expecting you to sleep for two more hours," I said, standing to kiss him.

"That would be two hours when I could be with you," he said with a smile.

"Oh, brother, he's got it bad," Billie said to me. She turned to Mike and said, "Want any coffee?"

He eyed the carafes near the breakfast bar. "I'm a tea man, if you don't mind." He headed off just as Inspector Holt and DC Kahlil entered the room.

"I'm gobsmacked," I said to Holt. "Does everyone over here get up as early as me? Is there something wrong?"

"No, not at all. The constable and I have some early-morning appointments, but I had two or three orders of business with you." She and Kahlil sat at a table beside us. "First of all, I wanted to bring you up to date with what has been happening with our detainees. They've all confessed, so there'll be no jury trial. Mr. Campos and Ben Purdue will be sentenced here in England, but Roy Burke's family has requested that he be extradited back to the States."

"His family?" I asked.

"Mostly his brothers, who work with him at his restaurants. They're in shock, as you might imagine. They knew about the lawsuit that Luella was threatening Roy's livelihood with, but they never dreamed he would do something like this."

"Well, the opportunity presented itself," I said, "but I believe it was more than that. In my conversations with Roy, I sensed his restaurants weren't just his livelihood—they were his life. It was everything he had struggled to build."

Holt accepted this assessment soberly, but was distracted by music and shouting coming from the front of the hotel.

My eyes lit up. "Wait a minute . . . I recognize that song!" The others followed me outside.

Marching up the street in front of the hotel was a small band of brightly dressed men and women, carrying signs proclaiming WALKERS WELCOME HERE! and ENGLAND LOVES ITS TRAILS!, followed by a small truck blasting the song "Walk of Life" by Dire Straits. People were coming out of their houses and businesses to cheer on the small parade.

One woman came up to me and handed me a flyer.

"Don't be afraid to walk our trails! They all are safe. Go for a walk today!"

The flyer showed a pair of boots under the banner WALKING BRITAIN'S TRAILS IS FUN . . . AND SAFE! It was produced by a citizens group called Citizens On Foot for England and Everywhere (COFFEE).

"Those trail incidents must have sparked a backlash," Holt said with a smile. "But the most immediate danger is no longer a worry. The LUAU group has disbanded. Lawrence Hancock was their driving force, and with him behind bars, their drive is gone. Jane Berry played her part, but she hasn't the will to keep it going."

Billie watched the marching band disappear into the distance. "So the pathways of Britain are once again safe for the walkers of the world. As someone who plans to be among that group again, that's good news."

"Indeed," said Holt, checking her watch. "DC Kahlil and I must be on our way. But there's one more thing, Chase. Both of us want to thank you for your help. We probably would have arrived at the same conclusion on our own, but you most decidedly speeded things up."

I gave her and DC Kahlil a humble nod of acknowledgment. "It's been a pleasure working with both of you," I said to the pair. "Forgive me if I don't say 'Let's do it again sometime.' But . . . can I ask one more favor of you?"

"Certainly."

I handed her a small note, gave her my request, and she nodded.

"What was that all about?" Billie asked as we watched them drive off.

"I was just acting on a hunch," I said. "I'll tell you all about it later."

Mike stepped outside, holding a teacup. "What on earth was all that commotion I heard out here?" I told him about the pro-walking group that had just passed through, and he laughed. "Some people have too much time on their hands."

I resisted commenting that it was far more encouraging than others releasing snakes on trails.

"After all that excitement, I'm ready for breakfast," Billie said. "How about you two?"

Chapter 30

**Saturday, midday,
The Carne**

Two hours later, our group (or what was left of it) collected in the lobby of The Carne, settling our accounts and saying goodbyes. If our walk had progressed as planned, without the shutdown after Luella's murder, we'd be finishing up that day in Looe.

I was pleased to see Rachel, Dave, and Ivy clustered together. For once, Ivy didn't look defiant. She shone a knowing smile at her mother that, if I was any kind of feeling person, said, "I'm so glad you're happy."

"Heading back home?" I asked.

Dave gave Rachel a squeeze. "No, we decided to see a part of England where murders aren't as likely to happen. Some place called Eastbourne. Ivy found it."

"It's on the coast farther east," I said, remembering a visit there with Doug. "But don't kid yourself. Murders happen there, too."

"Well, if one does, I'm going to stay out of it," Ivy said. "And guess what? We might see Taylor Swift, who's staying there with her boyfriend."

I looked her in the eye. "And where did you find out this piece of information?"

She averted my gaze. "My social media feed."

"What did I tell you about believing everything you see online?"

Dave placed his hand on Ivy's shoulder. "Whether or not we see Taylor Swift, it sounds like a beautiful place. Somewhere we can forget about what happened here."

Rachel tilted her head. "I'm not sure I'll ever forget it. I deal with the worst in human nature in my job, but this went beyond that."

Ivy gave an eye roll. "Get real, Mom. Don't you watch any TV? This happens all the time."

Rachel's phone dinged, and she looked down at a text that had just come in. "Listen to this. It's from Inspector Holt. She asked if we'd like to bring Ivy by the station so she can have a chat with their research expert."

"Me?" Ivy asked, wide-eyed.

I knelt and looked her in the eye. "Here's your chance. That guy will show you how you can put your interest in checking out people online to constructive use."

She turned a skeptical eye toward me. "This was your idea, wasn't it?"

"It sounds great!" Dave said. "We've got the time, let's do it."

Ivy's smirk turned into a smile. "Maybe I can be a detective, like you," she said to me. "I won't even need to go to college or anything."

I gave her a dose of side-eye. "Don't kid yourself."

"We'll keep you posted on Ivy's career choices," Rachel said with a laugh. "But we have other things to work out first. When we get home, Dave and I are going to have to figure out how to keep seeing each other even though Ivy and I live in Chicago and he lives in New York."

"Chase and I can give you some perspective on carrying on a long-distance romance," Mike said.

I laughed. "Our 'perspective' is that it's practically impossible. That's why I'll be moving to England permanently."

Mike's eyes widened. Perhaps I should have shared this decision with him first.

"Good for you!" Dave said. "At least Rachel and I won't be in different countries. And I'm thinking of getting into a different line of work anyway."

Rachel swung to Dave. "You are? This is the first I heard of it." I wasn't the only one dropping bombshells.

"It was going to be a surprise," he said. "But I've been considering it for a while now. We can—oh, here comes the taxi."

"I wish you all the best," I said to them as they placed their bags in the taxi's boot.

Billie was set to leave as well, her astonishingly small bag beside her. "I'm going with Dave and Rachel in the taxi, because *this* man's little car won't accommodate me," she said to me and nodding at Mike.

"The driver will drop us off at the police station on the way," Rachel said.

"I've got a flight back home from Heathrow tomorrow morning," Billie said. "No more sightseeing for me . . . I need to stay off my feet and give my knee a good chance to heal."

"See to it that it does," I said. "I'm expecting you back here next year for another walk."

Both Mike and I gave her a hug.

She smiled. "I'll definitely take you up on that, even if my knee turns out to be a new titanium one. But . . ." She hesitated.

"But what?"

She gave me a look of expectation. "Perhaps it can just be the two of us next year? Not with a large group?"

She was dreading another murder, and I couldn't blame her. "That's a deal."

We gave each other a warm wave of farewell as she boarded the taxi with Dave, Rachel, and Ivy. It always was difficult to say goodbye to Billie, knowing I wouldn't see her for another year. Perhaps she'd consider moving to England as well?

The taxi pulled off. Mike turned to me and said, "I hope you don't mind riding in my 'little car.' "

I laughed. "That's an interesting way of phrasing an invitation to spend more time with you."

He started to laugh as well when his phone gave a ding. He read the displayed message quickly and said, "Damn."

"Something up at work?" I asked.

"No. It's Randall. Elaine says he's refusing to get ready for moving to January House. She wants me to help."

"What can you do?"

"Randall eventually listens to reason. That is, he has until now. Perhaps that might be different given his current mental state, yet I must try." He paused, his expression not a hopeful one. Then he pocketed his phone, looked up at me, and smiled. "But we can worry about that later. Are you ready to go home?"

The word "home" had never sounded so good. I turned to give The Carne a farewell glance. While I'd never forget its remarkable views, they would always be tainted with the shadow of what had happened not far away.

And yet, happier times were in store. I turned to Mike. "I'm ready."